High Iron

By Tim Craire

White Cedar Press
New York - Miami - Auckland

High Iron

By Tim Craire

Cover art and map by Luka Cakic

White Cedar Press
New York - Miami - Auckland

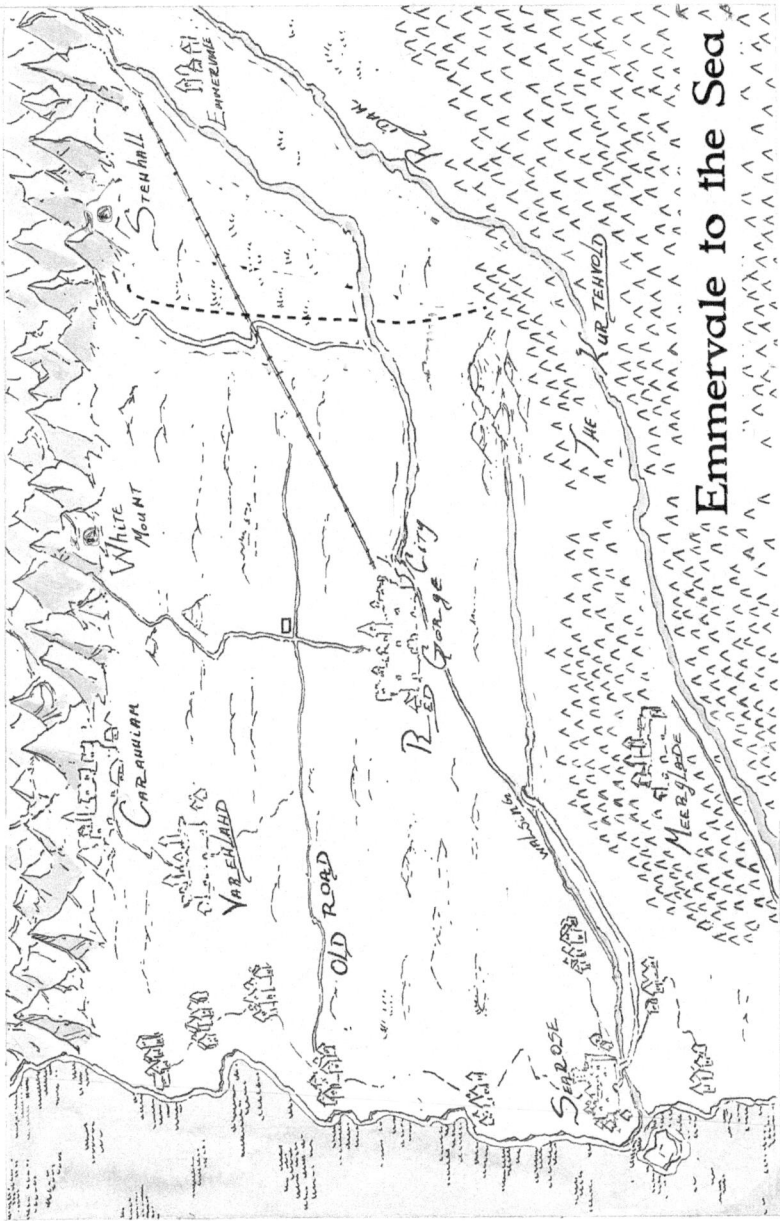

Stenhall

Emmervale

White Mount

Caraudan

Varehland

Old Road

Red Gorge City

The Yur Tehvold

Meerglade

Stenrose

One

I was fourteen when I first saw the wizards of Varenlend. Three of them appeared over a hilltop and walked down toward me as I sat cross-legged monitoring our sheep.

"Monitoring;" that was what my father called it. He thought that merely "watching" sheep, or "shepherding" them, made us sound like simpletons.

My two dogs had heard or smelled the foreigners long before I noticed them, and now trotted on either side of the three as they came down the hill. The wizards—two women and a man—paid them no mind.

The two women were younger than the man, and they walked in front. One of them was quite young, perhaps two years older than I. The other was an adult. The man looked to be around sixty.

I had seen them down in town in the previous week. Perhaps it was not these three, but some others in their party. A small group had traveled here, the first known visitors from their city we had ever seen in Emmervale.

All three smiled, now. They spoke among themselves as they descended the hill. They still ignored the dogs, whose ears were raised. The dogs maintained their distance, and were silent, but both would have tried to rip the strangers apart had they felt any threat.

I stood. The adult woman spoke first when they came near.

"You would be Aiman."

"I would be."

"Son of Anders, and family of The Marshal."

"That's so."

"Doing your family's work," she continued.

"A part of it," I said. "That's right."

"You'll pardon us for coming to you out here," she said. "We have questions for you, and perhaps an invitation."

"What sort of questions?"

"Personal questions. About your abilities, Aiman. And your learning."

They were too smart to look around condescendingly at the sheep. They kept their eyes on me. I should have told them to speak to my father, if they had anything to say to me, but that occurred to me only after. I was not used to dealing with strangers far up here in our hills as I monitored our walking wool.

I made no answer to her words about my "learning." They waited, and then the woman continued.

"We have come from Varenlend. I am sure you have heard of us already. I am Annira. This is my cousin Annelle, and this is Sokran, our chief instructor."

Annelle, the very young woman, nodded to me. She was smiling. Sokran stayed behind the two of them. I still did not say anything.

"Sokran is our chief instructor of mages," she added. "Aiman, we have heard of you in town."

I admit that, at age fourteen, I was not surprised to learn that someone had recognized my brilliance. I did wonder how exactly they had learned of me, but I did not think it unusual that they considered me to be out of the ordinary. I asked:

"What have you heard?"

"We have heard that you are possessed of a mind that is probably not challenged enough out here. You are a young man whose thoughts are on power; perhaps steam, or perhaps magic."

Annelle now spoke:

"We want to demonstrate something for you, Aiman. Our skills, and your potential."

These three were making no mistakes in their pitch to me—complimenting my formidable intellect and then having this sharp young woman take over. She was striking: tall, with black hair falling down her shoulders, and clear gray eyes. She addressed me with a slight but warm smile.

Their approach would have worked with any adolescent boy, of course. No such boy with even a handful of ambition would be content to sit and watch sheep for hours, and none would have minded being singled out by this lovely, urbane young enchanter (who was, for good measure—I eventually learned—likely to rule Varenlend one day).

She turned and spoke quietly to the man, Sokran, in their own language. We called this language Cranam, or Oppidan. I understood it, although I would not have wanted to converse with her in it. Everyone in my family learned Oppidan; my father made sure of that. She was quiet enough that I caught only the word "green."

She turned back to me, held out one hand, and extended her fingers. Suddenly the air around me was warm; as warm as an early summer day. In reality, it was just the beginning of spring, in fact one of the first days we had bothered to take the sheep out to graze. The ground cover was barely greening up after the winter.

For a moment I wondered if the warmth was just due to Annelle's eyes, and so on, but I realized the temperature was real. She, or one of the other two, had warmed up the hillside.

"You feel the air," she said. It wasn't a question. "You know we are able to do this in Varenlend. It is one thing we can do. One of many."

"I have heard as much," I said.

"Your animals are searching for grasses," she said.

"Yes," I answered. I wasn't sure of her point. "Grasses, weeds. Whatever they can find."

"We could help them find more."

This early in the season the flock was making do with the barest growth. Tufts of snowpetals had been out for about a week, and patches of what we called thaw grass were also now rousing themselves. But it was too early for much else.

Annelle glanced around her, then, and beds of hill mint, which were all around—and which had been pale and wilted—suddenly turned green. Like a carpet unrolling, but in all directions, the hillside jumped ahead a month in just a moment.

This included the ground beneath the sheep. They tore into it. I guessed they appreciated the change.

Annelle stood there, smiling. The white of her robe contrasted with the rich hill mint, now.

"That is impressive," I said.

"Aiman, we think you could do this, also. For example you could make it all wither again. You could do this right now. Try."

I had hoped to appear mature and confident throughout this encounter, but at that point I'm afraid I must have looked around in confusion, plainly bewildered. I took her word for it, that I might change the weather on this hillside, but of course I had no idea how to do so.

"Will it," she said. "Just channel the power. It is here already. Draw it back out of the ground and disperse it into the air where it came from."

I looked around at the mint and thought of it pale and matted. All of it promptly fell back to the way it had been. The stems drooped and the color washed out. This fade happened even more quickly than the original greening of hers.

"That was your doing," she said.

"How do I know you didn't just end it yourself?" I asked; but I knew the answer:

"Because you feel it," she said, and she was right. I did feel it. I had thought about all that growth returning to normal, and willed it, a bit, and it had done so. I felt that I had effected the change just as directly as when I whistled for my dogs. She was right: there was energy, power, in the air.

The three of them looked at me, apparently appreciative, as I stood there atop the fallen spring weeds.

"Aiman."

The voice came from further down the hill. It was my father.

I turned. He did not say anything further—no reprimand—but I saw concern in his eyes as he continued up.

"Anders Shearer," Sokran said. "Pardon our intrusion. This is gorgeous land you own."

"This is town land, here, not ours. But you are right. The views are very inviting, I know."

"You won't mind us speaking with your son. We knew we would have to come up here to find him. Your family is always working."

"As is yours," my father said. With these three simple words I understood that he was letting them know that he was aware their visit was carefully planned—carefully premeditated—with an important goal.

"Aiman here is very talented," Annira said.

"Indeed he is."

"I won't waste your time, Anders Shearer. We would invite your son to return to Varenlend with us. We believe he could learn very much there."

"You should speak with me about this," my father said, "not him. He is still a boy."

"Forgive us," Sokran said. "We wished to meet him."

Annira then said:

"You are beginning to prosper, here in Emmervale. We would like better ties between your city and ours."

"We have been prospering," my father answered, "since the day we walked down those mountains and reclaimed this town. And many thanks for calling us a city, but we know we are a simple village. We are content here."

"You may be a simple village, but someday you will be a target for the dunters to your west," Sokran said. "You cannot lard up too much wealth without drawing their attention."

"I have walked for days to our west and never seen a dunter," my father said. "The land between our town and their hovels is vast. It may as well be an ocean."

"An ocean they will cross. You won't want that, and we don't want it either."

Sokran sounded genuine, as he said this. Genuinely concerned for our welfare.

My father tilted his head. "Well. We are not unaware that they are our neighbors. Our distant neighbors."

Sokran raised his eyebrows briefly but did not pursue this, and neither did the other two. The three of them spoke a few more words and took their leave. They were very kind to me, of course, throughout. Sokran inclined his head to us, before they departed. Annira reached to touch my elbow, and Annelle actually took my hand and held it in both of hers. She was my height. Her eyes were a light gray—perhaps I have mentioned that already.

The three of them walked past my father and me, and headed down in the direction from which he had come, toward town. After they had moved well down the hill, my father spoke again. His voice seemed very spare there, just the two of us now with the heedless sheep and vigilant dogs beyond us.

"I'm sure it is very pleasant to be singled out for attention like that, Aiman. And you do have a fine mind. I understand that. But I'm afraid they were not coming to you because of your talents."

"I know, Father," I said.

"Do you?"

I shrugged. "I would guess they see me as one of their easier chances to wield influence here in Emmervale. A way to have a tie to you."

He looked at me and said nothing.

"They should have tried that wizarding invitation when I was a bit younger," I continued. "But I've seen them in town this past week, Father. They've nearly been weighing and measuring the place."

"Down in town."

"Yes."

"They haven't come up here before?"

"No. I've seen them down at our mills. And along the river. I suppose it is good news that they think us worth noticing. But from what I know of Varenlend, I doubt they are looking for equal partners."

"Indeed," he said. "And they know who we are, you and I."

"Yes. They mentioned our family."

"I think," he said, "that is more important to them than your formidable mind."

"I assume so," I said. "If they are looking for true brilliance they could speak with Britta." She was my cousin.

My father smiled, and shook his head once.

"Aiman. For all their words I think they have no idea just how wise you are."

All this was well and good, and I was glad enough—and am still glad today—that I did not pack my bag and march off with them back to Varenlend to be educated in sorcery. But I admit that those sheep never looked as gray, and our hills never seemed so far from the cities of our world, as when those three visitors turned their backs on me and returned to town. My father walked back down shortly after they did, and I was left alone again. My dogs were loyal, but their company was nothing like that of a gray-eyed young noblewoman. I thought of Annelle many, many times in the following years. After long days up in those hills I sometimes believed that I had imagined the visit. It seemed beyond reality that three such prominent mages would journey out there to the edge of Emmervale to address me. I sometimes wondered if it ever actually happened. But my father would occasionally tease me, during our more tedious chores, about the "job" I had turned down.

I walked to town myself, the next day, to watch them leave. Word had made it back up to us—to my father, this time—that I was welcome to present myself in Varenlend if I ever changed my mind. So I knew they were departing.

There were eleven in their party: the three I had met, plus four soldiers, and four others who looked to be more wizards, or perhaps Varenlend aristocrats. All wore white, and their horses were either white, gray, or black. They made a fine picture as they rode west out of Emmervale. I stood atop a low hill on the north side of town and could see them well enough. There was a sway to their movement, a confidence; it was hard to describe. Their horses' tails swished easily side-to-side, and those in front frequently looked behind them to chat with their companions. Annelle's waist bobbed slightly as she rode—but I probably just imagined that. I could not even be completely sure which one she was, from my distance.

After they left, I learned more about the three who had spoken to me. Annira was a niece of the current ruler of Varenlend, a powerful mage titled Vizer Ruhallan. He had appointed her to govern the urban center of the state; and given the prominence of that city, she was essentially in charge of everything worth directing. Sokran was indeed the master instructor of mages, and students from not only Varenlend's territory but even that of Caranniam came to him to study. The wizards of Caranniam had always considered themselves the finest in the world, so this showed the esteem in which he was held.

Annelle—her full name was Annelle WhiteStone Vizer—was the heir to Annira; this was because of her family but also her talent in wizardry. She would likely someday take over rule of the central city of Varenlend, and then eventually the entire state. She had been recognized at a young age as a gifted and clear-headed prodigy.

These were the people who had invited me to learn alongside them.

I sat up there in the hills instead, watching the sheep.

But I knew:

These were Mourno sheep, our finest. No one outside of Emmervale raised them, and even here there were only a few families doing so. Soon, later in the spring, we would shear them, and we would get an average yield of eight pounds apiece of the best wool in the world. We could trade this wool with elves for their steel, or with dwarves for their muskets. We could take the wool to Caranniam and sell it for forty crowns a bale, or to Searose or other coast cities for twelve skenders a bale, or to Varenlend itself for thirty bars a bale. With the amount of money we would earn we could rebuild half a dozen burnt-out houses, or put up a bridge, or start a school.

We had been free of the dwarves of Stenhall for twenty-five years. This was nearly twice as long as my entire life, at that point, but I knew that we were still a very young and precarious town—because my father and all the other elders drilled it into us. Everyone over thirty years old could remember the day our people had twisted out of the grip of the dwarves and walked down the mountainside to the remains of old Emmervale. All remembered how little they owned, back then, and what a task they had before them to rebuild. We never forgot that this work was still in progress. Some of our elderly remembered not only the day they had come out of the mines, but the day they had walked in. They exhorted us to build and rebuild, plant and grow, watch and multiply.

We were doing so. I was helping. Varenlend was a great city, but Emmervale would one day be great, also. And some of this progress depended on these sheep. I kept my post.

Two

Seven years later we were up to eleven hundred sheep, and I did not monitor them any longer; we hired for that. Emmervale continued to grow. We were adding not only our own children but also occasional migrants from Searose, Varenlend, Caranniam. Yes, citizens of Caranniam and even Varenlend itself traveled to our hills to start new lives. I wondered what Annelle and Sokran would have thought of that. Not bad for a "simple village," as Sokran had called us.

(One of those emigrants of Caranniam was a vintner whom my father hired to work our land. The hills around us were good for grapes, but I think my father also just wanted someone around who was fluent in Cranam. My father saw to it that I spent a lot of time with the vintner, and he was often invited to our meals. My Cranam became quite good, because of that, and I would not now have been reluctant to speak it with strangers, even the very beautiful ones.)

Our only real concern was a rumor of burgeoning growth in Red Gorge City, the nation of the dunters to our west. Sokran, it turns out, had been prescient. It had been only a few months ago that we in Emmervale were still assuming, as we always had, that the dunters would stay far away, as they always had. The truth hit us rudely:

First we were told that a sprawling army of them had departed Red Gorge and was marching toward Emmervale. This was in early spring, once again. The alarm was brought to us by a lone traveler from the west; we sent out scouts to verify.

These scouts reported news that was somewhat better: the army had indeed assembled, at the eastern edge of Red Gorge, but it was moving very slowly. It may have been only a war tournament, or perhaps a gathering for some cult ceremony of theirs.

The second wave of scouts, however, told us exactly why the dunters moved slowly, and it was not because of any cult meeting: They were protecting a new span of railroad that was being laid. The tracks, the scouts said, were aimed right at us.

"The dunters have an engine that's going to crawl all the way out here?" my cousin Britta asked. She and I were speaking with our friend Jed, who had ventured out as one of the scouts.

"It seems so," he said. "They're confident enough to be laying the track."

"They must have improved what they had before. I thought that pumper they had could barely haul itself from one side of Red Gorge City to the other."

"It barely could," Jed said. "They must have something better now. They may be dim, but they're not foolish enough to embark on all this construction if they have nothing to run on it." He seemed earnest, which was unusual for him. Usually he would not speak even this much about the dunters without ridiculing them considerably more. He stood before us with his arms folded, and his eyes slightly narrowed. We had gathered outside the fence of a paddock which lay between my family's house and Britta's. There beside our well-kept pasture it was hard to imagine the uproar of a swarming horde of dunters, and harder to imagine that they could ever threaten us.

"You did not see an engine, though?" I asked.

"No. Just horses and wagons hauling out the ties, and the rails."

"I'm surprised they can make such improvements to their machinery."

"They may have help. Outlaw dwarves, or who knows who. But Aiman, they were working in a fever. We were not very close to them, but close enough to see that much. Their kobolds were scurrying around, and so were they. It looked grim."

"I wonder how long it would take them to lay track all the way out to our borders," Britta said, "if that's what they're doing."

"It would take some time," Jed said. "Months. And even the forging of that amount of track would be a challenge for them, I think."

"They don't have the foundries for it," I said.

"I don't think so, no. But I'm sure they will labor day and night nonstop, if that is their goal. And they won't hesitate to work their kobolds to death and toss them aside all along that new line, if need be."

Now Britta's face darkened. She reached back absently to take her hair in both hands, pull it around front, twist it like a rope, and then let it go. She said nothing.

The two of them were understandably distressed, but I was thankful for the timing of all this. I thought I could at least take relief in that. It was well into spring, now, and our sheep had been shorn and had lambed. Any intrusion the dunters could manage—if that indeed was their plan—would not disrupt us too much. (I did not understand, at that point, the size and determination of that expeditionary army.)

I soon became a scout myself. I was curious to see this unprecedented rail project of Red Gorge and perhaps get a glimpse of what they intended to run on it. I took along Britta, and convinced Jed to head back out. Britta is my father's sister's daughter, two years older than I. She is well-respected in our family, and in Emmervale. Jed, for his part, is a lanky runner who covers ground like few others, whether on the longball field or out in open country, and we knew we would likely find ourselves on foot once we got close enough to the dunters. We loaded packs, took two muskets, and dressed to blend into the fields.

My father spoke to Jed and me before we left:

"Stay safe. Any glimpse of what these dunters are about should tell you much. You won't need to count their teeth. Remember, Aiman, you have a place here. Emmervale needs you."

"Emmervale needs all of us," I tried to correct him. "Or perhaps you are thinking of Britta."

"You, Aiman. You must understand this." He nodded, almost to himself, in support of something he was thinking.

"I suppose," he said, "you have never had to live through a time of darkness. In times like these, the people want leaders. Learn as much as you can, but stay safe. And then come back quickly."

As we departed, Jed turned to me and said:

"No weight on your shoulders, here." Now he wore his usual careless and contagious smile. "Once again I thank my parents for not bearing me into such a prominent family."

The three of us left early in the morning through the west gate of Emmervale town. I rode my family's saddle horse, and Britta had her own. Jed rode the same one he had just taken out a few days earlier.

We headed west. For some miles we rode past farms, and alongside planted fields. The houses we passed were whole, and occupied. Then, all too soon, the only structures we saw were burned-out, half-tumbled ruins. The land was still good—tall grasses and wildflowers grew—but there was no one to work it.

"We must send more people out here," Jed said. "Emmervale could double its size four times and still not lack room."

"Do you plan on turning up settlers next week?" I asked him. "We can hope that our children restore these homes and plant these hills. As long as no one else plants them first." I nodded toward the horizon before us, and the dunters beyond it.

Four days later, early in the afternoon, we were far to the west of Emmervale. From what Jed had told us about the location of the army when he saw it, we must have been close to the advancing eastern end of the new railway. We slowed, and kept our eyes open.

The land had flattened. We crept through a prairie. I knew the country, somewhat, because in better days I had traveled out this direction to sell wool to a trader from Varenlend. I had done quite well with those transactions, and had made a number of trips. But I would meet her by a certain hill, a landmark, which lay well to the south of us now. Up here the land was smooth, and largely feature-less.

"Do we ride all the way in?" Jed asked.

"As far as we can."

"We'll be visible from some way off. I would prefer to be hidden down there in the grass, if we want to get closer than I did the first time."

"We'll have to be more vigilant than the dunters," I said.

"Jed is right," Britta said. "If we come to a stand of trees, we should dismount. I would rather walk a distance than be seen by their scouts."

"If they have scouts," I said. "I'm not sure they're clever enough to watch a perimeter. But very well. If we come to cover, we'll stop. One of us will have to stay with the horses, though."

We did find a place to dismount, eventually; a small stream crossed our path, and there were trees growing along its banks. We tied the horses together, and then had to decide who would stay behind with them. We were facing each other in a triangle.

"Odd or even fingers behind your back," I said. We each hid one hand. "The odd one out stays here. Now."

We all showed our hands; each of us had just one finger out.

"We are all number one, clearly," I said. "Again."

This time Britta had chosen three fingers to my two and Jed's four.

"There we have it," I said. "Britta, you have the most difficult job."

"I will stay, then. See what is going on and then get back," she said.

"We shall."

"How about if we turn back to be here by dark, if we don't see anything?" Jed said.

"That's good. Britta, if we haven't returned by dark, lead these horses back. You might cut down south to the woods; better cover there."

"You will be back," she said.

We left behind our packs, and I left my musket. Britta kept hers with her. We wanted to move quickly, and we were not going to get ourselves into a situation in which shooting would do any good.

"You're sure you don't want them?" Britta said, as I stowed the gun in the scabbard on my horse.

"I can imagine our success if we have to shoot accurately, and then reload, as a squad of dunters runs at us," I said. "No, we don't need them. We are staying away from the squads of dunters in the first place. Isn't that right, Jed?"

"We'll give them a large berth, yes," he said.

We left her and started walking. The grassland stretched out before us, with a few easy rises now and again, and we saw nothing at the horizon. This land, just like that to the west of Emmervale, was unsettled. A hundred years or more earlier, kingdoms had held sway out this far, and there likely had been low houses and grain farmers. But in our time, after the plagues and then the fires, the land was unused. What farmers had lived out this way had tended to build out of wood, or earth and thatch, rather than stone, so we saw few ruins. The only crowds the endless green grasses might host were flocks of ring geese and bronzewings overhead, but we saw nothing. We covered some considerable distance.

"You might let me stand on your shoulders, Aiman, and we could see twice as far."

"Or I could stand on yours," I answered.

"No, I'm taller," he said. "So it must be me atop yours. We'd see farther that way."

"Impeccable reasoning," I said.

And after that, we did not have to wait long for contact. A small group of dunters—it turned out to be four—appeared before us, walking a route that would carry them just to our north. There were a few kobolds following behind them, also. Jed and I dropped to the ground. The grass here was thick, and green; a wild grain with heads of seeds. We raised ourselves up to peer through it.

Whenever I have a sudden scare, or see something which probably should have been scaring me all along, I feel a surge in my chest. It feels like quick heat, as if there is a small bit of lightning that strikes my heart. It hits me right behind my breastbone and front ribs. Perhaps it is a jolt of blood, but I feel it only in my chest. Maybe the heart pumps out something else apart from blood, some sort of firewater.

I felt this when I saw these dunters. They were dressed in uniforms: black jacks with a red stripe across the shoulder. That stripe marked them as belonging to the house of a particular warlord; we didn't know anything further about that heraldry, of course. Two of them carried muskets, and the other two, enormous broadswords. They looked capable. The picture of dunters I had held in mind was that of pale, spindly characters with long noses and awkward teeth, but these were meaty and stern. Their noses were indeed large, and their teeth so long that it made one wonder how they could eat; but they looked monstrous, not awkward.

The kobolds behind them seemed to be porters. They carried powder horns and shot bags on straps hanging off their shoulders. One of them had a spare musket, also, ready to hand to a dunter.

We nearly held our breath. They passed across our path. They seemed to be walking with purpose, although we could not tell to what end.

It took some courage, I must say, for us to continue. We knew that we could well be cut off from our route back to Emmervale by that group of dunters, and by who knows how many others which might be marauding. But we pressed ahead. We crawled on all fours for some time, and then raised ourselves to scan the fields; we saw no more of them. We stood, both of us crouching, and sped ahead as best we could.

In time we came within view of the black line on the horizon which was the main force of Red Gorge. I had intended to turn back, at this point, now that we knew how far they had advanced; but the land between us and that horde was vacant, a clear path. I wanted to bring back something more than the previous scouts had discovered. We kept moving.

"We can get quite a bit closer," Jed said. With that, I knew he also wanted to advance as far as possible, and it became out of the question for me to suggest we turn around. I could imagine Britta shaking her head at our risk, and of course she would have been right.

We trotted ahead in our crouches. Jed was in front.

"You mind to the right, and ahead," I told him. I tried to watch our left, and to the rear. In retrospect this was very foolhardy, but we made it close enough to the main lines to see the work on the rails.

The force did not look terribly organized. Some dunters just seemed to meander about, in groups or as solitary individuals. Some watched the work, and others stood in clusters and jabbered with each other. None of them—fortunately for us—seemed to be keeping formal surveillance. Most of the hauling, of rails and ties, was done by kobolds. They were tiny forms, slight but quick, among the larger dunters. Others of their kind were also shoveling, ahead of the crowd, in order to raise a bed for the rails.

Kobolds even drove the spikes. The largest among them—perhaps reaching up chest-high on a dunter—swung sledgehammers over and over again. We could see their short arms pumping. We could also hear the strikes. These were faint and out of time with the swings, due to our distance.

"Do the dunters do nothing?" Jed asked. "Their dog-boys even secure the rails."

"I'm sure the dunters are more concerned with putting their fine intellects to work directing all this chaos," I said. "And managing their supplies. Look at it all."

The rails and ties were piled up on wagons, pulled along next to the edge of the tracks by oxen. A line of the wagons crept forward, each waiting its turn to unload.

"They're not using their new engine to haul it all out?" Jed asked. "I assume their old ones could not have done it."

It had been three years since the dunters had rolled their first locomotive around Red Gorge City. They had made a show of it. They had done this for the pride and entertainment of their own masses, but made sure that a few straggling men—drifters and outlaws, for no one else would have gone near—had seen it also. Several of these observers had eventually made their way to Emmervale and shared this news with anyone who would listen. The locomotive had been rickety, apparently, incapable of pulling much more than its coal, but it was the first working invention of its kind.

"It could be," I said, "that they are saving their new one for a better debut. So it's ox power for now."

Then I noticed something about the line of wagons: standing atop a pile of rails on one of them were two elves.

Elves.

I stared at them a moment, disbelieving, and then grabbed Jed's arm.

"Look at that third wagon!" I said. "Do you see them?"

He lifted his head and peered.

"Somehow they look like elves."

"They are elves!"

"They can't be," he said. "The dunters would tear them apart. And the elves themselves wouldn't be able to stand their presence."

"It is! They are!" I repeated. "Look at their robes!"

He kept staring, but shook his head.

"Well, they are not dunters, clearly. But they must be men, then. There is simply no way."

It was obvious to me. The elves wore white, and seemed taller and thinner than men. They stood on the wagons, perhaps even directing the dunters and kobolds.

"You didn't see them when you rode out here before?" I asked.

"No. What would they be doing out there? Driving spikes for the dunters?"

"But yet there they are. They're on the wagons; maybe they're involved with the materials somehow?"

"Such as what—cutting down their trees for the ties?"

Now something ripped through the grass before us. Two booms on our left. We dropped to the dirt. It was bullets. We had been seen, and two guns had shot at us.

"I was to be watching the left," I said. I don't know why—I suppose it was an apology to Jed, but of course much too late.

I crawled forward a few feet and raised my head. Four dunters were coming toward us. I saw others behind them, busy with their arms; they must have been reloading.

"Up and run!" I told Jed.

He sprang upright and we raced directly away from the shots. Unfortunately this did not put us going back in the direction from which we had come, but rather to the northeast. This was not directly toward the end of the tracks, fortunately, but it wasn't toward Britta and the horses either.

Jed was a wondrous loper, as I said, and he surged ahead of me. We ran, having no better option; we had no cover, and we needed to get out of range of the guns, even if it drew the attention of that entire dunter army. Which is exactly what seemed to happen. I looked behind to see that the four dunters close to us were running hard, and far behind them more were splitting off that crowd. A few of the kobold porters scrambled along behind them, trying to keep up.

We flew through the grass. I hoped that we had the four pursuing dunters directly between us and their comrades with the muskets, so that the gunners would have no clear shots. Then again, knowing dunters, they might have fired anyway.

But they did not need to; another knot of them appeared now, to our left. We cut to the right. I saw a puff of smoke.

"Down!" I yelled, and we both dropped. I heard the slug plow into the earth to our left. We rose and ran again.

We raced over the waving tops of all that grass the way I imagined a hawk might swoop down over it to nab a mouse. But we, of course, were the prey.

And now before us appeared yet more dunters. Where had they come from? There must have been parties ranging about which we had missed, and they had been drawn toward the gunfire. We now had them on three sides.

"A plan?" Jed asked me.

"Pull knives and head toward the smallest group," I said. That meant the ones on our left; only three or four of them, and apparently only one gun. The odds would not get any better for us.

We carried long knives, and drew them. We turned and ran at

the dunters.

There were actually three of them, I saw now. They too wore matching jacks, just like the first group we had seen, but these were black with a white star. One of them was reloading; he looked to be ramming down the bullet and wad. The other two pulled swords. They seemed glad to have our challenge. Both wore banded helmets, and one now pulled his further down his forehead. Both smiled, showing their teeth—all their teeth, this time, not just the usual protruding fangs.

The gunner dropped his rod and dumped powder into his pan. We kept at them. Then he lifted the gun and aimed at us. We saw his hand on the hammer. We both fell to the ground.

There was no shot. We waited for it, panting with our faces deep in the grass. The two with the swords would be running at us.

"Up, now," I said.

We both lifted ourselves, barely. The two dunters were within forty yards of us. They held their swords out waist-high, each with both hands on the grips.

Smoke, and another boom; the bullet cut between us. It roared past like a giant hornet. The two dunters closed on us. Their broadswords against our knives; not a promising fight.

Then a hand took my shoulder and yanked me backward. I was powerless, back on my heels, and fell behind Jed. Another hand—of a woman dressed in brown—reached out, took him also, and brought him with me.

The dunters slowed and then stopped, suddenly, wide-eyed. One barked to the other in their language.

The woman holding us leaned her head between ours, released Jed, and pursed her lips to tell us to remain silent.

It was Ralenda, the trader from Varenlend who had sometimes met me down to the south of where we now stood. She let go of my collar but put her left hand back on my shoulder. She gestured with her right that we should back off. She then began to retreat, and we followed her.

The dunters now fanned out to search for us, but were still some distance away; they would not notice our trail through the grass. Ralenda had clearly made us invisible to them. We continued to tread backward, keeping our eyes on the frantic searchers. They dashed around in circles, shouting to each other. Several of them cut the grass with their swords, flailing. One of them with a musket was preparing to shoot, but a wiser comrade put a hand on the barrel to prevent him.

Ralenda watched all this and smiled. We were about sixty paces away, and the crazed dunters were not keeping quiet or looking for slight disturbances in the tall grass. She spoke:

"I think we may chance a word, now."

I was amazed by her rescue. I had never known her to be anything other than a traveling merchant. Varenlend was a city of mages, of course, but I assumed all those with such power would be content to confine themselves to their manors, plotting and throwing fire-bolts and so on. Furthermore she did not wear the usual white of the Varenlend magicians.

"Ralenda. You have some wizarding to you," I said.

"Not by the standards of Varenlend," she said. "This is nothing."

"More than enough to save us. I considered you just a wool trader."

"A trader of anything that can be traded," she corrected me. "Let's keep retreating."

We kept moving away from the dunters, and she continued.

"I never had the will or the patience, or the desire, to be a wizard. There are too many deals to be made, Master Shearer, and people to meet. Like yourself. And we all know that magic is not the life it once was." She nodded toward the crews still working on the tracks, in the distance. "Steam, machinery. Iron and gunpowder. The new powers in the world."

"Perhaps," I said. "But one spell from you has just defeated a dozen dunters and their muskets." Behind us, as we spoke quietly, they were still darting about.

"Ah, but just wait until they learn how to shoot balls more quickly," she said. "But I did get to you just in time, didn't I?"

"Indeed. We thank you. What were you doing here?"

"The same thing you were, I suspect. I wanted to see this railroad, their progress. So I took this turn south of my route. I was heading toward Emmervale."

"Were you?" I said. "That's a coincidence we meet here, then."

"Coincidences," she said dismissively. "Who is this with you?"

"My companion, Jed."

"Well met. Listen: I have been journeying out to tell you something. I was going to head all the way to Emmervale if need be, but here you are. I wanted to tell you, want to tell you, what is happening. I feel I owe you that much."

"What are you talking about?" I asked. "We can see what's happening—a dunter army building a railroad straight at us. And why do you think you owe me anything?"

"You were always an honest partner with me. You never packed any second-rate wool in with the finest, you know." She smiled.

"Of course not."

"I have come to talk to you about this entire war, not simply these tracks. We are an alliance, now, Master Shearer. Varenlend and Caranniam have joined with Red Gorge, and with the elves also."

"You've done what?"

"Our leaders are going to ensure that their magic—or perhaps our magic, I should say—allows us to retain our power. Now is the time. With the dunters, we have the alliance. We are assisting them with these tracks, and we have other methods, also, to keep them on our side. As for the elves, we have paid them handsomely for their iron—those rails they have provided—and afterward we and the elves will keep to ourselves. That is our promise to them."

"So those are indeed elves out there," Jed said. "Subjects of Alden Silvermoor?"

Ralenda nodded. "Indeed. You are thinking they must be from elsewhere, because Silvermoor would never do such a thing? But Caranniam helped arrange a deal by which they forged the rails for this new track. The amount needed was beyond the capacity of the dunters. And of course the quality of the elven steel is unsurpassed.

"And with the dwarves in the mountains," she continued, "and the men of Searose and the rest of the coast, and with—" she tilted her head— "and with you, I am afraid, we are extending our power, our influence."

"What are you saying?" I asked, although her message was clear enough.

"I am saying that this new rail line, here, is being built to reach Stenhall and the dwarven mines there. The first train out will carry the heavy weapons, cannon. And other ordnance, enough to take Stenhall. A contingent of my people, and also a group from Caranniam, will be joining this dunter force soon, to help them press their attack. Within a few weeks those mines, and their production, will belong to Caranniam, and to Red Gorge; and to us in Varenlend, also. And then these trains will carry back iron, gold. To Red Gorge City, and Caranniam, and my Varenlend. We are not aiming for Emmervale," she added, "but of course you are neighbors to the dwarves, and we understand you will not willingly accept the dunters in your land."

"Do you have some role in this?" I asked.

"No more than any citizen of Varenlend."

"And why are you telling us?"

"To warn you. And to explain. I feel free to speak because there is nothing you can do about this alliance, and this invasion. Not you, not the dwarves, no one. And again, I respect the trade you facilitated for me." She shrugged. "And Shearer, there will always be a need for sheep—for wool and mutton—no matter in whose borders Emmervale lies. You work hard; you will always survive."

"Even if we are vassals to Caranniam, or to you, or to—Red Gorge? I do not believe we would prosper under those conditions, Ralenda. We learned this in our years as servants to the dwarves."

"Ah yes, that. I had forgotten. Those memories of your grandparents are still dark for you, aren't they? It is unfortunate you never let them go."

"My own father nearly came of age in the mines, Ralenda."

"Did he? But Shearer, life under the governance of our cities will be stable. Orderly. You will benefit from our power."

"Benefit from it, or share it?" I asked. She ignored this.

"Now, the future of the dwarves," she continued, "under the domination of Red Gorge—that will be a different matter. The dunters hold the dwarves in very low regard, as you know. But that will not be your concern. I shall look for you when all this is done. You will always have a trader to count on."

"In that case it sounds unfortunate that all my people are not sheep herders," I said. "But we are not. I suppose I thank you for this news, and for seeking me out, Ralenda. But I will say that you sound extremely confident, and honestly you do not have so much to show right now. These tracks are not even halfway to Stenhall. And I wonder if any city of men can maintain an alliance with dunters."

"Nothing will stop the tracks," she said. "All the power of

Caranniam and Varenlend is behind them. And the dunters know better than to offend us."

"Very well," I said. "You may be counting unborn ewes. But I do value all the trades we made, and again I appreciate your journey."

"You are heading back to Emmervale?" she asked.

"Yes."

"You will be unseen past this horizon," she said. "I wish you safe arrival."

She made a short bow and turned. She began walking back toward Varenlend, a journey of several days. She walked with her head high on a path that would take her near the remnant of the dunters who had cornered us; she must have been keeping herself invisible, also.

"So that was Ralenda, your reliable trader," Jed said.

"Yes."

"All of that sounded to me as if she knows of what she speaks."

"I believe she does."

"Is she a woman of rank in Varenlend?"

"More than I had guessed, I suppose," I answered. "She always seemed prosperous, and could afford to purchase any amount of wool I could manage to bring. But now, with this magic of hers—she must be far more prominent than I thought. She spoke lightly of her power, but it is rare. It's not every shopkeeper, even in Varenlend, or in Caranniam, who can throw spells like that."

"If it's true they've made an alliance, and come to some agreement with the dunters, that was very wise of them. If it can hold."

"Wise? In the short run, maybe," I said. "But I agree it sounds like a clever plan. And the elves selling them iron? All that together can change history."

"We have to get back and share this."

"Quickly."

"Do you think the dwarves will believe it?"

I snorted.

"Well, I am sure they will want to send out half their number to see for themselves, and tap their axes to the rails, and perhaps listen for the steam rising. But eventually, yes, Stenhall will understand. I wonder if we will be able to come to some sort of agreement with them. And I wonder if it will do us any good, in the face of this grand alliance against us."

*　*　*

We reached Britta before dark.

"What did you learn?" she asked as she untied the horses.

"More than we hoped. And more than we wanted to."

We shared with her everything we had been told as we mounted and rode.

"This trader Ralenda," she asked, "sought you out just to tell you this?"

"Yes."

Britta shook her head. "Imagine what might have been had you been educated there, Aiman," she said.

Britta had known of my long-ago meeting with the wizards of Varenlend soon after it happened; I had told her about it before anyone else. She had thought I had made a mistake, at the time, and had never changed her mind.

"They were just trying to use me to get a foothold into Emmervale," I had objected.

"Yes, and they failed. Because you were smart enough to see through it. And you also would have been smart enough to see through it had you accepted, and learned from them. And then we would have a Varenlend-trained wizard with us."

"In any case," I said now, "my ties with Varenlend have helped us understand what's going on, one way or another. Maybe this was destined. I am afraid we are facing some dark weeks."

We covered the empty country back toward Emmervale uneventfully, largely retracing our path out. The flat prairie ended, giving way to modest swells and rolls of land.

As the sun was setting on the third day, we came upon a rare cluster of woods along a stream that crawled between two low hills. We faced another four hours of riding, we reckoned, to make it into Emmervale.

"Shall we push through, or camp for the night?" I asked.

"I am always ready to keep moving," Jed said. "But we might be dodging watchdogs if we get into town that late. The people are edgy, and no one is expecting me by dawn."

"Nobody is staying up gazing out her window for me, either, I'm afraid," I said.

"Don't be so sure, Aiman," Britta answered. Nonetheless we settled down by the stream and built a fire. Jed took out his kit to light twigs, as Britta and I gathered wood. Our food was dried fruit, and hard bread, so we did not really need to cook anything; but the fire was a welcome diversion after the day of riding. Eventually I unrolled a blanket, wrapped myself, and slept.

Some hours before dawn, Jed shook me.

"Aiman, wake up."

He said it only once, and then stood to look eastward.

I came to my senses quickly. That he made no joke about waking me so early, and said nothing about what he saw, alarmed me. I rose, blanket and all. Britta was already up.

There was a glow on the horizon before us, in the direction of Emmervale.

We could not run the horses at a gallop all the way to Emmervale, but we pushed them as much as we could. All the while the glow continued. The town was on fire.

"Who could have done this?" I asked. "Are there more dunters far to the east?"

"There must be," Jed said. "The dwarves wouldn't attack us."

Dawn came, and we neared home. The glow in the sky faded; in its place we could see smoke. We reached the outskirts of town in the light of morning, and every house and barn we saw was either burning or had burned down.

We could hear gunfire and a rumble of distant shouts from the center of town. We ran the horses hard, now, and tore down the grass streets through smoke.

Jed rode first. He had drawn his long knife. As we cleared one corner of a lane, at which a thatch-roofed house was aflame, we saw a dunter hurrying down the street before us.

Dunters in Emmervale. A force of them well in advance of the mob by the end of the rails. As I looked at this one running, I felt off balance, confused. If they were here on this street, who knew where else they might be. Across the river? Even up among our sheep?

We had surprised this one, and Jed surged forward to lean out and slash him as he ran. The knife struck the dunter's helmet, but the marauder kept his feet and bolted away.

Musketry was now right nearby. The shooting seemed to be coming from the far side of the river, and was pointed in our direction; this was some relief amid this nightmare, because it meant—we hoped—that our people still held the wall around the center. The town has walls, centuries old but restored, on the east side of the river. I prayed that the shots from that direction meant that the invasion, and the burning, had been confined to the west side. This would have been bad enough—about a third of the town lay on the west bank—but it might have meant that most of the people, at least, had managed to cross the river to safety.

"Jed, wait," Britta called. He heard and came back.

"A lot of that shooting sounds like it's aimed this way."

"It does," I said. "We can't just ride in there. Let's track back south, this side of the river, and then cross over."

We trotted past several rows of houses, all burnt out. Some were of stone, with the roofs gone and blackened holes where the windows and doors had been; others had been wood and were now only piles of charred beams and smoking debris. These fires must have been set soon after darkness, the day before, to have largely burned themselves out by now.

We did not see any bodies, outside on the streets at any rate. As we continued, we began to pass a good number of houses that the dunters had not torched.

"Lily's house?" Britta asked me. She meant my older sister, who lived on this side of the river. Her home was back in the direction we had come from.

"It's probably gone," I said.

We came upon a mill on the river which had not been touched. I knew there was a bridge behind it. We approached.

"Easy," I said. "We'll be in view of the wall on the other side of this building. They may be shooting at anything."

But before we could turn the corner around the mill, a man stepped out of it.

"Look—" Jed said, fearing a dunter, but caught himself. It was the miller, an older man named Sennet.

"Aiman," he said. "You all made it through. We've been worried about you."

"We just rode in."

"Watch yourselves." He nodded once as he said this. I noticed

29

that his hands and shirt were blackened with ash. He was a strong man, still clear-eyed after a long night, but exhausted.

"We've finally gotten up on the walls," he said, "and we're shooting. But it sounds like it's dying down—maybe the beasts have left."

"What happened?"

He raised his arm and pointed past us. "They came in from the west overnight. We heard a few shots, first, and then everything erupted. Have you seen many?"

"Only one."

"It's actually a blessing they stopped to burn as much as they did, I think. It gave people time to run. Crowds made it across the river to the walls. My family did."

"There was no resistance to them on this side?"

"No time," he answered. "People just woke up and fled, if they were lucky. I don't know how so many dunters moved across those plains without being seen by anyone. Friends of ours out there are sparse, I know, but a few must have seen them coming. And we had at least some people like yourselves scouting, as well. I'm afraid this army just overran dozens of farmers out there."

"They must have come in like a storm," Jed said.

"So they did."

"Your mill has not been touched?"

"The wall was manned by the time the dunters made it this far," he said. "I'm lucky I'm within range of it. A few shots kept them away. They came no closer than up that street, there. Their advance in town was slow, but I don't know how they came out here from their sties unseen in the first place."

"Caranniam and Varenlend," I said, "may have had a hand in covering their movements. They could manage that, I think. The wizards, Sennet, are working with Red Gorge. We learned this while we were out."

"The men of Caranniam? And Varenlend too? Were they part of this? I saw only dunters."

"Perhaps they are holding back," I said, "but they are allied with them."

"Allied?"

"Yes. We have learned this."

"Treachery from Varenlend," he said. "They had been holding

themselves out to be our neighbors."

"We need to find the councilors, Sennet."

"Let me help you get across the river," he said. "Here, wait a moment."

"You needn't—"

But he stepped inside the mill and then came out with an empty flour sack. He walked to the edge of his building nearest the bridge, and waved the sack around the corner a few times. He then peered out.

"Friends!" he shouted.

"Sennet, be careful."

"Follow me," he said. He walked out, still waving the sack. We followed on our horses. The bridge across the river was only a dozen yards long, and the city wall was not far beyond that on the far bank. We could see sentries clearly.

"We see you, miller," one of them called down.

He lowered the sack.

"I leave you here, then," he said to us.

The gate into the wall was offset from the road across the bridge. We rode closer to it, and the sentry called down again.

"Aiman, Britta. It's good news you've returned. Jed. Many were concerned about you."

"Who is this?" Jed called up. He squinted.

"Bollard. You know me from the ferry, Jed." He was a large young man, standing with his musket resting on a merlon. "Do you think they have pulled back? I don't hear much from them."

"Perhaps. We only saw one," I said.

"I'm not sure why they retreated, if they did. I'm afraid we didn't do them much damage. As far as I could see."

"Perhaps they didn't want to take on those walls," I said.

"I suppose not. They brought no cannons."

"So these walls were worthwhile," I said.

"Indeed. They paid for themselves today. I knew you would be glad about that, Aiman."

The council of Emmervale had debated restoring the walls for a long time, and it had been only within the past five years that the project had been completed. In the thirty years our people spent in Stenhall, many sections had deteriorated. Gates and sentry towers had been burned. Those who had spoken against their repair had said we were one hundred years too late; cannon could pulverize them. My father had supported the effort to build them, however, and now it was clear to me that he had been right. He had always said it was unlikely any invaders would haul heavy artillery along, if they chose to attack us, since there was so much empty land around us to cross.

"Can you have that gate opened?" I asked.

"Yes, but I think we are coming out ourselves." The wooden gate jolted and creaked, then. It swung open, and a handful of men on foot emerged.

The leader was Jens, a white-haired older council member who was well known to many of us. He was a mathematics teacher in a primary school. He barged forward, cradling an enormous wide-barreled musket.

"Gentlemen, and Britta," he said. His voice rasped, and his eyes were as tired as Sennet's had been. He barely looked like the calm teacher I remembered. "You're a welcome sight. We are going to sweep the city. The word has been passed to other gates also. It's good you're still on your horses. Join us."

"You made it behind the wall," I said. I knew that his house was on the west edge of town. "Did Ava?" This was his wife.

"She did. She still has some speed when need be, it turns out."

"How did you manage it?"

"The dunters made a racket, and they stopped at every home, every yard, to sack. They made off with hogs, milk cows, whatever they could lead or carry. And of course they burned, which took them time," he said grimly. "At many houses they would load up their kobold servants with our animals, and whatever else, while they themselves stayed to light fires. Let's move."

We crossed the bridge again and passed the mill. Sennet again came out. He and Jens spoke as more men and women issued from the gate.

"We need to get on with this," Britta said. "They may not have left. We'll have to flush them out if not."

"Let's tell him," I said.

We rode up and spoke to our old teacher. He took leave of Sennet and motioned for lines of people to move up different streets.

We moved north, first, along the river, while others spread into lanes that eventually led out of town to the west. As we guided our horses near the riverbank we passed three untouched houses but then the blackened ruins of another. A few more burnt houses, and then we came to a dry goods warehouse that had a dock on the river. It was smoking, and damaged, but still intact; a rolling pump had been moved up next to it, along the street side of the building, and was spraying water into the bottom floor through open windows. It was a hand pumper, and three men on each side worked its bars furiously.

We continued down the street, and now came upon another group which had been heading south from another gate.

"Aiman!" someone shouted; I recognized my sister Lily's voice. She ran through the crowd.

Her face was smeared, and she looked shocked, still, but she was unharmed. She pulled her hair back out of her eyes.

"You're safe," she said. I should have been worrying about her, not the other way around, since she was the one whose house had likely burned. But she spoke with relief and set her hand on my knee.

"We didn't know if you would be caught behind their lines," she said.

"We were not touched," I said. "What of Bron? And the children?"

"All well. Bron is up ahead, and the children at Father's, for now."

"The dunters didn't reach the farm, then? No one came down from the north?"

"No," she said. "My house is gone, but we have lost nothing else. The farm is whole. Not a sheep harmed."

This seemed to be good news, to her.

I pulled her up behind me. We rode to her home, picking our way along through the flattened streets. Formerly we would have passed by the fine house and shop of Sol White, a carpenter; and a row of narrow homes belonging to three of his sons; and also a large chicken house of a neighbor of Lily's. All were now destroyed. And then we saw that she had been right in her guess; her own house was burned to the ground. It had been lovely: a sprawling cottage of thick planks of ironwood, varnished red against the weather, surrounded by flower boxes and vegetable plots.

"Did you manage to take anything out?"

"Coats, each of us. We didn't even have time to find sacks. Bron took our strongbox. For once I am glad it is small." She smiled bitterly at this.

"Did you see them?"

"I did not. I ran out first, with Gaya. I held her hand. Then the boys, then Bron. Bron said he saw the dunters further down our lane. He said they seemed very methodical, torching the homes one by one. They let the people run, from what I have heard."

"I wonder why."

"People are thinking that they came to take supplies, more than kill. They carried off a great deal, everyone says."

"A great deal," I repeated. "They wouldn't need that much meat on the hoof if they were just raiding. It sounds like they intend to stay."

I rode across a good part of this side of Emmervale before heading back across the river to our farm. The large majority of the houses were burned. Numbers of people were making their way back, now, to see what had survived, and most were disappointed. Men, women, and older children picked through the remains of their homes—whatever remains were cool enough to touch—but could find little. From them I heard similar stories: they had managed to run, in time, but had mostly lost their homes. Any livestock they had maintained in their yards were gone. People in town did not have the number of animals that the farmers outside of it did, of course, but everything they did have had been taken. Horses, hogs; milk cows here and there. Later I learned that the farms outside town had been sacked in this way also.

And there had been deaths. Just as Lily had said, the dunters had apparently come with the intention of stealing, not massacring the town, but some of us did not survive the night. Burning homes collapsed on a dozen or more, mostly elders who did not hear the disturbance or were not able to flee in time. Several men who had confronted the dunters in the streets had been struck down, also. For our part, we had killed at least thirty of them, mostly in the shooting from atop the walls. Their corpses were dragged through the streets to a grave that was dug outside town. I assisted with this. The dunters were like those we had seen out near the tracks, with large noses and unbelievable teeth. The ones with their lids still up showed red eyes.

Later that day, in the afternoon, riders of ours brought word that the dunters had not removed themselves too far from our lands. They had set up a camp no more than a few hours' ride from our westernmost farms.

One of these men who had viewed the camp was Bollard. He spoke with us as we all strained to clear a street of the remains of a fallen warehouse, toward sunset. He had ridden up to us straight from his foray, dismounted, and set to work rolling a burnt beam off to the side. It was a long day of hard labor for all the town.

"How many would you say there are?" I asked.

"Perhaps two thousand. I did not linger to count. And there are some large tents in among them. The dunters seem to be just a crowd, a swarm, with no protection from the weather at all, that we could see. But there are fine white tents there also. Those are set at one edge of the camp."

"Those would be the personnel from the cities," Jed said.

"I assume so," I answered.

"The cities?" Bollard asked. "Caranniam and Varenlend?"

"Yes. While we were away, we learned that they are in on this plan of the dunters."

"So it's true. They are working together?" He paused, holding a blackened timber. "It must be the mages who have written the plan, I should think. That explains how the dunters came up with anything this ambitious."

"I wonder," Jed said, "if that trader, Ralenda, knew that this force was out here. If she knew it all along while she was speaking with us, but withheld it for some reason."

"I doubt it," I said. "She was so open with us. I think she would have mentioned this had she known. She would have told us to hurry back. It also seemed she didn't realize the wizards had joined in, yet. But that must be who is in those white tents."

"Perhaps including those who came to see you, years ago," Jed said.

"Perhaps."

Bollard shook his head. "We're up against something quite serious, then."

"More serious than this?" I asked, gesturing at the burnt ruins all around us. "But yes, we could well be."

The following day was one of more cleanup, and of burials. We posted armed sentries on the west side of town, but no dunters appeared. The previous night I had returned to our house to stay with my father. Lily, Bron, and their children had also moved in. Our farm was untouched, including our sheep. There at my childhood home and in the quiet pastures it seemed unreal that such a disaster had befallen, just a long walk away.

Our house was on the north side of town, as I have said; on the outskirts, just where the fields and pastures began their gentle rise up to eventually reach the foothills of the mountains. We were the edge, by our estimation and everyone else's. "Past the Shearers" was a local term that meant anything north of the town of Emmervale. There were a few more families who lived further up the rise, but they were considered frontiersmen. We enjoyed living close to people, but not shoulder to shoulder with them.

"Anyone who lives farther out than we do is a misanthropic hermit," my father liked to joke, "and anyone who lives farther in is an insecure worrywart."

Of course we needed to be on the edge of town to have grazing for the sheep. One might wonder if our fondness for open space developed because we depended on it in this way, or if our family chose sheep herding because we enjoyed the solitude.

That night I took a horse and rode out to see the dunter camp. I did not expect to learn anything that Bollard had not, or that any others among our scouts had not already observed, but I wanted to see for myself. Despite my contact with the mass of dunters out by the rail line, and their frantic kobolds, and the elves, their presence here still seemed unbelievable. I saw them burn Emmervale but I could still barely grasp that they were so close.

It was less than two hours' ride to the camp. I had expected to see scores of bonfires, and huddles of dunter faces lit by flames, but there was little of that. The dunters, I remembered now, could get along with very few comforts, and would have thought nothing of enduring endless cold nights. Then again, it was good enough weather now to sleep outside. Next to the white tents of the men in the camp, though, I did see a few fires. I wondered who might be around them. It might well have been some of the visitors who had come to us from Varenlend, seven years earlier. Sokran might be too old for the adventure, by now, but Annira and Annelle could be there.

I rode closer. Rahune and Rahira were both visible in the sky, this night, and both half full, so I could see well even without the fires. The dunter army spread out before me, a black mass against the gray nighttime fields. It was ominously large. At a few hundred yards away I could see pens they had built for our livestock they had stolen. Individual dunters were visible, sitting idly or going about errands. Spilling out around the edges of the main dunter mob were knots of kobolds who seemed tirelessly busy even at night.

I turned my horse. Our new neighbors looked to have set themselves down for a long stay.

The day after that, the Council of Emmervale convened. By ancient tradition—and when I say "ancient," I mean since we returned to the town, thirty years earlier—the Council met in the brewery. This was not meant to devalue the Council; the brewer had simply had the largest room available, back when the body was established. The original man's daughter, a councilor named Thona Hopper, continued the tradition today. She was the Meeting Master, for the assembly, but not its leader. The Council had no leader, in the custom of Emmervale. The forty councilors sat on benches amid the many barrels in the warm brick room. The meeting smelled of fermented grain. There was loud chatter.

But then Thona stood and announced:

"We commence."

Instantly the room quieted.

Councilors spoke in turn. Several from the west side of town, and from the western farms, spoke of their losses. Father—who was a councilor too, as was I, owing to our heritage—spoke about the dunter army. He gestured toward me.

"Aiman has seen them, as have some others of you. And you all have heard by now what Aiman was told: that this dunter army has come to attack Stenhall, first. But we know that this alliance of wizards and dunters will not tolerate a free Emmervale if they do defeat the dwarves. We must decide if we should attempt to remove them."

And with that, there was silence. The councilors mostly shifted on their benches and shook their heads. My father understood how hard it would be for us to attack the dunter army; I think he just wanted to be sure all of us were thinking the same way.

"But Anders, could we possibly push them out?" someone asked.

"We don't have the numbers, if they are two thousand," another answered.

"I would say they are many more than two thousand," I said.

"Very well," my father said. "It seems we agree. I am afraid we do not have the power to remove them." Emmervale was not large. We were growing, but we would be lucky to muster a thousand men at arms. Decades after the plagues, and the consequent explosion of dragons, we were still living the effects of those disasters. Our numbers had not yet recovered. There was a time long ago when we people of the eastern mountains would have smashed any dunters who dared come near, but now we were unable to respond. And now the dunters had guns and steam engines.

"If we won't attack, we have to defend," another councilor said. "I know many of us are passing nights awake as sentries, but we are not organized. I do not think anyone here could even tell us how many guard posts we have. I don't think anyone could really say if there is a system to raise a general defense, if need be, either. We have to organize."

This was all true. The Emmervale council worked together to run what needed to be run, in the town, but there was no military command. Such tasks as restoring the wall, as I have mentioned, had been a group decision. The council had hired the masons and overseen the work, but after it was complete nobody in particular had remained with any power over the wall.

"We have no captain in charge of our fortifications," this councilor continued. "No one in charge of defense in general, either. It's just as well we cannot attack their camp; we have no one who could organize the push."

Sennet, the miller, stood.

"We have many who could," he said. "We need one man, or one woman, to direct everyone, or at least direct our muskets. Until this danger is over."

I had attended these meetings for a few years, but had rarely said anything. This idea, though, I had to respond to. I stood and spoke.

"We have this council, not a hero. This is Emmervale. Our grandparents did not work so hard to return here, to a free town, just to see one ruler take over. They could have stayed with the dwarves if they had wanted that."

"Do not compare me to a dwarf," Sennet said.

"Come, Sennet, I am not," I said.

"And regarding our grandparents, and what they set up for us," he said, "they also did not lead themselves out of those dwarf halls all on their own. They had a leader. You know this better than anyone, Aiman."

"That was different," I answered. "Back then, in the mines, they could not call meetings. All was secret. One man had to do most of the plotting on his own, and take charge, or we would still be up there in that mountain today." That man, of course, had been The Marshal, my grandfather. "But that was an exigency. Now we're better off by sharing our ideas. Putting our heads together."

"We don't have time for that any longer," a woman said. I recognized her as one of those from the west side of town; her house had likely burned. The group rumbled assent to this.

"These torches," another councilor said, "these guns to our heads, change things. We make good decisions, here, but we're not able to act quickly."

"And we know that Caranniam and Varenlend are not going to waste their time having meetings like ours, before they decide to attack again," another added. "We have to be as nimble as they are."

Sennet spoke again, with a tone indicating he intended to prod us forward. "Let's elect a captain of the militia, then. He, or she, will answer to us."

"Very well," I said. "But let's call this person the dunter boss, or maybe the rail wrecker. This way it's clear that the job lasts only as long as the dunter threat."

"No one is going to be very proud of having a title like that," Sennet said.

"I know, and that's all to the good. One more reason for the person to drop the job as soon as possible."

"Very well, then," Thona said. "We will break for a few moments and talk. We will return and select a dunter boss. A rail wrecker."

Outside the brewery I saw my father take his leave from a group of other councilors. I joined him. He looked grim.

I asked him:

"Who do you guess this captain will be?"

He shrugged. "Bollard might do it. Sennet could; he is an organized man. We need to make sure it is a person with a sound livelihood, so there will be no temptation to perpetuate the post."

"Indeed."

"Or it may be you, Aiman."

"Or you, father."

He shook his head. "They don't need an old sheep herder."

"But a young one is ideal?" I asked.

"My irreverent son," he said. "We shall see. But you have to wonder how long this will last."

"This dunter siege?" I asked. "If this is a siege?"

"No, I mean our system. Our council. We are unusual, you know. An odd bird. Most cities through the ages have had a single ruler, one way or another. And this, here, what we're seeing now, is precisely why: there is a crisis, when quick decisions need to be made, and then one person gets into power and stays there. Or one family. The only reason we are not that way already is that the rule of the dwarves over us was so distasteful. Our ancestors valued their voices. All of them."

"I know."

"Your grandfather was lucky; his reputation was safe because there was no way he could seize power. No one would have stood for it. People tell stories of how he was committed to the council, and willingly gave up his leadership, but he really had no choice. The people would have bound him and thrown him out into the hills had he tried to just replace the dwarves and become another king.

"But there will be fewer and fewer left who will have memories of living under the dwarves. Eventually, few will have the old qualms about being told what to do. Someday a wise captain will come along, and people will appreciate the leadership, and that will be the end of the council. And the first one who succeeds in being such a leader may be very good and wise, you understand. He'll have to be, or the people will desert him. It's not him I worry about; it's those who come after."

"Well, there are still enough who do remember the dwarf rule," I said. "That will be a fight for another generation, I hope. Not ours.

"And this world is changing," I added. "There are trains, there are schools. One person will be less and less able to run everything. No single person will have the knowledge."

"Perhaps. Who knows what you'll see, Aiman."

"Enough to make me forget these dunters, one day? I wonder."

Once back inside, the council took nominations for dunter boss. The group variously called upon my father, Thona, my old friend Bollard, and others. And some nominated me.

Before anyone could suggest a vote, I noticed many faces turned toward me; and then most of them, and then all of them.

"Aiman, I think the council's wish is clear," Bollard said.

I shook my head.

"With your leave, I would do other work," I said. "I have a plan I think we need to execute. And I want to do it."

"All the more reason for you to be the dunter boss," Bollard said.

I shook my head again. "There is too much for one person. Listen," I said. "How is this: I accept, but I will take the title of rail wrecker and pass along the other one. Thona, you can run a brewery. You can also run our defense. I move that you become the dunter boss."

Now many of the faces in the room turned toward her.

"I will do it," Thona said, "if you have your plan. What is it?"

"To speak with the dwarves," I said. "Try to rouse them. Would any of you rather do that yourselves?"

No one volunteered, and most showed clear distaste. They lowered their eyes and again shifted on their benches. A few coughed and cleared throats in the silence.

"What could you have to say to Stenhall?" Sennet asked.

"I will explain. But first, the titles. I'll need one to do my work. So, do we have a Dunter Boss and a Rail Wrecker?"

The council debated a bit more but eventually agreed. We departed, leaving all the beer to continue fermenting in peace.

Later I spoke with Thona, Bollard, and my father.

"So what is this message you take to the dwarves?" my father asked. "I suppose I am proud of you for coming up with such a forward idea without running it by me first."

"I should have raised it with you, Father, I know. But I believe we have to tell them about this. Tell the dwarves. I mean about the alliance between Caranniam and Varenlend, and that railroad coming for them."

"Will they believe you?"

I shrugged. "We have to try, regardless. If they take any action, it will help us."

"What do you expect them to do? Withdraw from their lowermost gallery and lock themselves in further back?"

"Yes, I know it's unlikely they would ever do much more than simply wall themselves up in their tunnels. And they are certainly not going to lift a finger to aid us. But it can't hurt to inform them what we've seen."

"I'm sure they've had a grand view of half of our town on fire," my father said.

"But the railway, they don't know about that. They might act."

"Act? By doing what?"

"Well, let me speak with them first."

"Aiman, think," he said. "You know that their entire lives, all their decisions, are based on just living apart. And protecting their own."

"I know, Father. But we can't be sure what they'll do. This is unprecedented in our lifetimes, or even The Marshal's. When is the last time anyone declared intent to march on Stenhall? It's worth a trip up there."

Three

Britta, Jed and I walked up to attempt to speak with the dwarves the next day.

Stenhall lay a few hours' ride north of town, up through our family's vale and then across an expanse of rocky foothills. After the days of discussions and fear in town, it was good to get out. The grass was now dotted with spring flowers, yellow and white. I felt guilty for enjoying the clean and quiet views, but out here it was difficult to worry too much about the dunter camp. We climbed up the gentle slope, eventually leaving Emmervale far behind and somewhat below us. From this distance the burnt dwellings on the west side of town—well, they could still be seen, if an observer out here was looking for them, but they were not so obvious. They might have been missed altogether by someone unaware of what had happened.

I spent the ride telling Britta and Jed about the talk of the council the day before.

"Rail wrecker, is it?" Jed said. "Will you make yourself a seal with this on it?"

"I won't hold the post long enough to need anything like that."

Britta, as usual, was more serious:

"So Caranniam and Varenlend both have forces with that dunter mob."

"It seems so," I said.

"You know where I am going," she said.

"Of course."

"If you had lived years in Varenlend, they would have kept the dunters away from us, now. They would have—" she tossed her head— "invited us to join them, more likely."

"You can hardly think that would be a good—"

"Of course not," she said. "But the world would be a different one."

"It's long past," I said.

Jed spoke.

"Aiman, do you see movement, up that hill? Just a few specks?"

We were up now on an incline that had little vegetation. Jed had good eyes. I scanned the rock and crevasses.

"I don't. Britta?"

"I see nothing either," she answered. "Are you certain, Jed?"

"Yes. Something coming down toward us. Several things, I should say."

"Well, let's keep going," I said. "We can outrun them if need be. If it were a wyvern it would have taken wing already."

"It's no wyvern."

"Is it dwarves? Coming to see us?"

"It could be. It's been a long time since they've sought us out, though, hasn't it?"

"A very long time."

We continued ahead and soon I could see the figures, working their way down.

"Definitely dwarves," Jed said. "And they have an animal, hauling something. I think they're pulling a sledge."

Soon I could see it, also. Three low shapes—the dwarves—bobbed around a mule and its load. They dropped down the hillside in fits and starts.

"What's on that?"

"Some carcass. It's bigger than a stag."

"Did they kill an ansark?"

"Perhaps. Why would they be hauling it down here?"

Our two groups neared each other. The dwarves did not slow down as they came closer. They were thick and powerful, swaying side to side on posts of legs as they descended. All three had shoulders as wide as a wheelbarrow lengthwise.

They looked so much alike that it seemed to me they could have all been brothers; and this struck me even when they had come up to stand directly before us. They had similar eyes, dark hair, long beards. Each dwarf wore a wide leather skullcap, black in every case. Only their jackets differed; two of them wore dark brown, and the third, simply a lighter shade of the color. This one carried a musketoon slung over a shoulder. This is a short weapon we in Emmervale refer to as a mountain gun, since it is common among dwarves. The other two wore axes at their belts. One of them led the mule, and the other two walked behind the sledge holding onto ropes that were tied to its rear. Parts of the slope were steep enough that they would have to be cautious about the sledge slipping forward and crushing their mule.

They smelled, of course, like dwarves. Their scent always struck me: leather, and smoke, and deep sweat mixed with stone and dust. The mortar of bricklayers was one thing that always reminded me of dwarves. And they smelled of age. These were old stonecutters before us, each of them likely with more years than the three of us combined.

On the sledge was the dead body of an ansark. It was a large one, the jaws of its long head looking perhaps two feet wide. The mouth lolled open, displaying the razor teeth. It was on its back, tied to the sledge, its four thick legs sticking up in the air. Enough of the fur on its sides was exposed to show the well-defined gray and brown stripes of a mature adult.

The dwarf with the musketoon nodded toward the animal.

"I am Hrond. We took down this beast up in the hills. A bit east of here. Not so far away from your sheep grazing."

I was taken aback at this.

"You know I raise sheep?"

"I meant your town's. But if they are yours, all the better. You have respectable flocks. You won't want this out there." He gestured at the dead ansark.

"Indeed not," I said. "Thank you. I am Aiman Shearer. This is Jedrek, of the house of Blackwater, and my cousin Britta, also Shearer." The dwarves had not seemed concerned about introductions, but then Hrond did ask:

"Shearers, both of you?"

"Yes."

"Very well." He nodded again toward the carcass. "This was a large one."

"Certainly. You brought it down by musket, I presume?"

"Yes. Not even we relish getting close enough to one of these to dispatch it with spears. It was several muskets. I was there, but the other hunters have returned."

I had assumed that they had intended to haul the thing down into the valley, for whatever reason, but now they seemed to regard their journey as complete. One of the two in back moved up to the sledge and pulled a knife to cut a cord that bound the ansark. They did not speak. I found it curious.

"And what," I asked, "are you going to do with it now?"

"Leave it here for the wolves. This mule will be glad to be free of it." He took a step back to watch his companions both place a boot on the dead animal, now, to push it off the sledge. "We don't eat ansark steaks. I don't know if you do."

"No."

"You are hunting, yourselves?" he asked me.

"No. We were coming up to speak with you."

All three looked at us, then. The two behind Hrond froze, each with a boot still on the ansark. Their faces instantly became more guarded, if this was possible for these dwarves with heavy eyebrows and beards up to their cheekbones.

"Speak with us? Concerning what?"

"This force of dunters camped out beneath your foothills."

"Of course we have seen them," Hrond said. "And it looks to us more like they are camped outside your town. We don't believe we are their target. We saw that they did much damage to you already."

"They did, yes. But we have learned that they plan much more yet, directed at all of us," I said.

"How can you know that?"

"We have spoken with someone from Varenlend who knows. A trader I meet with. And Varenlend and Caranniam are both involved, we have learned."

We shared what we had been told by Ralenda, days ago out by the tracks: the alliance, the railroad, the elves. The dwarves listened with a tilt to their heads and a squint in their eyes that told me they were skeptical; but they were gravely silent all the while.

"And this trader was certain that the dunters are coming for Stenhall?" Hrond asked.

"That's what she said. And she seemed to be in a position to know. She had magic."

"She did? What sort?"

"She made us invisible. Jed, here, and me."

"Well, then. We might assume she knows of what she speaks. Mightn't we." He shook his head and continued:

"We will blast them down the hills. We will blast them all the way back to Red Gorge."

"They seem to be preparing for that," I said. "This is quite a collaboration of theirs, with those cities and the dunters as well."

"And the elves," Hrond added. "I was not surprised to hear you say that, Master Shearer. We have always known they would take whatever opportunity against us they could, and this seems a good one for them." He nodded once and scowled.

"So this is what you were coming to tell us?" he asked.

"Yes. And to ask you to make a plan with us. With all these powers lining up against our vale, and these hills, we should coordinate." I nodded further uphill, in the direction of Stenhall. "Begging your pardon, we were hoping for an audience with your leaders. Perhaps Ghranam, if we might."

"Speech to us is speech to us all," Hrond said, indicating himself and his two companions with a flick of his hand. "I don't doubt the gravity in all this, but what would you propose? With all respect for your new town—" he regarded Emmervale, now a full generation removed from our time indentured to his people, as still a "new" venture— "your numbers are not sufficient, even with ours, to hold off the cities and the dunters. If this is indeed their plan."

"We want to hit their rail line," I said. "You are right, we could not defeat all of them out in the open. But if we can break their line, even before it starts, that could save us."

"They would just repair it. Build it back."

"But that would give us time. Time for you to speak with White Mount, and for us to ally with Searose or others."

He considered this. The other two stood silent by the ansark.

"This would be a war of all the North," he then said. "Everyone involved." He shook his head. "No more time for the dwarves to isolate themselves in their halls and watch the winds blow down below, eh?"

"That may be the size of it, sir."

"Well. We will want to confirm all this ourselves."

"I'm sure."

"We have eyes of our own, and ears. And many who would want to be heard, about this." He straightened, now, and adjusted the musketoon's strap over his shoulder. "But I take you seriously, Aiman. Aiman Shearer." He showed a slight smile. "I believe you should have taken the name Marshalson, young man."

"I shear," I said. "And people know well enough who I am."

"I am sure they do. Off with it," he said; this was to the other two. With their boots they shoved the ansark off the sledge. It rolled over and hit the ground, belly down. It had one bullet hole in the side of its head, and at least two others in its back. Its eyes were open. Even in death it looked wild, threatening, ready to tear a horse in half with its crusher jaws.

"We will send word," Hrond said. "I will send it, at least, no matter our answer."

This was all. He took the lead of the mule and the three of them headed back up the slope.

We were left with the dead predator.

"Big one," Jed said. This was an understatement, but someone had to say something in the silence.

"Quite." I nudged its snout with my boot.

"I don't understand why they brought this thing to us," he said. "It's good they took one down, of course. But what were they doing? Giving us some sort of spring gift? A dead ansark?"

"I don't know, either," I answered him. "Are they feeling concern for us? That seems unusual for them. But I don't know what else it would be. Do they feel they should have come down during the fire, and this is their way of making some sort of effort, late? I don't know."

"And these things are just as likely to take their hogs," Britta added, "as our livestock. They know we know that. It's not as if they were out here hunting for our benefit."

"Certainly," I said. "Well, I delivered the message. Now we wait."

"What do you think they'll say?" Britta asked.

"He seemed to take us seriously," I said. "I was actually glad he was as skeptical as he was. It shows he was listening."

"Do we come back up here in a day or two?" Jed asked. "To get their response?"

"I'm not going to do that," I said. "I'm not desperate for their help, and don't want to appear so. They can find us."

We waited two days. We did not have the numbers to attack the dunters alone, but at the same time no one in town was much inclined to flee. For one thing, Emmervale was surrounded by barren mountains on all sides but our west. We had never before seen this isolation as a problem; no one had believed the dunters would bother reaching out this far east. But now many were regretting that we had no easy escape route.

We sent messengers to Searose, although we were grim about the odds of those coast people taking an interest in our plight.

"We should have been reaching out more, all these years," Britta said. "We could use alliances with other people. Searose, or the peoples to the south on the coast. Or some of the vassal towns to Varenlend or Caranniam, even. Anyone, anywhere in the Open Lands. We should not be alone the way we are."

"Well, Varenlend tried to forge ties," I said. This was grim humor, of course.

"I mean partnerships, not exploitation," she said. "We've been busy rebuilding Emmervale these three decades, but we should have made time for relations."

"We should not criticize ourselves too much, Britta," I said, seriously now. "All those places you mention have been rebuilding, themselves. Not even Searose escaped the plague. We would have found poor pickings for any grand alliance of our own, even if we had tried."

On the third day after we had spoken with Hrond on the hillside, he showed himself at my father's house. He came in the morning, alone, and announced himself to my niece Gaya, who was picking early greens in the garden. She was a very self-possessed ten-year-old, now, and told us of our visitor with a calm that made us all stop eating our breakfast and wait for her to repeat herself.

"A dwarf has come here?" my father asked.

"This must be an answer to our walk up the mountain," I said. I rose as she brought him into our house.

It was Hrond. He was wearing his brown coat again, but had left his musketoon behind. His shoulders stretched across our hallway.

A dwarf in our house: I would not have guessed such a visit might ever happen. We were all silent, perhaps to the point of rudeness, but Hrond pressed ahead.

"Pardon me, Aiman. I hope I find you well. And you would be Anders Shearer," he said to my father.

"Yes."

"I have been sent to speak to you about your proposal."

"Very good," I said. I motioned him to come in. "May I offer you tea?"

"No thank you."

"Will you sit down?"

"I will not stay long. Thank you for this welcome into your home. I have another question. You've seen this railroad?"

"I have."

"Personally. Very good, then. We will help you take it down."

"All right," I said. I had expected tougher questioning. "That is good news."

"Yes, well. Some of our blasters, our tunnel-borers, are always glad for more work. When shall we go?"

He was not dawdling. Fortunately I had been mulling over the timing.

"On one hand," I said, "we have been thinking we might give it another week, or two. That would give them awhile longer to build more of their line, so we would have more targets. And that would also mean that they would have poured more time and work into it. But of course we can't wait too long. Their army hasn't raided us again, but they're still out there."

"And where were you planning on striking that line?"

"As far west as we can safely go, without getting too close to Red Gorge City. We hope to find a place between the city and their army that is unwatched. It shouldn't be difficult. I was able to ride out there once myself already, and we've had more scouts make it through."

"They continue to lay the track?"

"Nonstop," I said. "With their kobold labor, and the elves still riding out to them with the steel."

"Elves," he said. He shook his head.

I was surprised by something:

"Hrond, I must ask—you have not been out there yourself? Or others from Stenhall?"

"No. We take your word for it. And of course we can see that expedition of theirs they are trying to link up with."

"I admit, some of us assumed you would need to see the tracks yourselves before you agreed to assist."

He shrugged. "If we hike out and find nothing, we can hike back. We're not going to allow ourselves to get waylaid by dunters.

We don't intend to leave this world that easily, Master Shearer."

"I'm sure. We will need to meet to lay plans, then. We'll want to bring a small party, and I would guess you will do the same."

"Yes. But I have been sent to complete all plans. We would propose meeting one week from tonight along the remains of the old road that led from our west down to the Kurtenvold. You know it."

"Yes."

"And the track is there? It stretches at least that far east from Red Gorge?"

"Yes. Actually it now comes even closer to us than that."

"Very good. At full night, in one week. The intersection of the railway and the old road. We will approach from the north. If there are dunters guarding the tracks in that spot, we will meet as far north along that road as need be."

"Good. And what will you need me to bring?"

He shrugged. "Yourselves. We shall bring supplies to ruin a good length of their tracks. The dwarf you will meet there is named Maghran."

Maghran: he rolled the *gh* in the back of his throat. It was a fine dwarven name.

Four

I emerged from the trees into the moonslight. Rahira had barely cleared the horizon, but Rahune was high and nearly full. I saw
the dwarf sitting up on the train tracks. Next to him were bags,
which I knew held the explosives. The days since my meeting with
Hrond had passed slowly, with all of us in town feeling we were
nearly in the sights of the dunters. I walked to him quickly.

"You would be Maghran," I said. I did not bother with any
greeting beyond this—he had seen me approaching.

"I would. Master Shearer," he answered.

"Yes."

I stood directly before him now, two heads taller but perhaps
half as broad in the shoulders. I held out my hand.

"Thank you for meeting me," I said.

He clasped my hand. I am sorry to say that I jolted, somewhat,
because I realized he was missing a finger. He held up the hand; the
smallest was indeed gone.

"Lost in the trade," he said. "Hope you don't mind."

"Of course not," I said.

"We were diggers, once. Now we are blasters as well. I could
greet with my left, but that's no improvement," he said. He held up
that hand, and it too was short a finger, or most of one—the point-
er in this case. He nodded down toward his explosives. "There's the
problem. But they have not taken the rest of me yet. Let's move.
We should have met farther down the rail line."

"This is where it was arranged."

"I know, for the landmark. But further down there is a fine target. You've seen your spotters?"

"A few times."

"And I've seen mine." Both of us had companions along who
had been walking well ahead of us, and on our flanks, scouting for
dunters. Jed and Britta, once again, were mine. They had signaled
to me a few times in the night; all was clear. "We should move
down some distance to a bridge. We have the space open before
us."

"A bridge?"

"Yes. It will slow them down much more. It's not far, we have time. Can you take these?" He picked up a shovel, and also a battle axe that had been lying between the rails. "I'll take the bags."

The axe was a cruel but beautiful thing, sharp and broad with etchings and runes. "You trust me with this?" I asked him.

"More than I would with what I'm carrying."

Without further words he started down the tracks, westward. I followed him. His hair flowed down over his almost impossibly wide back. His boots stomped along the ties.

I wondered what my grandfather, the Marshal, would have thought of the scene. Not so much the railroad, that's not what I mean; the Marshal had been an educated man of science, and I'm sure he would have listened along intently as I explained the mechanics of mounting a steam engine on a carriage. I mean the scene of this dwarf and me sweating together all night to collaborate on this operation. The Marshal had led the return to Emmervale, a move made precisely in order to remove us from the thrall of the dwarves.

And here I was, his grandson, carrying my comrade Maghran's axe for him so it would not continually bump up against the canvas bags of explosives. I think—indeed I hope, for the sake of my pride —that Grandfather would have understood the urgency of our times. Those who remained free now had to unite.

"Lovely steel here," Maghran told me. He walked in front and barely twitched his head sideways to let me know he was speaking to me, and not just to himself. "It reflects the moons so beautifully." His voice was a growl, his bitterness clear.

"High quality from the elves, as usual," I answered him.

"As much antipathy as I hold for them," he said, "I still cannot believe that their Lord Silvermoor went through with this. They have always been insular; that's fine, so have we. They have never come to our aid, but again I understand this, for we have not aided them either. But to go out of their way to sell rails to dunters? I do not understand. They have surprised me, and I have not been surprised for a long time. A very long time."

"We were also shocked."

"And to do this when Red Gorge is expanding, and gaining the upper hand already. And when any being with eyes and ears knows that we are the next targets of their conquest." He shook his head. "After we blast these tracks, we may well blast the elven furnaces, and then blast the elves themselves."

"We understand."

"Have you done any demolitions before?" he asked.

"I have not, no."

"I don't suppose you have many opportunities," he said as he walked. "Yours is a quiet town. Well, it's not difficult. And we have enough power here that we don't need to be too particular about where it all goes. It's not like this in our quarries, you know. There, we need to be careful, because too much blasting reaches all the way to our halls. It can shift them, shake them. But here—we'll put on a show. Too bad only you and I will really see it. Perhaps our spotters will catch a view."

"What do you use, exactly? Regular blasting powder?"

"That's right." He nodded; I watched the back of his head bob up and down. "Have you heard of niter-glycerol?"

"I have, yes. A clear liquid."

"Very good. Not too many people know of it."

"I have been asking about what I might expect from dwarves. Ever since Hrond and I came to the agreement about this project."

"Very well. At any rate, we shall not use the glycerol. Too difficult to transport. Our regular powder will serve us quite well."

"We'll start soon?" I asked.

"We should be at the bridge in just a short while," he answered. "That will be harder for them to repair than just these open tracks."

"I understand."

I kept my eyes on the ties beneath my feet as I walked—and at this moment I came up upon Maghran and nearly strode into him. He had stopped.

"Look there," he said, just barely loudly enough for me to hear.

Far down the tracks I saw a gray shape, a blur in the night. Its movement was barely discernible, at first, and I wondered if it might be an animal. Soon its gait was obvious; two legs.

"Dunter," Maghran said. He pulled a knife and moved it behind his leg to conceal any gleam it might throw. "Lower yourself. You stick up like a sunflower."

I complied (and ever after knew a bit more about what dwarves thought of our appearance). Maghran lay down on the ground, also, his eyes not leaving the figure.

"I don't believe that's a dunter," I whispered. "Alone like that, so far out here."

"Who else might it be? Some Emmervaler out for a stroll?"

I didn't answer. The figure neared as we lay motionless.

"You may be right," Maghran allowed. "Looks like a man. In flight."

The person trotted quickly along the tracks. Soon it was clear that it was indeed a man, in tattered clothing.

"Safe to stand?" I asked.

"I have no fear of this one," Maghran answered.

We stood. The man continued to rush toward us, not running but picking his steps quickly and carefully along the tracks. He walked with his eyes down and did not notice us. He was almost near enough that I was about to call out to him to get his attention when he finally saw us and stopped.

"A dwarf and a man," he said to us, squinting to make us out.

"So we are," Maghran answered. "Where do you come from?"

"West of here. From east of Red Gorge City. And you?"

"Mountains, for my part, as you could guess," Maghran said. "What are you fleeing?"

"The dunters and this railway."

"Very well—why have you waited until now to flee it?"

"I've been a captive of those things," he said. "I had lived on the plains east of them, and they took me two months ago. When they started their line. I went to see what they were up to."

"What do you mean," I asked, "living on the plains?"

"Just as it sounds."

"No one lives there."

"Dunters do, now, and I did before that. I was alone, on a river bank. It suited me. But they caged me in one of their jails for these weeks. I slipped out when they forgot about me for a day."

"Good tidings for you," Maghran said.

"But not for you," he said. "They were distracted because they were celebrating these tracks. They are about to start this thing. Their locomotive will be along in a day. It may be straight behind me know, for all I know."

"You've seen the engine?"

"Yes. It's not much to see, don't get me wrong. But it will carry them out here."

"And it's ready?"

"They intend to start it this day. This is a festival day for them, do you know that?"

"Because of the train?"

"No, I mean a day in their calendar. Fire Day, they call it. From some ancient lore of theirs."

"I don't concern myself with dunter high days," Maghran said.

"But it means their train starts at dawn. They boasted to me of it, when I was in their cage. Through those teeth of theirs, I could still make out their words. When darkness fell, two nights ago, they began their rally. They intend to launch their train today, and conquer with this line." He nodded once. "They intend to conquer for and with this line."

"And then they let you go?"

He shook his head. "I forced the cage. It was the first time they had left me alone. I crept out and haven't stopped moving since. I did not linger, as you can imagine, but I did see immense fires. They'd had their kobolds hauling wood for days to fuel them."

He looked behind himself now, as if expecting to see the engine chasing him. He was haggard with flight, and wide-eyed with his story.

I was still struck by the life he had claimed before he had mentioned anything about the dunters.

"How long," I asked, "had you been living close to them?"

"Years," he said. "I fished, I gathered. The countryside there is spare, but one can live off it."

"Along the Walsing?"

"The Walsing," he repeated. "I always knew it as the Vacing, but yes."

"Have you been a holdover out there since the sickness? And the burnings?"

He shook his head. "I hope I don't look that old. But there are a few such persons."

"Where are you heading now?"

"East of Emmervale."

"My city."

"Is it? You know you are in their path."

"We have already been in their path."

"But you have come out this direction, instead of retreating toward the other. Well, you are braver than I. I must move along."

"You say you are bound east of Emmervale."

"Yes."

"You know there is nothing much east of there. Mountains, and wilds."

"I have no other direction to go, now."

"How are you eating?" I asked.

"Not well."

"Take this," I said. I pulled out a pack of food from my bag. "I am Aiman Shearer, of Emmervale. To the north of the city you'll find my father's farm. Anders Shearer. You can tell him I sent you, and he will put you up."

"Obliged," the man said. "Aiman Shearer, and Anders. Very well. I am Korben. I will call on your family, but I will not stay long. Farewell. And I would take care of myself near these tracks."

He nodded to us and then continued east.

"We seem to have timed this well," Maghran said.

"Just in time to stop their train."

"Yes, that. But also I mean that we let the dunters spend much energy building this thing. This will be a larger blow to them. Wonderfully timed."

After a long walk beneath the stars we came upon the bridge. At this point in the railway a small river, a tributary of the Walsing, cut through the land and formed a ravine. The dunters had built a wooden span across. It was a rough structure, but sturdy and serviceable; typical of them. Or more accurately, typical of their kobolds.

"And here we are," Maghran said, setting down the bags. "I'll take that shovel and set some sticks in this bank, if you can step out and tie a few in among those beams. We'll twist all the fuses together. A few may be thrown when the first ones blow, but what goes off at the same time will take this down. Here you are."

He pulled six sticks of the explosives from a bag and handed them to me. Each had a long fuse coiled.

"Does it matter where, exactly?" I asked. "I have not done this."

"Lower is better," he said. "But of course the fuses must reach up here to me. Tie the sticks into joints. You have cord, or rope? Good. Press them into cracks as much as possible. Their force should be driven into the wood, and not allowed to dissipate into the air. Do you follow?"

"Yes."

He set to work at the end of the bridge, digging holes among its foundations. His arms seemed as thick as the ties beneath him, and he cut into the ground with that shovel as if he were parting snow. I stepped out a few feet and then climbed over the edge and down, to be able to reach among the supports beneath the rail bed. The fuses were around fifteen feet long, only, so I could not move out very far, but I made sure that the first two large columns were mined. I jammed the blasters into the wooden joints of the columns and their cross supports, and then tied them in place with cord.

"Those are good placements," Maghran said to me. I was not aware that he had been checking from above. I climbed back up on the tracks and uncoiled the fuses. Maghran was finishing burying his share of the sticks. The bridge was heavy and formidable, with spikes driven everywhere—the typical overbuilt effort of lashed slaves—but from what I knew of dwarf explosives, it would soon be splinters.

"The ends of the fuses, please," he said.

I handed them to him. He twisted them together with the fuses of the sticks he had buried.

"It will be a race," he said, as he knotted them. "A race to see which spark gets to its charge first. We hope it will be a twelve-way tie."

"Yes, we do."

He set the bound ends of the fuses on the ground.

"There. All is ready. Let's eat something before we set it all off. We may find ourselves running for some time, very shortly."

"I thought you were confident we were not being watched."

"I am. But this explosion here will draw very quick attention from a long way around. We dwarves need ample fuel to move like that." I thought I saw a slight smile through his beard. "And at any rate, the dawn is coming up. We will call this a very early breakfast."

The sky was indeed beginning to fade from deepest blue to

daybreak at the horizon. He reached into one of the bags and pulled out wrapped food of his own; it was dried meat. He handed half to me.

"Since you gave yours to that traveler."

"I kept plenty," I said.

"I'm sure. You are all eating well, yourselves, in your town, we understand," he said.

"We are."

"Very good. And I have been told that you are a son of the Marshal himself."

"A grandson," I corrected him.

"All the same to us," he said as he chewed. "The Marshal's plan worked, then, I suppose."

"Our town is prospering."

"Good. But you might have stayed with us."

Our history of indentured servitude to the dwarves was not something we liked to discuss, especially with, of course, the dwarves themselves.

"We paid you well," he continued. "We gave you a share. You were no kobolds."

I felt my face grow red, but it was probably still not light enough for him to see it. I chose not to argue.

"That was before my time," was all I answered. Then something occurred to me:

"Did you know the Marshal?"

"No," he said, shaking his head. "I saw him, you understand. But I did not speak with him. But perhaps I am meeting him here in you. You're clearly a leader."

"I have no ambition to direct anyone the way he did."

"Hm," Maghran said. "New times forge new ambitions. And I like you, Master Shearer. You are good enough setting explosives, and you eat well. We dwarves do not demand much." Now I saw clearly that he was smiling. He ate the remainder of the meat and wiped his hands on his breeches. "Very well, let's light this and move."

I saw just a glimpse of yellow-white behind him before tight arms slammed around me and pulled me away. I heard blows, and a scuffle, from Maghran as I was lifted off my feet and carried forward a few paces. I tried to match the fight that I could hear

Maghran putting up, but it was no use against many strong arms. They planted me down before an elf.

It was three other elves who held me. One of them breathed down my neck, literally. They pulled my arms behind my back and tied them together as the one before me spoke.

"Marshalson Shearer," he said. "You should pick quieter companions. You yourself might have eluded us, but for this one." He nodded over toward where Maghran was being bound. "But you needed him for the blasting expertise, I know."

He looked me over. He was tall, of course. He was dressed in what looked to be a light gray cloak, rather than the usual white; I supposed this was as close as elves ever came to wearing, or needing, a concealing garment. His hair was blond. He was a typical elf but for lines on his face. The lines surprised me: for an elf, he looked much too young to have such wrinkles.

"You are with Alden Silvermoor," I said.

"I am. We are. I am Aladar Silvermoor."

"Here to ensure the dunters get to our towns on your steel."

The elf shrugged. "We are here to ensure our rails work as they should. What the dunters do with them is not our concern. Is that one bound?" he asked the others.

He meant Maghran, of course. The flash of white I had seen behind the dwarf was from one of a larger group of elves who had pinned him down and tied him up. This took them time, and half a dozen elves, and much rope. I managed to turn enough to see Maghran, now. He was bound, still struggling, and snarling with anger.

"You forest dirt," he said. He jolted his shoulders violently in an effort to throw off the ropes. "If you want to annihilate us, come try to do it yourselves. You should be warriors enough to try, not go through the dunters."

"We do not want to annihilate you, my friend. But we do want to sell our steel. It is the finest in the world, you know."

"And the dunters would be hobbled without it," Maghran snapped. "And you provide it to them."

"Yes, and we make it from ore which your cousins, the White Mount dwarves, sell to us," Silvermoor said. "Or which Herrar sold to us, we should say, I suppose—in the past tense."

Maghran shuddered at this.

"Perhaps you should speak with them," the elf continued, "before you complain about us. All these parties in a chain thinking of nothing more than their next sale, and the end use be damned, and look where it gets us. Look where it gets you."

"You cowards. You—" Maghran started. At the mention of the other dwarves he had lurched forward and nearly broken free from the arms holding him up. Silvermoor interrupted him:

"Gag him," he said. "I regret this, Maghran, but I cannot have you drawing more attention than you have already. We have a strong force with us, but yet we must be quiet."

I assumed these elves would have their fingers bitten off attempting to gag this dwarf, or any dwarf, but their method was a bit of elven handiwork: one of them took out a long scarf, already tied into a loop, and lowered it over Maghran's head. The scarf covered his face from the nose down to his chest. There it remained, and the dwarf could no longer be heard. Maghran quivered, and apparently tried to shout. He shook with rage—silent rage.

Silvermoor addressed me:

"Our cloth can keep you nearly invisible, and also nearly silent. I don't suspect we'll need this with you."

"If I am not killed, here, my people will hear of all this," I said. "I am in no position to make threats, with my town facing obliteration by Red Gorge—but those of us who remain will remember."

"I am sure," the elf said. "I expect no less."

He turned and walked up the tracks a few yards. One other elf joined him, and they spoke quietly. No one made any effort to remove the explosives that we had laid. The other half dozen elves merely stood where they were, preventing Maghran from hobbling away and also keeping an eye on me.

Time passed. Our group was quiet enough that a knot of deer came into view in the ravine and worked their way northward along the riverside. Far, far away I thought I heard the bark of a dog. I fancied it was from Emmervale, but we were much too distant for that.

The sky was now an early morning blue, and becoming gold at the horizon as the sun rose. Silvermoor walked back and stood next to me. He faced the tracks.

"Dawn," he said. "And now, in the heart of Red Gorge, the train will be raising steam."

"So that is true," I said. "A wandering man passed by here a few hours ago and told us."

"Korben, the odd fisher," he said. "Yes, we saw him pass by and speak with you. He was correct. We will be done here any moment."

"Any moment? It will take the dunters hours to get here."

"Watch closely, Mr. Shearer. The rails."

I watched the rail bed; nothing happened. Far to our west, in whatever foul outpost of Red Gorge served as the mustering point of the dunter army, I imagined an engine being loaded with coal, and smoke beginning to belch from a stack. I imagined the loading of troops, and spears, scimitars, muskets, cannons, all intended to kill my people. Soon a stinking engineer would push a throttle forward.

I heard a tiny metallic crack. It snapped me out of my daydream. There was nothing more. I looked at Silvermoor. He stood motionless, still gazing straight ahead.

Then another. This one was a creak, again of metal.

Then many creaks, and cracks. They came from the railway, all up and down its length. The rails were creaking, sounding as if they were buckling—every single one of them. All these hundreds, thousands, of rails which the dunters and their kobolds had emplaced so carefully.

Then more clear groans cut through; metal being extracted from wood. This was from the spikes, I realized. I saw now that each end of every rail was beginning to turn upward. Each began to warp. As the ends lifted, they pried up the spikes that had held them down. The ends of the rails hauled out spikes like the claw of a hammer pulling a nail.

And soon the spikes began to pop out. They jumped into the air like fish leaping from water. Dozens and dozens did this, all up and down the railway as far as we could see.

Now Silvermoor was smiling.

Free from their spikes the rails continued to curl up, lifting on either end. They bent more and more, until they were nearly half-circles.

And then they rolled to their left, each one the same direction, all of them now tilting toward their ends. They balanced, impossibly, and at the same time continued to bend.

It struck me then, and I gasped: The written symbol of Lord Alden Silvermoor in the elvish language was a character, nearly a circle but open on its left, with a short vertical line bisecting the top curve. This is what these rails were forming. Every single one of them, all in unison, in two long, long rows stretching all the way west to Red Gorge and all the way east nearly to Emmervale and the foothills of Stenhall.

The rails now grew circular, except for that gap on the left of each.

Then bulges formed at their highest points. These bulges grew, and extended upward and downward, the steel growing like a magic vine until Silvermoor's symbol was complete.

The creaks and groans stopped. The rails stood still, silent, and upright; thousands of the signs of Lord Silvermoor stretching to our right and left. They ran like a sort of silver chain from horizon to horizon.

"Bless them," Maghran said, in awe. "Bless those cursed pale ghosts."

I looked over at him; his scarf had been removed. He was no longer bound, either. The elves were gone, of course. He turned to look for them in the clearing behind us; I did not bother.

Five

Maghran was silent just a moment longer and then seemed to shake himself back to his senses.

"What a thing we have seen," he said. I heard the grudge in this compliment to the elves.

"Indeed, Maghran."

"We have to retrieve the charges. We can't leave them here."

"Should we blow the bridge anyway?" I asked.

He considered this. "The dunters will not be able to obtain this much track again anytime soon. Given that, I can't see how this bridge would do them any good, even intact. And I don't want to draw attention to ourselves if we don't need to."

"Our capture by those elves probably has drawn attention already," I said.

"You believe so? From the deer, perhaps. The elves were quiet, even given the noise I tried to make. As they always are. But a detonation here would be noticed. Trust me."

"Very well."

He started for the bridge, and I followed. I had expected him to speak more about the elves, but he said nothing.

"Those were many strong arms they needed to hold you," I said.

He was silent, and then made just one more comment about them:

"It is well for Silvermoor and his company that they destroyed their steel."

The bridge was not at all affected by the twisting of the rails. Spikes had been pulled from it, and the rails on it were bent into upright characters just like those on the ground, but there was no other damage. I climbed down, cut through the cords I had laid, and lifted out the explosives.

"Nothing volatile about these?" I asked.

"No. Or nothing very much," he added and shrugged. "I suspect my companions will be here soon. The elves must have ambushed them just as they did to us—otherwise they would have come."

"How many are you?"

"Four others. And you?"

"I have two companions out there. We will be returning to Emmervale. What are your plans?"

"We must speak of that, my companions and I," he answered. I recognized this as a non-answer; he probably had firm plans, and just did not want to share them. The camaraderie of dwarves went only so far. I did not press him further.

I did ask him about Herrar, however:

"May I ask—what did that elf mean to say when he brought up Herrar, of White Mount?"

Maghran stopped cold when I said this. He was silent. It was clearly a grave topic with him. I had considered that before bringing it up, but I had hoped he'd be able to speak of it with me.

He eventually answered, roughly:

"She was outside of our territory."

"When? What do you mean?"

"You have not heard? About her disappearance?"

"No. I barely knew of her, Maghran. And I'd heard nothing recently."

"You barely knew of Herrar?"

"Only that she is the leader of White Mount. She has not ventured out for us to hear much. To my knowledge."

"Well," he said. He paused to consider this. "This was great news among dwarves, but I suppose not so much to others. You may all feel the repercussions, I will say. In fact we have all been feeling them already." He nodded toward the tracks.

"Herrar," he continued, "departed the White Mount to visit us, some ten months ago. We were not aware that she had done so. She left with a small party; three others. She did not send word to us. Our territory well to the west of Stenhall is protected, and secure, but we would have sent an escort out to meet her had we known she was coming. We do not know why they did not inform us of their embassy. But they did not, and they all vanished."

"Why were they traveling to speak with you?"

"To talk about this war. The alliance between Varenlend and Caranniam and Red Gorge. They had heard rumors of it. It concerns them greatly. As long as those parties were at odds with each other—or at least two of the three of them—and of course as long as they did not, could not, unify against Searose, the White Mount dwarves felt secure that they would always have the men as trading partners, and would be able to deal with either Varenlend or Caranniam at any time."

"Very pragmatic of them."

"It is a dangerous world, Master Shearer. I don't need to tell you. And no people have ever gone out of their way to advocate for our welfare; we have to do that ourselves. You yourselves have benefitted from your understanding with Varenlend, I believe."

"Any ties we can maintain with Varenlend give us, or gave us I should say, an ally on the other side of Caranniam. A potential knife in their back."

"Exactly. And our cousins in White Mount were thinking along similar lines. But then Varenlend and Caranniam appear to link up —this alarmed them. Herrar led a party to confer with us. A camp of theirs was found eight days east of White Mount, well into the wilds between our realms, but nothing more. White Mount believes that the party made it into our territory before they disappeared, but we know that is not true."

"Why do the White Mount dwarves think the party made it that far?"

"Simply because two days' walk—a long two days—would have put them past our border. And they assume Herrar must have made it that far. They have offered no reasoning beyond that."

"And you know her party did not make it into your lands—"

"Simply because we would have seen them. A rabbit does not run in our hills without our knowledge."

I knew that some hunters and travelers from Emmervale occasionally passed through that area without being seen by dwarves, or at any rate without being confronted by them, but I did not mention this. If the White Mount and Stenhall dwarves were set on feuding about the fate of Herrar's expedition, there would be nothing any outsider could do to dissuade them.

"What do you think might have happened to them?" I asked.

Maghran shrugged. "There are dangers in the wilds. There are wyverns, and other predators. You know this. And we allow those dangers to exist, in part, to help us patrol that border."

Again this struck me as a curious portrayal of the realities in those mountains; not even an army of dwarves would relish an attempt to exterminate a wyvern. But again I said nothing. If this dwarf wanted to portray wyverns as border guards that they tolerated, I would not argue.

"For one of those dangers to eliminate a party of four dwarves with no trace would have been unusual, certainly. But that must have happened."

"Do you reckon a raid from Red Gorge might have ranged up that far?"

"Not likely. They do not typically travel up that way, and certainly are not known for traveling quietly. But no matter what happened, Herrar is gone, and we have been blamed. This probably explains why White Mount sold that ore to the elves, even knowing that the elves might turn around and sell steel to Red Gorge."

"And Maghran—what do you think Herrar would have proposed to you, had she made it out to meet you?"

"Well, that is the tragedy, isn't it? We don't know. But obviously we think she wanted to discuss turning our combined powers against Varenlend or Caranniam. Probably Caranniam, since they are closest to both of us."

"If you believe that alliance is obvious, you could still pursue it, no?"

"Yes," he said. "We may well yet. This is going to be the last throe of the wizards, I believe. There is too much power, now, too much steam, too much steel, for them to control the Open Lands much longer unless they conquer all right now."

"Ironic that they are using rail and guns to do so," I said.

"Ironic indeed."

I had gathered all the charges which I had set, and handed them to him. He carefully rolled up the fuses and returned them to his bag. His eyes were on his work, but partway through he spoke to me:

"These are my companions. Behind you."

I whirled; four dwarves were nearly upon me.

"We're no elves," Maghran said, "but we also can travel quietly when we have a mind to, eh?"

One of them was Hrond. Again now, just as he and his companions had struck me on the hillside some days earlier, they looked so much alike that it seemed they could have all been brothers. This included Maghran as well.

One of them walked slightly ahead of the others. He was

dressed in black, whereas two of the others were in dark brown and Hrond again wore a dun cloak. Hrond looked to be the youngest, and it occurred to me that all five of these dwarves seemed to wear darker clothing the older they were. Maghran himself wore very dark brown, but not the black of the dwarf out in front. This must have been a custom of theirs, although I had never heard it from our older Emmervalers who had lived in their mines. I suppose our old folks were too bitter to be inclined to share stories of dwarf culture.

Maghran came to my side now and nodded to this first dwarf:

"Master Shearer, this is my brother, Ghranam."

So that's who Maghran was—brother to the leader of Stenhall. He had given no indication of this before.

Ghranam slid his eyes toward me and nodded once. Hrond did the same, I saw, but the others did not, and none spoke. This group was not expressing the relative warmth, if that's the word, of Hrond and his companions with the ansark.

All carried battle axes, worn snug against their sides, with the heads above their belts. Two of them carried guns; Hrond had his musketoon, again, and another of the younger ones hauled a very long-barreled musket, quite heavy and as accurate as they came.

All four of them wore rucksacks. Three of these had iron helmets tied onto the bottom. All wore heavy boots like Maghran's. These were heavy, but still potentially quiet, as I had learned.

Ghranam stood out for his black cloak but also for a broad silver belt he wore around it. His face was almost unbelievably grim; I would hate to think what his mood would have been had the railway aimed at his people not just been ruined. He spoke:

"I am much inclined to find and kill these elves, brother."

"You were also taken by them," Maghran said. It was not a question; he knew this party would have come to our aid had they been able.

Ghranam nodded. "Cursed elves. They fear to show their faces until we are bound and helpless. They are underhanded."

"Well, we can be glad they have been underhanded with Red Gorge as well," Maghran said, nodding toward the tracks.

"This must have been months of work for them. I do see that," Ghranam said. "Even for elves this measure of magic must have cost them dearly."

"They must have extracted a high price from the dunters," Maghran answered.

"That's so," Ghranam said. "Very well. Perhaps they are not on our side, but we can see here they are not on the side of Red Gorge either."

"Anyone who did this much to block the attack on Stenhall," Maghran said, "I will consider to be on our side."

"I hear a herd of tundra oxen," Ghranam said.

I had heard this also, but had hoped the dwarves had not. After their quietness in their approach, and that of the elves, it was embarrassing that my own spotters could be heard quite a distance away. I looked over Maghran's shoulder and saw them coming into the ravine.

Jed came first, and then Britta. Both of them watched their steps but also glanced at our group warily. There was little warmth between us and dwarves, and now that the dunter tracks were ruined—the common threat we had both faced together—much of the motivation we had felt to cooperate receded.

Just like the dwarves, these two were well-armed. Britta carried a musket, and Jed a longbow. Jed also had—quite usefully, it soon turned out—a quarter-staff.

"And now I introduce my cousin Britta, and my countryman Jed," I said to Maghran.

The dwarves barely looked at them.

Jed was still gathering himself, I would say, for the same reason that Ghranam had been. He seemed more sheepish than bitter, though, about the capture by the elves.

"The elves bound us, for a time. Both of us separately."

"We assumed," I answered. "They took all the rest of us, also. Of course."

"But they performed quite a bit of work here, with these," he said, putting his hand on a bent rail. He pushed it gently, and then a bit harder.

"You know, I don't think these can even be pushed down. Or not easily, at least."

Maghran was not interested in chatting about elven handiwork. "Well, we part here, Master Shearer," he said.

"This is a Shearer?" Ghranam asked him.

"Indeed. And that means apparently we have two of them."

My cousin Britta barely nodded.

"Royalty, then," Ghranam said. This might almost have been taken as a sarcastic insult; but I could tell, and I think the other two of my comrades could also, that Ghranam spoke with some genuine respect. The Marshal had walked a careful and successful line, in his day. He had freed us from our servitude to the dwarves with a combination of guile and bravery—but without enough fighting to kill any dwarves and thereby start blood feuds that would have still been boiling today.

Suddenly Jed said:

"Horse. Get down."

He nodded to our west as he dropped to the ground. The rest of us lay down, also, and we crawled back toward the slope of the ravine by the bridge.

The odds were against us encountering a friend—someone like our refugee Korben—out here twice in one day. I glanced down the line of upright rails, for that was the direction Jed had nodded, and saw him: A rider wearing red, on a brown horse.

Maghran looked out, too.

"That's a Caranniam rider," he said. "Perhaps a messenger."

"Yes." The red clothing, which in this man's case included a cloak, was the mark of the rulers of the city.

He continued coming our direction, toward the bridge. He was still some distance from us, and he rode on the north side of the rails. We had been standing on the south side, and that must have been why he did not notice us. As far away as he was, the upright rails had concealed us.

"Why do we hide?" Hrond asked. "He is one, we are eight."

"He is mounted, Hrond, and will flee if he sees us," Maghran growled. He then spoke to me.

"Can your tall man there wield that staff?"

"Yes," I said, and then I in turn spoke to Jed. "You could knock him down, and out?"

He nodded, but added:

"But shall we just shoot him down?" We had three guns among our group, so this gave us a good chance of sending at least one ball through him.

"I would rather tumble him from his mount," Maghran said. "Messengers, if that's what he is, often know more than what is written in their letters."

"Very well," I said. I told Jed: "I would guess he will slow down a bit as he comes to the bridge. Can you get beneath it, and around it?"

"Now? Yes."

"Then I'll turn him toward me once he's here," I said.

Jed scrambled over to the foot of the bridge and passed under it, out of my sight.

I was correct, it turned out, that the rider would slow at the bridge. He had been moving at a trot but nearly stopped the horse completely as he came to the planks. He wondered about the integrity of the bridge after the elf magic, just as I had.

In addition to his red cloak and clothing he also had a fine saddle, spurs, and a breastplate that shone; but all this, unfortunately for him, had only served to mark him as a target. I got to my feet, now, and stepped out, on his right side.

"You, there, traveler," I said, loudly.

He turned toward me immediately and put his hand on the hilt of his sword by his side. This was good news, for me; it meant he probably had no magic. He began to advance.

"Hold there," he ordered. He spoke not in Cranam but in the standard Valley Lower.

Jed now appeared behind him, raising his staff in the air. I stepped toward the rider, Jed closed the gap, and then he swung hard.

It hit the man on the back of the head. He was knocked forward in his saddle, but not out of it. Instantly Britta and Hrond were out and at him, and the other dwarves followed. Britta pulled him down, and the dwarves held him. He did make some efforts to free himself from their grip. These were useless of course.

"Insolent highwaymen!" he snapped. "Common thieves!" He seemed high-born, from his language and his apparent indignation.

"You might save your strength, and mind your manners," Maghran said. "This is war, you are a soldier, and you were close to encroaching on our land. You're a captive now. Show us what you are carrying."

"Your land, you say," he sneered. "You are hill people. And I carry nothing."

"Nothing? Just out this far from your city, heading toward a dunter encampment, for diversion. Very well. And furthermore we see your saddlebag, sir."

We pulled down the bag. It did indeed contain a letter; just one. We found nothing else of interest on the animal or the man. He made some show of resisting the dwarves' search of his person.

The letter he carried had been folded and sealed, with a stamp on the wax.

"Two crows," Maghran said. "This is from Somoroveln himself then, it seems."

"It's not addressed to anyone," I said.

"No. I suppose this man here was to deliver it in person."

"Do we mind breaking the seal?" I asked.

"We must."

Maghran opened the letter. It was a large sheet of fine paper. It rippled a bit in the breeze. He held it so that I might see it also.

He shook his head. "What odd runes. These look like the decorations of children. Nothing to me."

The characters were nothing I recognized, either. I could read some of the old high script of the wizards, as well as Cranam and our own language, but this was different. These runes were mostly based on squares, and had only tails and crosses on the corners or on opposing sides to set them apart from each other.

Maghran turned to the captive messenger and pointed at the letter.

"What does this message say?"

The man shook his head slightly.

"I would not share it with you even if I knew."

"I suspected not," Maghran said. "Who is it for?"

"That I do know, but again I will not share it with you."

"Right," Maghran said. He turned back to me. "It must be code, I would think. Not a real language. We have scholars who might read it, but it could take weeks."

"Scholars," I repeated, and I thought about it. Then I turned to Britta.

"Do you fancy an excursion?"

Her face fell.

"Not her," she answered. "Really?"

"Quiet down and come over here. Jed, you also." I motioned them closer to Maghran and me, so that the messenger would not hear us.

"Yes, her," I said. "She's not so far away from us, here, you know."

"I'm afraid she isn't," Britta answered.

"Who is this you speak of?" Maghran asked, quietly. We stood in a tight square, and he was expressing more interest in what we had to say than he had up till now. "There is some learned woman out here?"

"Learned, but that's not the half of it," I said. "Duchess Wilhelmina."

"Duchess? Of what? Not anything out here?"

"Not here, exactly. Down in the Kurtenvold. But no, there's nothing of importance there either. Nonetheless it's what she calls herself. You must meet her."

"Is she some sort of necromancer?"

"No. She would be glad to have you believe that, though. Just a hermit who lives out near here in the Kurtenvold."

"In truth? When I think of a hermit, it's always a male," Maghran said.

"I don't know how else to describe her. She passes through Emmervale now and then—"

"We have seen her perhaps once in the past five years," Britta interjected.

"Yes, well, she has passed through a few times, but mostly stays out here. For years at a stretch. She is aged, and knows many languages, and fancies herself knowledgeable about magic. I think she would be able to help us read this."

"You'll seek her out now?" Maghran asked.

"Yes."

"We'll accompany you, if you'll have us."

"I thought you had some other errand?"

"Plans change."

"Very well, then."

"What will we do with this one?" Britta asked, inclining her head back toward the rider.

"Take him along. Perhaps we can find someone to leave him with, but we can't free him. And we ought to keep him alive. If nothing else, he looks like he must be worth something."

All four of us turned and regarded him, at this moment. The other dwarves guarding him had allowed him to stand up. I imagined what was going through the unfortunate fellow's mind: It was probably obvious to him that we were sizing him up to determine if he was best suited to be captured, or captured and beaten, or fed to ansarks.

We turned back to one another.

"Very well, he comes along," Maghran said. "Bound, of course."

He turned and walked over to the man.

"Your name?"

"It's the reason you will be struck down," the man said.

"Is it, now." Maghran pulled a knife from his belt. "Handsome cloak you have there," he said. "Vibrant dye."

He took a corner of it and cut off a wide swath. He then reached up, grabbed the man's tunic, and pulled him down to his knees quickly, easily, as if he were bending down a twig on a sapling. Britta, Jed and I pinned him, and Maghran gagged him with the cloth.

We told the others about our plan. The dwarves then withdrew to talk with each other. After a few minutes Maghran spoke to us again.

"Ghranam and one other are going to return to Stenhall. The other three of us will stay with you."

"Very well. We welcome your company."

"Two of us shall leave so that we can get the explosives back home, in part," he said. "It's either that, or destroy them, and this is a good amount. I don't want to be carrying them around lest they fall into ill hands. Those elves, among others, could decide to try to take them. Although I don't intend to let them surprise me again. But regardless, Ghranam is carrying that load back."

The dwarf who departed with Ghranam was one of the pair in the dark brown cloaks. We were left with Hrond, and we learned the other was named Inman. Inman was the one who carried the long musket.

"Let us move," Maghran said. "I would suggest we stop in the late afternoon. That will be far enough for this day. Perhaps you agree with me, Master Shearer."

"I'd be glad to stop then," I said. "None of us slept last night."
Maghran nodded at this.

Six

We were seven and a horse; three dwarves, the three of us from Emmervale, and our gagged prisoner. Jed was last in line, leading the horse.

"You might as well ride it," Maghran told him. It was a tall and powerful gelding. Dwarves, of course, preferred to stay on their feet.

But Jed shook his head instantly:

"I shall walk with the rest of you."

Maghran and I went first. Behind us, Hrond and Inman prodded along the messenger. Maghran had told them:

"Keep a club about you, the butt end of something. If anything happens to us—begins to happen—you have to knock out that man, quickly. We can't have him assisting our enemies."

We started away from the tracks and the bridge, due south. We would be walking through open grassland for some time, seeing only occasional clusters of trees. It was well into the morning now, a fine day with a breeze.

The double row of Silvermoor's sign behind us made me think he was forever watching me over my back. I stopped and turned to look at the rails.

"They are so odd, I feel they may disappear," I said. "But I suppose they won't go anywhere."

Britta answered this:

"Perhaps we can roll one home with us when we are done."

"We should keep moving," Maghran said.

"Should we?" Jed said. "No one on any train passing by is going to see us." I saw him shake his head, and he seemed to be rolling his eyes; I didn't know why. But we resumed our march.

The terrain continued as before: green, and no signs of habitation. We would see a bird of prey circling high from time to time, looking for rodents in the fields, but no men or elves.

"What sort of dwelling does this woman live in?" Maghran asked me.

"An old keep. You would think it is ruined, to see it. If you can see it at all. It's covered with vines, and concealed. I have not been there for years, mind you, but I doubt it has improved, or that she has trimmed back anything."

"It's in those woods, then?"

"Yes. The Kurtenvold. We'll cut into them eventually."

"Where is she from?"

"Caranniam. Long ago."

"And why did she leave?"

"Some sort of falling out with their council."

"So she must be a friend to us. Or close enough."

"Yes."

"I suppose she consorts with elves, what with living out here?"

"Yes. They come out this far."

"I wonder if they watch us even now."

"I would not be surprised if they do."

We kept on, past mid-afternoon. Eventually we neared a stream which came from the open land to our left and cut in front of us. Beyond it—well beyond it still—we could see a wall of dark green; this was the Kurtenvold.

"That is our goal, then?" Maghran asked, nodding toward the forest.

"Yes. There is some more walking even once we are in."

"Then let's cross this and then set up our camp," Maghran said. "We've traveled a good distance. We can enter tomorrow."

"As you wish," Jed said from in back. His voice was sharp. I noticed this, but Maghran did not seem to. Then I heard the horse snort behind me. I looked, and Jed was tugging the lead and hurrying to the water, passing us. He was shaking his head. I touched his arm as he came abreast of me.

"Jed, what is it?"

He threw one hand up in the air. "Why does he give the orders? Why is he the leader? We've done just as much out here as they have."

"Jed, it's not important. He's an old dwarf; it does no harm to respect him. And he brought the explosives."

"Which ended up making no difference, for all their boasting of them," he said. "And they are the ones who told us that they wanted you along to help. Why does that mean that he is in charge? It's not as if it was our idea to assist them. And why is it that they guard the prisoner? And why do they invite themselves along now at all? Wilhelmina is our acquaintance, not theirs."

"Jed. Let's just walk, and take care of this letter, and get home. We may be very glad to have these companions along, before we return."

He passed me, and said nothing.

We crossed the stream all too soon, and Britta and the dwarves began dropping their bags. Britta was near Jed, and Hrond spoke to them.

"We did not come stocked for an extended stay in the wild. Did you?"

"We did not," Britta said. "We brought enough food for the return home, but not for this detour here."

"We'll have to see what we can find, then."

"We are nearing dusk, and there's the line of trees," Maghran said. "Perhaps a deer will come along."

"That must be our plan, then," Jed said. Again no one else seemed to notice his tone.

"Can we shoot out here?" Hrond asked. "Is there any reason to stay quiet?"

"I believe we can shoot," Maghran said. "If you feel you can hit anything between the two of you."

"Between Inman's barrel, and my shot, I'm sure we could."

"You're not the only ones with a gun," Jed said.

"True," Hrond said. "Or perhaps you could catch us some fish, young man. Just like the old times."

"Catch them yourself, dirt-eater," Jed said, and he swung his fist at the dwarf, and connected.

I felt a quick shock.

Normally a strike from Jed landing on a dwarf would have essentially bounced off, but Jed had been standing a bit higher than Hrond to begin with, and also he stepped firmly into his swing. He landed his punch on the left side of Hrond's face, and he snapped the dwarf's head sideways a bit. The sound was like a potato masher hitting tough raw meat.

"What's this!?" Maghran roared.

"Jed!" Britta yelled. She threw her arms around him and pulled him back.

"We are your fishermen no longer!" Jed shouted.

Hrond brought his face back around, darted toward the two of them surprisingly quickly, and swiped at Jed. He hit him in the lower ribs, with one swing, and knocked him over along with Britta as well. His blow made me think of Maghran pulling the messenger down to his level, earlier; neither dwarf seemed to put much effort into the action, but both tossed around the bodies easily.

"Come now," Maghran said. He stepped toward Hrond and pulled him back as I went to my two fallen companions and shook my head.

Long ago in Stenhall, of course, one of the chores of our grandfathers and great-grandfathers had been to catch fish for their dwarf masters. The dwarves would not deign to do it; and they ate fish only occasionally, and then only thoroughly dried until it was satisfactorily tough for them. But they had taken pleasure in ordering our forefathers to fish for them. And not only had the dwarves found fishing disagreeable in the best of times, but in those years a fishing trip out of their mines and down to a river meant potential attacks from the scourge of dragons and wyverns. These were very dark memories for Emmervalers.

Maghran held Hrond back with one hand, and spoke past me to Jed. "Listen, young man. You fish for no one; we know that. Your two companions here are of your proudest family, and we are indebted to you yourself for that strike on the messenger. Hrond was not insulting you. We are out here together, and we have five thousand dunters a day's walk away who want all of our heads. We have to leave this behind us."

"Then leave it," Jed said; but he did turn and walk away. He disappeared into the woods.

Maghran looked at me.

"A proud young man," he said.

"To a fault," I said.

"If he can keep his fists to himself, his strength should serve him well."

Hrond stood there—not, I noticed, rubbing his face.

"So," Maghran asked him, "when's the last time anyone struck you?"

"Not since I was a lad. A fight among youth in some forgotten hall."

"You can forget this?"

Hrond nodded. "I think this man Jed here may be even younger than that lad of ours who last struck me, in that brabble long ago."

Britta, Inman, and Hrond took their muskets to try to hunt deer, or anything else they might find, to the south, closer the edge of the woods. They saw nothing. I located some splitleaf plants, and dug up their roots; we ended up roasting those and also eating the considerable rations which the messenger had brought along. We bound his legs, untied his gag, and allowed him to drink water and watch us eat.

"We will let you wait to eat until you are with your friends the dunters," Maghran told him. "They should have some food you will enjoy."

The man did not answer, probably assuming, rightly, that we would gag him again and take away even the water if he objected.

"Would you want to tell us your name, now?" Maghran asked him.

"No."

"How about your message? Your errand?"

The man did not answer.

"We are going to keep you alive, sir, but I reckon you will not see your countrymen until this war is over. You have nothing to say?"

"I do not."

"Your railroad has failed. The elves you assumed were working with you, are clearly not. You have been robbed. Your dunter armies are far from their bases, with no reinforcements coming. Any men of your acquaintance who are with them are now subject to whatever preemptive raids my families, and those of Emmervale, will mount. You have nothing to say?"

"Nothing."

Maghran's warning about the attacks from Stenhall and Emmervale was optimistic, I knew, and the messenger probably knew it also. Emmervale could not defeat that dunter force, and it wasn't probable that Stenhall could either. Furthermore the dwarves were not likely to even bother harassing the dunters as long as they were not under imminent threat. The messenger said no more.

*   *   *

Britta and Jed ended up building their own fire and sleeping some distance away from us. Britta had asked me what I thought of this, and I encouraged her to stay with Jed. I remained by a second fire, with the dwarves. We soon set watch and slept.

In the morning we rose early and set off quickly. We went without breakfast, just drinking water from the stream. The three with guns kept them ready.

"If we see anything to eat, on hoof or wing, we can stop and roast it, I would hope," Britta said.

"If you can bring it down," Maghran said.

Jed joined us again, and we walked in the same order. Jed and Hrond did not speak to each other. Maghran did not seem to pay them any mind, and I tried to do the same.

We reached the Kurtenvold fairly quickly, but along the way the messenger began to flag a bit. Hrond and Inman had to prod him more frequently. Maghran spoke to me.

"Our friend did not sleep well, it seems."

"He can rest more once we are with the Duchess."

"The Duchess of the wild," Maghran said.

"And this reminds me," I said. "I wish I had a gift. I didn't know I'd be coming down here."

"It's necessary to bring one, for her?" Maghran asked.

"No, not necessary. She'll still speak with us, I'm sure. But it never hurts to smooth the way, with her."

"I may have something." He swung his rucksack around and reached into it.

"You carry gifts?"

"Small wealth. For such occasions."

He produced a deep red gemstone. It lay rich in his hand, diverting one's attention even from the missing finger.

"Arovis," I said. "I've seen them in Emmervale."

"From our mines. We charge dearly for them, for they are rare."

"You'll part with it? I think she will be pleased with that," I said.

"She very well should be," he answered. "Many hours go into

finding these and polishing them. Many hours."

Finally we came upon a sort of protrusion in front of the woods, a small hill. It was just a bit higher than the rest of the rising land around it.

"Here," I said. "We cut into the woods here."

"Very well," Maghran said. "And is it far in?"

"No, not far."

"Not too thick in there for the horse?"

"No."

Inside the trees, the woods quickly became dark. But they were not tangled; our progress was easy across the forest floor. Ferns grew, and became larger as we continued. We soon had to cross a river. This was the Ridan, the same one that ran through Emmervale miles to the northeast. It was shallow enough that we did not have to walk far to find a place to ford. The river bed held piles of smooth rocks. Britta stopped to skip one as we crossed.

We continued due east, through the trees. We heard the echoing calls of birds high above us, and they parted as we passed below. Eventually we moved up a slight ridge. The undergrowth rose up quite high, suddenly, and vines and low branches from the trees came down to meet it.

"This is it," I said. "Over there."

I had taken care to point out the keep before it could be easily seen, but Maghran did not admit to being unable to find it. I had hoped to get a reaction from him. At any rate we advanced, and soon it was obvious: dark green walls stood before us. A carpet of vines grew up the sides. Only at the top did stones emerge so one could see that this was an old tower. It was wide, but not tall, just twice the height of a man. Crenelations, unmanned for who knows how many decades—or centuries—looked down us.

Two large trees had grown up within the walls, right in the middle of what had previously been a formidable defense.

"One could certainly walk quite near it and not notice," Maghran finally said. "Who lived here—is it known?"

"One of the great families of this region," I said. "I do not know the name. Long ago, of course, well before the emptying. These woods were not here, then; at that time their edge was to the south, and this land was productive."

"Just a single tower? It must have been long ago indeed." He meant that larger castles had been built in this area, in later years. But this was just a tower—what was left of it. Its modest heights had broken down in a few spots.

We walked around the wall to a gate. The heavy wooden door was intact, but the lintel piece above had collapsed onto it, and some of the surrounding stones were loose, also. A second, newer, smaller door had been cut into the original.

"Empty hands, everyone," I said to the group. I then called out: "Duchess Wilhelmina, friends call on you."

We waited.

"You reckon that's enough to bring her?" Maghran asked.

"I believe so."

We waited longer, and then the smaller door did click, and rattle, and open inward.

She stood there. In her youth she must have been striking. Even now, she was striking still. Her face was lined, but her dark eyes were still penetrating; her hair was unruly and unkempt, but still mostly black and full. She had some sort of scent about her, that of a spice tree or some mix of herbs. She wore a blue robe—it was rather fine for a hermit, thick and clean and whole.

"There were two more dwarves with you, earlier," she said.

Maghran and the others were taken aback, at this; they looked at each other.

"They have gone back to their home," I said.

"Which is?"

"Stenhall."

"Very well. Why have you come? And you are a Shearer, I believe. An Emmervaler."

"I am. Aiman. I was hoping you would remember me. Thank you for opening your door to us, Duchess. We have come into possession of a letter written by Caranniam. It was being taken to the dunter army which is camped at some short distance from Emmervale. We want to know what it says, but we are unable to read it."

"My guess," she said, "would be that it commands that army to take and burn down Emmervale."

"Yes, well, milady," I answered. "It seems a long letter for that. There is much writing on it. And also we assume that those would have been the orders known to that army all along. We think there must be more to it."

"I suppose this bound man here is the messenger himself."

"Yes."

"And nothing from him. Well, you must have time now, or perhaps a reprieve entirely, what with the ruin of the railroad tracks."

"We hope so, of course," I said.

"I will ask you to come in," she said. "This is not precisely my battle, but I always enjoy a disguised message, if this is indeed what you have. And I would miss Emmervale somewhat, if it were eradicated." For all I knew, this may have been the strongest statement of allegiance and affection she had ever made for any city or realm. She beckoned us inside. We entered, pushing the messenger along with us.

The inside of the old keep was one large space. Ages ago there must have been guardrooms, hallways, and other chambers, but now the inner walls were gone. A few broken foundations of them were still in place—and a few columns, to support what remained of the flat roof—but otherwise the space was open.

Open, but not empty. The great room was decorated with old tapestries along most of its outer walls, and in a few places they hung down from the ceiling to create partitions. There were also a few old, broad tables, and wardrobes here and there. It would have made quite a grand hall in the palace of a king—save for the trees, of course. As we had seen from outside, the two large trees grew right in the middle of the hall. The apertures in the ceiling left a large gap around the trunks, but Wilhemina did not seem to worry about any intruders climbing down. Grass grew beneath the openings where the sunlight could enter. Near one of the trees was a tall, freestanding brick fireplace, which made use of the opening in the roof for the smoke to exit.

Wilhelmina also had benches strewn around, seemingly at random, and several very worn chaise lounges and upholstered chairs. There was a cluster of chests near the fireplace. The furniture was kept on areas of broken stone and tiles, but some areas of the floor were dirt.

Britta and I had been inside the keep before, but all the others stood and took it all in. It was a singular home.

"You have this letter?" Wilhelmina asked.

"We do," Maghran answered. "But first, if I may ask for a moment from you, I have a gift I would like to present. A token from my family in Stenhall."

He held up the arovis gem and gave it to her.

"Very handsome," she said. "I know the value that dwarves place on such jewels, so I appreciate your gesture."

I suspected she was insinuating that she herself did not place value on such things, but Maghran bowed.

"You are welcome," he said. "And now the letter."

Britta handed it to her. She walked nearer the light, by one of the trees, and held it up before her eyes. She seemed to relish it.

"The seal of Somoroveln himself," she said.

"So we saw," Britta answered.

"Very good," she said. She scanned the letter. "Very good. Written by a clever man, or a clever woman. I would guess it was not actually written by Somoroveln. I don't know that he is a cryptographer."

"You can read the letters?" Britta asked.

"They are not letters," she said. "They are parts of words. There may not be enough words in this message to tell me how many characters are being used, and that is one way to distinguish letters from syllables. But there are few characters to each word, and that is another way. It is not likely that a message would be composed completely of such short words." She barely nodded and repeated: "One, or two, or three letters per word? Not likely. So therefore each symbol must stand in for several letters. Several letters."

She continued to read, and began to move her right hand in the air, absently; she was apparently drawing the characters, and also making occasional circles. Then she began to sway back and forth, very slightly. Britta glanced at me. The dwarves stood, unmoved.

"This writing," she then said; but she caught herself, and glanced toward the messenger.

"Shall we enclose that one in a chest?" she asked us.

"Well," I said. I looked at Maghran to try to gauge his opinion; he seemed to raise his eyebrows.

"Honestly, we do not feel a need to antagonize this man if we don't need to," I said. "Not any more than we have already, that is. We could take him outside, if you like."

"Let us just speak quietly, then," she said. "There is an easy clue to the code here. The dunter army is outside of Stenhall and Emmervale. Between them, is that correct?"

"Yes," I answered.

"There are two words which occur next to each other and repeat themselves several times, in the beginning. If I suppose that these are Stenhall and Emmervale . . . and I assume that they are writing in the language of Caranniam . . . " she trailed off and was silent a moment.

"It will do for a start," she said, almost to herself. "It will do for a start. For a start," she repeated, her voice quieting even more. She raised her fingers to twirl her already unruly hair, absently.

"What tails and crosses we have here," she murmured. "Tails and crosses, indeed . . . and crosses and tails."

Then she called out to all of us, abruptly:

"There is bread in a shelf by the fireplace. Other food. This will take time."

She said no more. She began to pace, now, still holding the letter before her.

When she was some distance across the room, Maghran spoke to me in a low voice.

"You say she is no wizard, but there is magic in this place."

"You believe so?"

"Look at its stones. I can't believe these walls are still standing."

"Some of them are not."

"But it's remarkable that any of it at all is still upright."

"It was built solidly."

He shook his head. "Just gaze around you. You build a bit in stone, also—even your masons could see how weak these walls are."

I let this slight pass, and he continued.

"They should have fallen. Large sections have bowed in so much that they should have collapsed."

"Maybe the vines hold it firm."

Maghran shook his head. "And she has no protection. Any fool could drop in near those trees. And she is clearly no fool herself; so she must have reason to feel safe. Some reason that we cannot see. This is quite an odd friend you have, Master Shearer."

By now the Duchess had sat down at one of the tables. Britta and Jed walked, somewhat slowly and shyly, over to the fireplace to see about the food she had mentioned. Soon they found it and offered it to all of us.

"Is there a well here?" Maghran asked.

"I haven't seen one."

"She might have it in here, and not outside, as large as this place is. I will search."

We ate, and then waited. Maghran found water and shared it, even with the prisoner. I watched as we made ourselves more and more at home in this ancient hermitage. It was not hard to do so, what with all the chairs and lounges. Britta lay down to nap. Even the prisoner sat down, though of course we left his hands and feet bound.

Jed busied himself picking up leaves and sticks which had blown in through the holes in the roof. The sticks he piled by the fireplace, and the leaves he threw outside.

Through all this the Duchess did not move from her seat at the table. Her long hair had fallen forward to the point where it looked as if she had drawn a curtain around herself.

The afternoon wore on. Britta, Hrond, and Inman again took their guns and set out to search for game.

"Will she mind if we shoot?" Britta asked me.

"We have to eat," I said. "And of course we'll share with her."

"I mean, will it break her concentration?"

"Ah, that's what you mean. Well, if the noise of six of us and a prisoner rambling about her home doesn't bother her, I don't imagine she'll be distracted by hunting."

They left. Some time later we did hear three shots; the Duchess flinched a bit but did not take her eyes off the paper, and did not move.

"I feel useless," Maghran said. "Had I known it would be like this, perhaps she could have ripped that thing in half and given part of it to us to sort through."

"I don't feel I'm up to it," I said.

It turned out that the hunting party had taken down a deer. By now it was nearly evening, and most of the party—everyone but Maghran and me—moved outside to start a large fire to cook dinner.

We ate a prodigious amount; we roasted a portion for the Duchess; we looked about for any ice room or ice cave where she might store such things, but found none; we put out the fire, moved the remainder of the carcass well away, and returned back inside; and still she worked on the letter.

The night was well into darkness, and the Duchess had long since lit a lamp, when she suddenly stood. Only Inman and I were awake. Inman nudged Maghran, who was on the floor beside him.

She glided back toward us. She still did not seem to move her eyes from the letter.

The she looked over at the prisoner. He was now lying on the ground some distance away.

"You understand," she said to us, quietly, "that there is a grand alliance between Varenlend and Caranniam."

"Of course," I said.

"Unprecedented in our time. An alliance which, combined with the masses of Red Gorge, can level your cities, and neutralize Searose, and isolate the other dwarves and also the elves."

"Such is their plan," Maghran answered. "Isolate us, or worse." Inman, standing next to him, nodded.

"Yes. But this is quite a letter you have intercepted," she said. "Do not look back at that messenger as I say this, just in case he is awake. Now. This letter is directing the Caranniam army at your doorstep, once they have massacred you, to march back to Varenlend and destroy it."

I was astounded at this news.

"You have been able to read everything?" Maghran asked.

"Yes. I can show you. See these here? These words are the names of Stenhall and Emmervale, as I said. And then we have a bit of quick luck: the first symbol in the code for Stenhall starts the salutation of the letter; this might mean it is addressed to a lord. A lord of Caranniam."

"Lord Sterovannar, the leader of their guard."

"Yes. Exactly the man we would suspect to lead the dunter army and the other men who direct it," she said. "And he has a long name, with several symbols. One of which is similar to another in the word Varenlend, which occurs further down the letter. This confirms my guess.

"Only one other especially long word occurs repeatedly in this letter, and I surmise that to be Caranniam. So you see. We can make five educated guesses about patterns we would see with these five coded words, and that gives us the symbols for a number of syllables already. Over a dozen of them.

"This is a direct coding of Cranam. And one word we can put together from the others is *vacar*, war march. Its components we know from the code for Sterovannar and Caranniam. And it appears before Varenlend; further confirmation that we are making the right inferences, and that Varenlend is to be attacked. This is how I decoded this. There were many more steps along the way, but this is how.

"The alliance is over after your towns fall. Or that was the plan, at least, until you came across this. Tell me: Is it known if that army from Red Gorge has units attached from both Varenlend and Caranniam, along with all the dunters? Or is it only Caranniam?"

"It sounds as if you may know as well as we do, Duchess," Maghran answered. It was the first time he had used her chosen title, I noticed. "But our understanding has been that yes, elements from both of the wizards' cities are in that army."

"That would make sense, from this letter. And that means there will be a hard night for the Varenlend contingent when this message is received. Or there would have been."

Maghran shook his head and said:

"We must positively thank these fool wizards for dissolving, on their own, this alliance which might have allowed them to conquer all of us. This is more than we could have hoped to engineer ourselves."

"And now, what shall we do with this knowledge," she said. "Or what will you do with it. It belongs to you. Your captured messenger, your letter, your towns under attack."

"We must get the letter to them, of course," Maghran said. "We might send this messenger straight off. With our blessing and a bottle of spirits for his trouble."

"We can keep our spirits," I said. "But of course we might be able to make even more of this."

"How do you mean?"

"We have their messenger and their code."

"Yes. Well?"

"Do you think we could alter it? Alter the message? Could you change just a few words in the beginning, Duchess?"

"To what?"

"Keep in all the bit about marching to Varenlend, but instruct them to call off the attack on our cities. Instead of 'after destroying,' change it to 'leave immediately.' Something along that line. And then we could get this new message to them."

"Get it to them," Maghran repeated. "You mean to that army camped out by our homes? Directly?"

"Yes."

"Well," Maghran said. "That is a fine idea. That is genius, young man. If the Duchess can help us write."

"I can, yes," she said. "They will never know my version is not straight from Caranniam."

"Perfect," Maghran said, and he bowed. "Although the delivery might be difficult. We would need someone to attempt to pass himself off as this gentleman messenger of ours. Someone who looks a bit like him. A man, of course."

He looked at me and continued:

"Someone who might wear that fine red clothing."

"You are mad," I said. "You want me to pretend I am him?"

"You're just a messenger, who would know? It's only a scourge of dunters. They won't look very hard at you."

"Only a scourge of dunters," I repeated. I imagined myself riding alone into that camp. "First, thank you for your confidence in sending me into a crowd of savages as an impostor with a forged message. Second, we know that this message will not go to just anyone, but rather to the command from Caranniam."

"So you would speak with them. You could pull it off."

"Perhaps—unless they know this man. And I would guess it is quite likely that they do. He is likely a noble, and they probably are, also, and I would think they all know each other, Maghran."

"Hmm. Perhaps."

"We'll need another way."

"We could send in the horse, with no rider, but carrying the new message in the bag. We could drench the saddle in blood. Someone in the camp would get the letter to the command."

"Unless the horse turns around instantly and heads back to Caranniam," I said. "But you are right; something like that is the thing to do. We would have to make them think that they had recovered the letter untouched."

"We would want to get close to the camp in order to pull this off. Make it more likely the horse and message would end up there."

Inman, still with us, shook his head.

"But Maghran, and Master Shearer," he said. "We must take this false letter to the camp, or close to it, so that it will be captured."

"Yes."

"But obviously we must not be captured ourselves. And this delivery must look like a genuine loss, a genuine mistake of ours. Genuine enough so that the dunters, or the men, who recover the letter do not suspect it is fake."

"I doubt the dunters would have the acuity to suspect anything," I said.

"The men, then," Inman said. "It could be a man we encounter. And we are supposed to pretend to run away in a panic and drop something this important. And to mishandle a horse, if we have it along. There is too much that can go wrong here."

"Inman is right," Maghran said. "We can't afford a mistake."

"I think Master Shearer has to ride it in," Inman said. "But perhaps he could simply thrust it into someone's hands and then turn back. You could just bark orders to deliver it and then leave, comrade. I think that's what we might expect from our high-born friend here anyway," he said, nodding toward the messenger. "I don't believe he would stop and chat with any dunters."

"And in case some Caranniam noble in that camp is expecting you to pay him a call and stop for tea, you could let it be known that you must rush, due to the very news you carry," Maghran said. "You can just snap at them in Lower and depart. It's what this man would shout at dunters anyway."

"I do speak Cranam, if it comes to it," I said.

"Well then, all the better. And once they see that letter, no one will question why you rode off quickly," Inman seconded. "They will see that the war is continuing."

I nodded. "Very well. I see the sense in this. So our journey here would once again become longer. Duchess, we might trouble you to ask for some food to take along. Can you write this new message for us tomorrow?"

"I can do it tonight," she said. "I can sleep the day after."

"The paper will have to look right, of course." Maghran said. "And it should have that seal of Somoroveln copied."

"These are no obstacles," she said.

She set immediately back to work, this time with a paper and ink. We woke Britta and Jed, and Hrond, and spoke with them.

Then the Duchess sat at a table and wrote as Maghran and I reviewed the words.

"There is no elaborate penmanship with this code?" Maghran asked. "Yours will look the same?"

"The same," she said. "You see the characters; there are no flourishes, no ornament. Merely shapes, with some legs and tails. I shall tell them to call off the attack?"

"Perhaps simply 'leave forthwith.' Or 'right away'—is the rest of its language more formal, or informal?"

"I would say formal," she said. "Written by a learned man."

"Very well, 'forthwith,' " I said. "You can piece that word together from the symbols you know, Duchess?"

"Yes," she said. "And should we supply a reason? They might be suspicious, without one."

"Yes," Maghran said. "How about if we tell them that Varenlend has attacked Caranniam? That would explain the quick move. And it would sow confusion, and discord—something I would like to see as soon as possible."

"Good," I said.

Again we found ourselves biding our time in the keep of the Duchess while she labored for us at something with which we could provide her no help. A few of our party dozed. Inman produced whetstones from his pack and sharpened his axe, which I doubt needed it.

I had enjoyed the quiet time, in this strong and eccentric ancient tower of the Duchess, during the hours she spent deciphering the letter; but now that she was altering it, an obvious plan formed in my mind and occupied me. If she were successful, and we were successful, in inducing the invaders to leave our land, our work would not be finished. I tried to ignore our opportunity, but I could not.

"Maghran," I said. "If we pull this off—if this united army of Caranniam and Varenlend and Red Gorge really abandons its attack—we will have to take the attack to them."

"I thought the entire point was to let them fight each other," he said.

"Caranniam and Varenlend, yes. But think of Red Gorge. It will be wide open if Caranniam takes all those dunters to the battle of Varenlend."

"And what would we do, the six of us? Install ourselves in the main hall of Red Gorge and bar the door?"

"Of course would have to send for our own armies," I said. "Of men and dwarves. And we could then march into Red Gorge and dismantle it."

"You mean cart away all their bricks?" he said.

"Come, Maghran. I mean spike their mills, ruin their foundries. Take over their city, if we can. At the least, demolish their industry."

"It seems the elves have already done that," he said.

"And you want to leave that work to them?" I asked him. "You are depending on elves? It seems unlike you." I smiled.

"Yes, well, perhaps you are right," he said. "But we do not prize battles out in the open. We have built our halls strong for a reason, and we are glad to stay in them. In any case, all of that hinges on this woman here pulling this off," he said, nodding toward the Duchess. "I do not want to get ahead of myself."

She had the new letter finished some time well after midnight. We set watch over the hungry prisoner, and slept. The Duchess extinguished the lamp and disappeared into the shadows.

Seven

In the morning we woke and soon were all examining the Duchess's new letter, comparing it to the old one. We all were struck at how similar the two were; the characters, and even the paper. She had a supply of paper and parchment stashed away in that sprawling keep. Then she spent another hour replicating the seal and the stamp of the two crows; she did this with her own wax, and a knitting needle, and a thin knife.

Maghran spoke to me:

"It would be best if we could leave this silent messenger of ours here. Nothing good can come of his traveling with us. But I don't know if she could watch a prisoner."

"I don't think she could, Maghran."

"Are there any rooms in this place? Anywhere she could lock him up? She mentioned putting him in a chest, but that will not work for the long term."

"I don't think there are any rooms, no. Perhaps a cellar we missed when we were looking for that ice room? But I doubt she could keep him alive, safely. And she should not kill him. Even if Caranniam loses their war, their noble families will likely endure, and harm would probably come to her eventually if she abused him."

"If anyone knows where he is," Maghran said. "But I think you are correct. We are responsible for this man. There is no reason for him to become her burden."

Soon we were packed and ready to leave. We spoke to the Duchess before we stepped out. She appeared no worse for having spent so many hours awake.

"We thought of asking you a favor, milady," Maghran asked.

"Keeping that prisoner of yours."

"That's right. But we shall take him along."

"As you should. I could not guarantee that he would be contained here. I am alone."

"And so we shall leave you."

I was not glad to leave that keep and the quiet, heedless hospitality of the Duchess. I looked back at it one more time as we moved away, and so did all the others. Even the dwarves were impressed, I think, with her isolated and undisturbed hideaway; something they could appreciate.

Our walk toward the dunter encampment would be two long days. We began by heading north-northeast through the woods. The dense Kurtenvold proper was soon behind us, but lands which were mostly wooded stretched farther and farther north as one headed east. We would cut through them for some distance, as a direct route to the encampment and also a way to avoid any dunters who might be ranging this far south. All was quiet in the woods; it was midmorning and any animals that would have been about in the early hours were holed up again. We picked our way between towering trees, on a floor of fallen leaves. After a short time we banked to our left, making our way due north.

The Duchess had given us bags of wheat, and we also took game as we marched. We fed the prisoner enough to keep him alive. Most of the time he walked. For some stretches we would throw him over his horse, on his stomach, not wanting to give him the dignity even of riding sidesaddle with his legs bound.

"At least we will still get to take away those fine clothes from this buffoon," Maghran said. "I think you will cut a fine figure in red, Master Shearer."

During the second day the woods began to grow less dense, and there were clearings here and there. In one of them we came upon a sign of the roving dunters: a ransacked farmhouse. It was the first dwelling we had seen since leaving the Duchess, and the first regular house we had seen in days for that matter. Its door was wide open, and the interior was in disarray. Remains of a bed, and broken barrels, littered the yard. Two outbuildings were also deserted. A paddock behind one of them was empty. As we passed it we saw a dead cow, partially butchered.

"Did the dunters kill it and not take it all?" Inman said. "Fools."

"The dunters may have done this, but I blame the men of Caranniam, and Varenlend," Britta said. "Were it not for them, the dunters would have never left Red Gorge. There is no way they would have ventured out this far."

"So we know that we are nearly out of these woods, now, and the dunters are close," Maghran said. "Let's be aware of patrols. And if we happen to run into a war party, we should fire off a few shots, but drop that letter and get away."

We nodded at this sensible advice, made our way across the clearing, and prepared ourselves to be alert when we finally left these woods.

And at that moment, at the clearing's edge, a pair of amvizons screeched and launched themselves at us out of the brush.

They looked like starved bears and attacked the way a starved bear might. They were as tall as the dwarves and came at us with wide-open jaws of knife-teeth. They were sleeker than ansarks but had a spring to them from their thick haunches. They killed with their jaws but could grapple with their front claws.

One crashed into Inman, who threw up his arms and fell backward. The other aimed first for Maghran but then darted at Britta. She had her musket slung and reached for it, not to shoot but just to get the stock in the way. She stepped sideways and managed to hit the bear-dog in the snout with the butt of her gun. This did not slow the animal, but it did have to turn again to reach her. This gave Maghran a second to step in with his axe. He swung and missed, still not close enough. I pulled the long knife I carried, but of course Maghran with his axe would swing again first.

Inman heaved himself backward on the ground and the first amvizon closed in. It snapped at his leg and caught his boot. He tried to kick himself free.

Hrond had now leveled his musketoon. He fired. The blast from two paces away knocked Inman's beast over.

Jed stepped up on the far side of Britta and brought his staff down on the neck of that amvizon. This did no harm to the animal but again we had at least stopped it for a moment, and then Maghran was able to sink his axe into its right shoulder. It was a cleaving swing that cracked bone and ran deep. The bear-dog jolted, struggled with spasms for a moment, and then fell.

Inman's attacker stayed down, too. Hrond's shot had opened up its side.

Then we all flinched at yet another shriek, again from the brush. A third amvizon jumped up, but this one ran back into the woods. It was a young one.

"The cub of these two," Maghran said. "Tragic for them they felt they had to defend it. I would have stayed clear of it anyway."

"They must have been drawn by the butchered cow," Britta said.

Inman stood.

"Thank you for that shot," he said.

"Your leg?" I asked him.

"No damage. We make our boots to last."

"Let's continue," Maghran said. "The way will be clear of predators, now, after all this noise. Dunters are another matter. We shall see."

Then we heard a scream from behind us. It was muffled; or, more accurately, gagged. A raiding party of small forms were running away from us, south into the woods. They were kobolds, and they had our prisoner—their prisoner now—dangling hogtied from a beam they had shouldered.

Eight

Five of us immediately took off running after them. Jed stayed behind to tie up the horse but soon caught up.

"We all took eyes off him?" Maghran shouted.

"Of course," Hrond answered. "Who would have watched him amid that?"

The kobolds dashed between the trees, pulling away from us.

When I thought of the little dog-men I always pictured them dirty, and worn. They were either servants of the dwarves, filthy from digging in mines, or else slaves of the dunters, even filthier and envious of their dwarf-owned cousins. There may not have actually been any dog in them, of course, but many referred to them that way because of their fur, and ears, and their harsh speech which often came off like yelps and snarls.

We would see the occasional runaway or free kobold in Emmervale, and they were uniformly haggard. But this little group we saw now were dressed in very serviceable clothes. Above their furry ears, which stuck straight out from their heads, they wore sturdy helmets which fit them well enough not to bounce off amid all the jostling. They wore real boots, all of them. There were perhaps eight, in total. Four carried the pole, and three or four others ran beside them and in front of them, and barked at their laboring comrades to make better speed. The ones off to the side continually looked back at us, to see if we were gaining. The ones carrying the pole kept their heads down and plowed ahead.

We were weighted down, but so were they. The long pole to which they had tied the baron, even though they carried it on their shoulders, was not high enough off the ground to prevent his rump from dragging. They shouted as they ran, exhorting each other.

We all followed close behind, and began to cut the gap. Britta, Jed and I were faster than the dwarves, especially Inman with his recent boot-mauling and also his long-barreled musket to carry. Within two hundred paces through the woods we had moved well ahead.

Now one of the kobolds came to a dead halt, pulled out a pistol, and aimed at us.

"Around!" I yelled at Jed and Britta, but I didn't need to; they had already swerved. I had been half-expecting one of the raiders to make a stand like this, in order to gain time for his comrades, and I think Jed and Britta had, too.

I ducked, moved to my left, and heard the boom from the pistol. I may have also heard the bullet rocket away through the leaves of the trees; at any rate, it did not strike any of us. Now Britta swerved back toward the brave kobold and, before it had a chance to pull a blade, literally ran him over. Britta kicked him aside like a longball. We followed her.

We kept on. Jed and I now outpaced even Britta, who was carrying the musket and of course also had lead and powder. The two of us stayed close to the barking knot of dog-men and their quarry.

A thicket of narrow trees appeared before us, and the kobold raiders made for it. They ran straight into a slight gap between the trunks. Again the baron was the worse for being dragged through. Jed and I crashed in after them.

We found ourselves in a small clearing with a dozen other kobolds; or perhaps more, many more. It was a camp, or actually a tiny village. In the middle was a large fire. That was where the raiding party stopped, dropped their pole, and drew swords. The baron struggled on the ground and eventually managed to sit upright. He had slid his hands around the end of the pole. His wrists and ankles were still bound, however, and he was gagged.

A relatively large kobold had been sitting by the fire, roasting something on a stick, and now he stood. He wore chain mail, unlike the others. I guessed he was their leader. He sized up the baron, and us.

The group of them could have attacked Jed and me at once and probably dispatched us quickly, but fortunately the kobolds who had been in the village all seemed taken by surprise by the prisoner and our pursuit. As they looked at each other, and at the raiders, and the baron, Britta burst through the thicket and quickly knelt and aimed her musket at one of them.

If the flint of her gun was still in the clamp, after all the jostling from her run, and likewise if the ball and wadding had not been knocked loose, I would have been surprised. Furthermore she was breathing so hard that I doubt she could have hit much under the best of circumstances. But nonetheless the kobolds were wary of her. It was a standoff, for a moment.

I examined their little village. What had looked at first glance like piles of brush were sturdy little houses, carefully concealed with branches and saplings. They were made of stone, or rammed earth, and had sloped roofs. They had doors, short chimneys, and windows. There were a few pens with pigs. Beyond the central area, a stream ran through the clearing.

"This is quite a little town they have for themselves," Britta said.

"And well-hidden," I said. "They must have been in this place for some time."

"And unbeknownst to us." In Emmervale we had never heard of such a warren, not really too far away from us.

Again we heard noise behind, and now Hrond emerged from the trees. He surveyed us quickly, understood the standoff, and swung the musketoon around. I noticed that he aimed it at a kobold who stood next to our prisoner. Given our distance, and what with the width of the barrel of that musketoon, he would have blown as much shot into the Caranniam man as into the kobold had he pulled the trigger. I pictured the possible end to our crisis: the kobolds might panic, and one might swing a sword; then Britta's musket would misfire as Hrond promptly blasted the prisoner. All quite heroic.

But the kobolds saw Hrond now switch his aim to their chief, and they instantly shrieked, all together in a howling group.

This, I thought, was an unnecessary risk and provocation on our part. I did not want to tangle with this proud little town of dog-men if we did not need to.

"Hrond, aim elsewhere," I told him. I don't believe he heard me. And amid all that screaming and baying we did not notice the next entrant into the clearing: the kobold that Britta had kicked aside, earlier during the chase. He came sprinting in—brandishing a knife, and heading straight for Hrond.

I had not seen this runner until he had passed me, but somehow Jed had. As I turned to my right to look at the kobold, and the knife, I noticed a blur coming from my left. This was Jed; I have no idea how he moved so quickly. He cut to his right and dived between the kobold and Hrond. He knocked over the kobold—the little dog-man's second takedown in ten minutes.

Jed rolled and then was up on his feet. The kobold tried to raise itself up but Jed stepped over and kicked the knife out of its hand. The blade flashed away through the air, end over end.

Hrond had turned, at the noise behind him. He saw the collision, and then saw the kobold disarmed. He regarded Jed, and then quickly turned back around.

Britta and I had also turned our eyes to the kobold, just as Jed and Hrond had. We turned back around to again look at the prisoner and the apparent chief, and now saw the entire group withdrawing into the houses. Four of them had grabbed the prisoner by his arms, and by his hair, and quickly slid him toward a doorway.

Hrond again leveled his musketoon at them.

"Hrond, don't fire," I said. "No sense shooting that man."

Britta stood, and Jed stepped forward.

"We need to retrieve him," he said.

We moved toward the house. The kobolds had melted away into all the buildings in moments.

And now Maghran crashed through the canopy, trotted into the clearing, and came up beside me. On the way he had to step past the disarmed kobold; it sat there in the grass, breathing heavily, gathering wits, as Maghran moved by him with barely a glance.

"Where did they go?" he asked.

"That house there," I said. "With the prisoner. Come."

We advanced, the five of us, and saw no eyes in doorways, no musket barrels protruding from windows. It was suddenly quiet in the clearing.

"It must be a tight fit in those homes," Hrond said.

"I would guess they have gone underground," Maghran answered.

We came to the doorway through which the Caranniam man had disappeared, and entered the little house. The door had been left open, and we peered in and saw that Maghran was right: stone steps descended into a tunnel. This house, at least, was nothing more than a roof over a tunnel entrance.

Maghran, not breaking stride, rushed to the stairs and dropped down.

"What about Inman?" I asked Hrond.

"He'll take care of himself. Too slow. He'll be along."

"Hrond, you next," Britta said. "This will be useless." She meant her long musket; Hrond's musketoon would fit more easily down the passage. She followed him after he disappeared, and then Jed and I went.

The steps descended perhaps thirty feet. The air went cool and damp as I hustled down. The stone floor at the bottom was barely illuminated by light from a shaft above. We were in a tunnel perhaps forty paces long, with a torch at the far end.

I was surprised, but should not have been, to see that the tunnel was small, no more than five feet high. Ample head room for a kobold, but not for us. Britta would not be able to use her musket, and Jed would have to crouch down to the point where would be waddling.

She handed him the gun.

"Why don't you go back up," she said. "Watch out for that beaten one up there."

He looked down the tunnel, nodded, and held back as Britta and I followed the dwarves. We trotted after them as quickly as we could.

At first glance I had taken the tunnel to be irregular, but now saw that the side walls had small alcoves carved into them. Within these were decorations, mostly shields. I was struck by this, and by the smooth floors, and the lighting which was dim but adequate.

"Kobolds must have done this," I said to Britta as we moved. "I'd have guessed they took this over from someone, but dwarves and men build larger tunnels."

"I wonder if it's wise to chase after them down here."

But we continued down the halls, tailing the dwarves. Maghran and Hrond seemed much more fleet here than above ground. We followed them around one corner, then another. The passages sloped downward. We heard the chatter of the kobolds some distance ahead of us.

"Maghran," I called. "How far will we pursue them?"

"No one is going to lose me underground," he answered.

Each new hall was illuminated by a torch on the wall; and now, in addition to the alcoves and shields, we passed fine mosaics and carvings. I noticed that some of the shields on display were accompanied by swords—swords of men, too large for these kobolds. I was surprised, yet again, to see this, because these weapons had value. All of the few free kobolds I had seen before passing through Emmervale were such paupers that I'm sure they would have sold such prizes for whatever cash had been offered. These raiders down here were prosperous enough to keep them.

At the end of this third hall the passage gave way into a large chamber. We could not see much of it, and I would have liked to peer in before charging. But Maghran and Hrond did not slow down, and neither did Britta and I.

The four of us entered this large room, and stopped. It was well-lighted by torches, and held dozens of kobolds. The chief stood to our left on a sort of stone stage. Next to him were the Caranniam prisoner and a clutch of other relatively large warrior kobolds. Around the hall were many others, standing amid tables.

The prisoner was on his knees, next to the chief. He was looking more and more like a pile of wet wool with each new leg of this sad journey of his.

The hall was loud. As soon as we had entered, the kobolds had begun yowling at us. It was a fearsome racket, and the commotion seemed to shake the walls themselves. Kobolds jumped up and down and shook furred fists at us. A few young ones darted back and forth and barked.

The only calm ones were the chief and his guards, up on the stage. The chief held a knife to the prisoner, and watched his people with seeming pride. Hrond had leveled his musketoon at the group, again, and I feared that might prod the chief to give an order to overwhelm us. But he said nothing, and I think he was enjoying this show of force from his tribe. At some point between our first view of him outdoors, and now down here, he had donned a sort of crown. It was a simple black circlet that seemed to be made of stone. It came down as far as the tops of his ears.

Behind him I noticed a standard leaning against the wall. It was a black pole with spikes at angles, at the top, looking like dunter teeth. Above the spikes was a small platform capped with a large iridescent stone. It was indeed a dunter standard. I was amazed. As loose and chaotic as the Red Gorge hordes were, it still would have been quite a feat to capture this from them. I wondered if the kobolds had really done so.

Britta had noticed it too.

"These little ones captured a dunter prize?" she asked me.

"It looks that way."

"That's astounding."

"Perhaps they just found it?"

"How would anyone just find a standard like that?"

The chief and his chattering tribe were making no effort to communicate with us, yet, so I leaned forward to ask Maghran:

"Are these tunnels dwarf-built? Do you have relations down here? Or did you?"

"No," he said. "We would have made everything larger. I suppose these beasts dug all this." He seemed to speak with grudging respect.

Now their chief raised his hand, and the ruckus quieted somewhat. He lifted the knife he held and waved it. The kobolds holding the prisoner shook him and pushed him toward us a foot or two, I suppose just in case we had not noticed that they had him. The chief now spoke to us in his own language, and jerked the knife back and forth again.

"He overestimates our interest in that man's safety," Maghran growled.

Then one of the larger kobolds next to the chief translated:

"Chief Korf says this man is now our prisoner. You can either leave now, or we shall dispatch him."

The chief barked a few more words.

"Chief Korf says you should back away carefully and lift your gun."

More barking.

"Chief Korf says you should do a better job guarding your prisoner."

Then the laughter started up again. It sounded like a group of curs fighting over a sheep carcass. They did not stop even as the last of our party, Inman, now ran up behind us and joined our little group.

Britta spoke to us:

"Should we just leave him with them? We could do without the burden. And he seems to have nothing to tell us."

We considered this. It was true that we were fatigued of hauling him around.

"But do you think they could hold him?" Maghran said, quietly so that the translator could not follow. "Beyond their hall here I don't believe they are demonstrating much competence. They should have cut us down one by one as we came into their clearing up there, for one thing. He might well find a way to flee. And he needs to be held until that army is long gone. After that, they could trade him for a side of bacon for all we care. But I think we need him back."

"Do you think that army of Caranniam would really turn back toward Stenhall if he were to escape and tell them what had happened?" Inman asked.

"I don't want to risk it," Maghran said. "There's no sense in doing so. We can drag him along behind us like a sledge if we have to."

"Very well," I said. "This man should be grateful to us. How do we extract him? We need to hurry."

"Sir," Maghran said, more loudly now, to the translator. "We will pay you for this prisoner. He is worth something to us."

Once again I watched Maghran shift his pack to his side to pull out a gem. I knew what he was doing, but of course the kobolds did not. Several stepped forward menacingly, and Chief Korf waved his knife again.

Maghran held out one hand, palm open, at this, and said:

"I have a jewel to exchange for that man. As much as you will get from his city, or his family." He nodded to the translator, who repeated it in their language.

"You have another?" I asked him.

"Small wealth, as I said. Easy to carry."

He pulled out a second stone of arovis and held it up.

"You know what this is?"

"That is arovis, the rose-stone," the translator said. He nodded, and suddenly he looked bitter, and weary somehow. Up until then I had not noted his face at all, but now he struck me. He seemed a bit older than the others standing next to the chief, and his eyelids dropped down to narrow his gaze.

"I," he added, "dug those stones for you in White Mount."

"Not for me," Maghran said. "Not us. That is not our home. But this is arovis I have, and I will give this to you for that man."

The chief promptly lowered his knife, dropped down off the podium, walked up to Maghran, and snatched the stone. He raised it up to a torch on the wall and peered at it.

He jabbered something, and the translator said:

"This man is important to you?"

"Important enough for this," Maghran answered.

The chief kobold lowered the stone and looked at Maghran. He spoke to the assembled crowd of other kobolds, and there was some back and forth between them. Then, the issue apparently settled, he spoke to the translator, who told us:

"Chief Korf will take stone, and also your axe."

Maghran shook his head very slightly.

"I'd sooner part with another stone. This was my father's."

The translator did not bother running that past the chief, but just responded, again with a sober look in his eyes:

"Chief Korf will also have axe. Or no trade."

Maghran sighed.

"The mongrels," he muttered. "Well, it was I who wanted to liberate this man of ours. They have their price."

He drew the axe from his belt and stepped toward the chief with the handle held out.

"Use it well, please."

The kobolds erupted in a screeching cheer, then. They waved knives in the air, and their whelps danced around. Maghran seemed taken aback. Had he known what a prize the kobolds would consider that axe, I think he would not have given it to them, just out of pride.

But it was done. Chief Korf grasped the handle of the axe, and then turned to signal to the others by the prisoner. They lifted him to his feet and pushed him toward us. He was the worse for his capture, and for being half-dragged through the woods and along these stone floors. He stumbled, but he did move in our direction. His hands were still bound behind his back, as we had left him.

Hrond, only now, finally lifted the muzzle of his musketoon. Inman had brought his gun with him but had never bothered to shoulder it.

"Let's just back out of here," I said. Maghran snatched the arm of the prisoner, and the six of us began to move. We stepped to the entrance of the hallway and slipped out. The last image I saw of the kobold mob was many of them approaching the chief to admire the dwarven axe, their tongues lolling out of their mouths.

Nine

One more sign of the power and confidence of that group of free kobolds was the fact that they did not bother trailing us as we left their tunnels. We had the place to ourselves as we picked our way out. We climbed the steps into the stone house, exited, and saw Jed.

"You all return sound," he said. "And we have our hero back with us."

"They had their price," I said. "And Maghran had the payment."

"We must move," Britta said. "We need to get that message to Caranniam. Who knows how delayed it is already."

We left the little kobold village and continued north, retracing the way of our pursuit. We passed the clearing of the raided house again, with no incident this time. Jed untied the horse, who perhaps had enjoyed the break from the walk. We made our way past the last of the trees, and then crossed a wide stretch of open country.

"What did I miss down there?" Jed asked.

"It was impressive," Britta said. "A very tidy stronghold for the kobolds."

"Are you joking?"

"No. They are well-armed, orderly, with a strong leader. They've lined the walls down there with their plunder."

"You are serious?"

"I am."

"I should have seen it."

"You should have."

Eventually we neared Emmervale, approaching from its southwest and reaching the Walsing river again. We must have been close to the enemy army.

"This should be our camp," I said when we reached the river banks. The land was still basically flat, with just a slight fold downward where the river ran through. It was shallow, and dark with the stones beneath. There were trees along the turf banks. We could smell the water.

"Yes," Maghran nodded. "We may not find anything as good until we reach their expedition. Or until you reach it, I should say."

"It's odd hiding here when we're so close to home," I said. I remembered how close the dunter encampment was to Emmervale; it had not taken me long to ride out to it, when I had gone to survey it some weeks before.

"Close to home, indeed," Maghran said, "but with some very inhospitable neighbors between, now."

We dropped packs and set the prisoner on the ground. We tied up the horse to a tree on the south side of the river, with a long lead so it could graze. Maghran, Britta and I then crossed the water to look north from the other side. We were on the edge of the broad prairie that lay between Red Gorge and Emmervale. It stretched to the west and to the east for many miles; land which was good for farming, but poor for concealing our party. There were slight rises here and there, nothing more. The prairie ran uninterrupted as far as I could see, but we knew that to the north, and the east, there were farms not too far away.

"I will leave in the morning," I said.

"And then come back here, and I suppose we wait," Maghran answered. "If all goes well, we will have a fine show to watch."

"And then our next step?" I asked. "On to Red Gorge with our people?"

"If this works, and the army breaks up? Give me another day to think about that," he said. "We want to get home. I suppose you can take that prisoner to Emmervale and lock him up as long as you wish. And we can let Caranniam and Varenlend deal with each other. If they all fight a noble war valiantly, and defend their beloved homelands, they should bleed each other pretty well."

"We should try to get word to Varenlend just before the attack," Britta said. "They would last longer, and take more Caranniam forces down with them, if they have some time to prepare."

"That's brilliant," Maghran said. "You can send a few riders out from Emmervale with that intelligence. You might even drop off our messenger friend along the way so that he can join his comrades and fight the good fight."

"But Maghran," I pressed him again. "That cannot be the end for us. Or we could see this army outside our gates again in a few years time."

"Another day to think, Master Shearer," he repeated.

In the morning, after we had eaten, we relieved the messenger of his garments. I gave him mine; breeches, a loose shirt that had been white at one point, and the light coat I wore to keep off rain on warm days when I surveyed our sheep. They fit him well, but were clearly several steps down the ladder for him.

"He looks like someone who might earn an honest living, now," Maghran remarked.

"And I look like a noble messenger, ideally," I said. I had put on his red finery. "I hope to come back soon."

"We will help if we can," Maghran said. This was obligatory of him, but of course there would be nothing they could do if I was taken somehow.

I mounted the horse and rode out. The gelding seemed glad to have a rider and a purpose, after days of being led, and he moved confidently.

"You yourself seem a Caranniam noble," I told it. He had smart and welcoming eyes, I thought. This was the only Caranniam citizen I had ever taken a liking to. (The Duchess, as an exile, did not count as a citizen any longer.)

I scanned the land before me as far ahead as I could. I was looking for the camp, of course, but also thought I might be able to see the eastern terminus of the ruined railway. I could not make it out; it must have not quite reached this far, or else it was more to the north.

In a few minutes I approached a farmhouse. It was abandoned, and had been burned by the invaders. Its stone walls still stood, but the roof, shutters, and doors were either blackened remains or missing altogether.

The house had a barn behind it, also stone and also burned out. A fenced area showed that the family had kept some livestock, but all were long gone. I rounded all this, and came to the other side— with a clear view of the encampment.

It lay perhaps half a mile before me, and it was far, far larger than I would have guessed. It seemed to have grown since I had seen it last.

It roiled like an anthill. One small section, at an edge, had white tents; the personnel from Caranniam and Varenlend. Most of the camp, however, was a swarm of dunters in disorder, and an enormous swarm it was. I tried to estimate the number there, but it was not possible at that distance. Perhaps—I said to myself—it was five hundred there, five hundred more there, and so on? But there was no way to count them all. For one thing, there was constant motion. It was, certainly, many more fighting dunters that I had assumed Red Gorge was able to give.

I had assumed I might see patrols issuing out of the camp from time to time, in formation, but in reality small groups and individuals were continually splitting off, apparently on their own. It looked as though I could put myself in the way of marauders within a few minutes. In fact it surprised me that no dunters had stumbled upon me yet.

I gently spurred the horse, easily the hardest thing I had done in my life. But I kept on. I took strength somehow from that fine clothing I was wearing, and from the role I was playing. I did not have to give orders and demand respect as Aiman Shearer; I could do it by pretending to be this haughty noble who was at that moment tied to a tree. The handsome horse I rode helped, also. I wondered if a grand mount and grand clothing were in themselves much of what it took to feel the confidence of a ruler.

I could not spend much time on this reflection because there now appeared before me two figures—dunters. The first was perhaps two hundred yards away; the second was some distance further. Both were coming toward me.

The second, the farther one, looked larger and showed a glint of armor. I avoided the first and rode to this more imposing character. Perhaps he would have to pass the message through fewer hands to get it to the recipient. The first eyed me as I rode by. He was not tall, dressed only in rags with an iron helmet, but he had a fighting look in his eyes.

The larger dunter behind him had wide shoulders that made me think of my dwarf friends, and a steel breast plate that shone. He carried a broadsword slung across his back, and a heavy pistol at his waist. He had the usual protruding lower jaw and sharp teeth reaching up from it. He wore a nose ring, had a thick black tattoo on his neck, and showed a horrific scar over his left eye from some blow that must have nearly torn off his forehead. But for all that, he did not have the defiant sneer of the first one. He did not speak as I approached. Perhaps he had more to lose than the first if he were to disrespect this noble messenger from Caranniam that he saw before him.

I withdrew the letter from the saddle bag as I rode, and held it out to my side so he could see it, lest he think I had pulled a weapon. I snapped at him as I approached, before he could say anything to me:

"You there. Take this to Lord Sterovannar. Tell him I was here. I must turn back directly. He will understand why when he reads."

I had spoken in Cranam, as the messenger might have, and I had no idea if the beast would understand. But he answered in kind.

"Your name, sir," he croaked. He spoke with the usual dunter lisp through all those teeth.

I finally reached him, now, and thrust the letter at him. He put out a scarred hand and took it.

"He knows who I am. Be off," I barked.

I turned the horse and spurred it. The smaller dunter had been watching me all along, but I did not meet his eyes as I swerved around him again.

I did not look back as I departed. I kept the horse at some speed; not a gallop, for I did not want to suggest fear, but quick enough to get out of there and discourage anyone from attempting to catch up with me.

Would it work? Would the dunter take the message where it needed to go, or would he get caught up in some quarrel or brawl along the way? Would he try to read it himself? Few of them could read, so there was little chance of that. Of course it would have been gibberish to him even if here were literate and tried. All in all I thought he was a responsible-looking chap and would deliver the letter directly, if he could. I hoped that it did not need to be handed through some hierarchy of dunter lieutenants and warlords to get to Sterovannar. I kept up my pace as I approached the burned-out farmhouse.

Two mounted men then moved out from behind the barn and stood in my path. One was dressed in the red of Caranniam. The other was in brown, but carried a musket.

114

Ten

Both of these men were tall, with long noses and black hair. In other words, they both looked like our captive messenger.

"Baron Laurent," the first said. He spoke the name slowly. Although I understood the Cranam he spoke, it took me far too long to realize that he was not starting a story about a Baron Laurent but rather was asking me—confirming with me—that this was my name.

"Yes," I said. I could hardly deny it and come up with something else. Baron Laurent I was. I hoped this was indeed the name of our captured messenger.

"We did not expect you. You were in the camp?"

"Not all the way in, no. I brought a message to be delivered."

"You took it to Lord Sterovannar?"

"I did not. I had no time; have no time."

"You did not see Lord Sterovannar?" he exclaimed. Both looked at me queerly, now. "What did you do with the message?"

"I gave it to that dunter captain," I said. I turned and pointed toward where he had been, but he was no longer visible. I had no idea if he was a captain, of course, but I decided he could do with a promotion if not. It would sound better than handing the message to a dunter sergeant.

They looked even more appalled at this. Their faces fell.

"A dunter?" the first said. "To take responsibility for a message for the Lord?"

I saw it was time for me to take command:

"We have no time for protocol," I said. "This attack is called off, and the attack on Varenlend starts now. That is the content of the message. I must get back myself immediately, and you must of course also complete your work here and then pull out without delay. This exercise here is at an end, and now our real campaign begins, gentlemen."

Would they have known of the treachery against Varenlend? I figured that if they did, my knowledge of it would help convince them that I really was the messenger; and if they did not, the shock of it might cause them to forget any suspicion they might have about me.

They took me seriously, it turned out.

"Attack on Varenlend?" the first said. "So it is true. The rumor."

"Indeed. You understand my haste, then. Good day."

Again I spurred the horse, and again rode off with some speed. A speed that was confident—and got me out of there—but not rushed, I hoped.

I made it back to the outcrop of trees and was congratulated.

"You dealt with dunters and men from Caranniam?" Britta asked, after I told them what had happened.

"Both. Had I known that, I would not have gone. But I am back alive."

We settled in to keep watch to see if the expeditionary army would indeed pull up its stakes—or gather up its rags, as the case might be—and march back to Red Gorge, and then Caranniam, and then Varenlend.

I gave the messenger his clothes back, and took mine. I had considered just keeping his red garments—they were very well-made—but it would have felt odd to dress like a Caranniam noble indefinitely.

"So, Baron Laurent," Maghran spoke to him. "Now we know your name."

Fatigued and hungry as usual, the prisoner did not reply. He stood to dress himself, seemed to sway in the breeze somewhat, and then collapsed again.

"If the letter works," Maghran asked me, "I suppose they will not move until the morning."

"And perhaps not even tomorrow," I said. "Although we did try to be clear with the Duchess to give it a sense of urgency, didn't we? We shall see."

"The letter alone does not even have to do the job, now," Britta said. "If the men you spoke to believed you, as you think they did, they'll inform the forces of Caranniam themselves. They would not want to wait around for the Varenlend fighters to catch wind of this."

"True," I said. "I wonder how easy it will be for these leaders from Caranniam to order around the dunters. It might be difficult to pull them away, when they were looking forward to an attack and spoils."

We prepared to sit tight in that cover for a few days until the army, we hoped, moved away. Jed and Britta and I did not want to risk being run down by a dunter patrol, had we chanced an immediate return to Emmervale, and the dwarves stayed for the same reason.

That narrow stretch of woods turned out to be a providential location for our wait. In addition to the concealment, the river there had ample fish. (Jed, who usually would have caught some, stayed away from them, after his altercation with Hrond; but Britta took a number out and the three of us all ate them.) I also found more splitleaf roots to eat. We risked fire during the day to cook. We only worried that some dunters or enemy men might come to the river for water, but none did.

But of course our wait felt like no picnic, as we kept watch for the large army to move west. We guessed they would keep to our north, if and when they marched; but we were wary about them heading toward us, and we stayed ready to flee.

We waited patiently that night, and the next morning, and into the afternoon. At this point Inman and Hrond grumbled about the lack of progress with our plan. Maghran upbraided them:

"We don't know yet that we failed. It will take time for them to get that horde moving."

It became time again to eat, and I think Jed and Britta intentionally made a fire which was larger than it should have been, and threw off more smoke, and lasted longer into the twilight, because they half-wished that some dunters would come investigate and they would thereby have something to do. (The dwarves, for their part, for all their strength and weaponry, seemed glad to spend the days unnoticed and eventually return home having done nothing more than lay down some explosives and pick them up again. This adventure, for them, would have then been just an extended hunting trip, and they seemed content with that.) But we were again left to ourselves.

Something like a crack of thunder and lightning woke us well into the night, however. It was not natural lightning—the sky was clear. We darted up from our sleeping rolls and joined Britta and

Inman, who had been standing watch. They were on the other side of the stream, looking north.

"That flash came from there, from the enemy camp," Britta said. "And there were some others before it, not as great."

More silent flashes now lit up the sky to the north. One was blue, a second red; then a larger white flash flared, and a moment later we heard a blast.

"This could not be an attack on our towns, could it?" Jed asked.

"I don't think it can be," I answered. "Emmervale would be to the east, and Stenhall would be farther north than what we're looking at. It must be the camp."

"I suppose the Caranniam contingent did not get the drop on those from Varenlend, as they would have hoped," Maghran said. "They must be having it out."

Britta shook her head.

"Just imagine what they could have done to us with that power," she said. "We've escaped a disaster."

"We could make plenty of noise of our own if they brought that to our gates," Maghran said. "But it's good they waste it on each other."

The flashes and bursts continued. Some lights brought explosions, and others did not. They continued for perhaps a quarter hour, and then began to diminish. Some became more quiet, as their frequency dropped off, and then all of it ceased altogether. The night returned to its usual stillness. Some frogs along the river began to strum their calls, and insects chirped.

"Now we must truly be alert," Maghran said. "There may be men fleeing that battle, and I would guess the main army will move out soon."

We neither saw nor heard anything, for the remainder of the night; of course that does not mean that no one ran across the fields before us. Varenlenders may have fled in the darkness, heading west. All was quiet, apart from the frogs, and I even dozed.

It was in the gray dawn that Jed called to us. Inman, Hrond and I stalked up to his position, beneath low-hanging branches of a tree on the edge of the stand. We half-dragged the baron along with us. All the others were already there.

Jed pointed. I saw tiny figures moving, from our right to our left; from the camp toward Caranniam and Varenlend, just as we had hoped. There were only a few. They seemed to be men, not dunters.

We saw no more for some time. The light of dawn continued to build, and we could see more clearly when the main force of the army of Caranniam—for that is who they were—passed before us. The riders out in front wore red, and immediately behind these nobles were the standard-bearers. Then came a few dozen more riders, and after them, a score or so of wagons. After the wagons, the soldiers on foot. All were men.

"Will we see any of the force from Varenlend?"

"Perhaps they fled at night. Or perhaps there are none of them left to flee."

"Where are the dunters?" Jed asked. "We need them to follow along."

But there were none. The Caranniam march numbered only a few hundred, much as we would have guessed.

When the small army had passed, Jed looked at me gravely.

"A fine force, but nowhere near everyone we hoped to see," he said.

"So the dunters remained," Inman said. "With no allies, and no railway. They must still be bent on taking Stenhall, and your Emmervale, if they don't intend to starve."

"We will have to flush them out," Jed said.

"They will be a much easier force to defeat, without the help from the wizards," Hrond said.

"We could still use your assistance," I told him.

"You must speak to Maghran concerning that," he said. "Our march back home will begin now, in any event."

We walked back to the camp site. The dwarves strolled with little care, not betraying much concern with the dunter army that remained out at the foot of the hills of Stenhall.

"And now home," Maghran said. "Hrond, have you kept your powder dry, through all this?"

"I believe so. It's a good thing we've had fair weather."

"Quite."

We reached our packs and bedrolls. The dwarves said a few more things I did not hear, but it was obvious to me that they were celebrating the end of their mission—and its several detours—and that they were not readying themselves to follow up on our success. There was none of the grim reticence from Maghran that I had seen during our operation at the tracks, and in our dealings with the Duchess.

"Maghran," I said.

"Yes, Master Shearer."

"You all seem to be in good spirits. Aren't you concerned that we did not see the dunters leave along with the contingent from Caranniam?"

He shrugged. "The dunters will always plague us, whether they are in their city or camping out beneath our mountains. I can't say we feel much threat from them. When the wizards were there to guide them, that was different. But now, I don't believe they'll dare march up toward Stenhall."

"We had spoken of how we might take advantage of this flight of Caranniam."

He did not answer.

"That is," I said, "how we might gather expeditions of our own to expel the dunters."

"We did have a few words about it, yes," he now said. "Shearer, I must tell you. It will be difficult to convince my people to risk themselves against that swarm. We can wait them out. We have food, and they will be scavenging."

"Scavenging from Emmervale, that is."

"I believe you can protect yourselves quite well. Truly. The dunters will have to abandon their campaign within a few weeks."

"And then next spring, when they come at us again?"

"We don't know that," he said. "With Varenlend and Caranniam fighting one another, there is no one to direct them. And even if this conflict between those cities ends up being only skirmishes, they will not lead a combined force against us again."

"But Caranniam will eventually come after us. If they intend to rule with sorcery, they will have to try again, keep us off balance so our progress does not overtake them. And if they intend to adopt industry themselves, they will need your riches."

"That's a supposition."

"It was important enough for them to put that horde of monsters on our doorsteps."

Maghran thought about this and then said:

"Master Shearer, you performed a very brave deed, delivering that letter. And you thought to find the duchess yourself, and you stood up to that band of hounds back there and freed this dead-weight baron of ours. You have acquitted yourself well. You should enjoy the calm, now, and get back to your farm."

"I am not doing this to prove anything to anyone, Maghran. I am not concerned about my place in history. I'm concerned about my town's future. My children's future."

Again he was silent, as were his companions. Finally he said:

"We need to get back to our families. I will speak to them of this. I give you my word about that."

This did not sound promising. The dwarves packed their belongings. I fumed, silently, but soon the dwarves were again speaking to each other, quietly, apparently about nothing of consequence; I heard an occasional laugh from them. We still had thousands of dunters on our doorsteps but yet these dwarves seemed to content to chat about—who knows what. Perhaps the scenery, and boot repair.

Eventually we were packed and ready to head north. Britta and I glanced through the trees to see if there were any dunters marauding, or perhaps the Caranniam contingent changing their minds and heading back east; but there was nothing. We untied the horse.

Then there appeared before us, once more, Aladar Silvermoor. I would say that he materialized from the shadows of the trees like a spirit.

Many more elves instantly appeared behind him, and then one dwarf. It was an older dwarf, distinguished-looking and dressed in black, and female. She wore a heavy brass circlet. I had never seen anything like it on one of them. It was not ornamented, nor even polished, but it looked to be a sign of power.

All of us were stunned. Aladar and the other elves said nothing. They seemed to think the dwarf they had along with them would make an impression, and they were correct.

"Who in the furnace of the earth do you have here with you?" Maghran said.

"We have brought one you have missed," the elf said.

The dwarf nodded, and allowed a thin smile. She was proud,

and regal.

"So this must be Herrar," Britta said.

Aladar nodded to her. "The Lady of White Mount."

Herrar looked much like the other dwarves, as usual, although her hair was white and she seemed older. Her black clothes reminded me of those of Maghran's brother Ghranam. She dressed like the male dwarves. She was set apart only by her shoulders, which were narrower—although still just about as broad as mine— and her lack of a beard.

At her side she wore a battle axe that seemed impossibly heavy and broad. It was shining steel, laced with engravings. She also carried a short spade, strapped to a pack she carried; it was small, and had some ornament to it, with scrolls and other metalwork at the handle. It looked almost ceremonial, but well-used. I wondered if it was something traditional which a dwarf in her position would carry.

"How long have you held her?" Maghran demanded of the elf.

"Easy, cousin," Herrar answered.

"We recommended," Aladar said, "that she wait for you to complete your work at that bridge some days ago, and then you might escort her back to White Mount. We were not willing to make that journey, and we thought she would be safer in a group."

"So you have been following us, all this time?" Maghran shouted. "Watching us, still? And you knew of those kobolds?"

Aladar nodded. "It is a fine village they have. We admire them. We don't believe they know that we are their neighbors. Are their caverns pleasant?"

"We might have died down there!" Maghran roared.

"We don't believe you will end your days in a kobold warren, sir," Aladar answered.

"And now, with Herrar," Maghran snapped; something had occurred to him. "You had her days ago when you ambushed us by that bridge!" he stormed. "Did you not? Anyone with honor would have brought her then!"

"They had me when they met you at the bridge, yes," Herrar answered. "I was in Meerglade, and it took us time to get that far east. By the time they took me out this far, you were done with the bridge, and well on your way back to the dunter encampment. They have lost no time, Maghran."

Maghran stood silent at this, seeming unwilling to admit that the elves had acted honorably and reasonably. He finally asked Herrar:

"What of the other three who were with you?"

"Still imprisoned in Red Gorge."

"Imprisoned by dunters?" Maghran asked. He sounded truly shocked.

Herrar only nodded.

Aladar added: "We obtained the best price we could. It was part of our deal with them for the steel for their railroad. They would release this dwarf, but not the others. We spoke of it at length, with the dunters, and even canceled the transfer, for two days. But it was clear they would not negotiate further, so we then accepted and took Herrar. And the gold."

"They would not agree to pay you less gold in exchange for giving you the prisoners."

"No."

"So they are still held."

"We must go release them," Herrar said. She sounded very matter-of-fact about it; she and Maghran and the others would simply retrace her steps—apparently into the very heart of Red Gorge—and liberate the imprisoned dwarves.

"I would think," Maghran said, "that those dunters will not be inclined to treat our cousins well. If they ever were so inclined. After what has happened to their rails, and this transaction the elves made with them."

"It will leave a sour taste indeed in their mouths," Herrar said. "But I believe our kin will still be worth enough to them that they will not be harmed."

"Perhaps, although the dunters will now be wary of trades," Maghran said. "Herrar, how did they manage to capture you—four dwarves? This has never happened."

"Wizardry," Herrar answered. "They had assistance. It has never happened before because Red Gorge has never allied with Caranniam before. There was a mage with the dunters. We were walking, and then it was as if we had become submerged in the earth. We could not move our legs, and they took us."

"And transported you?"

"It was a large group of dunters. And this mage of theirs kept us down."

"Where did they take you? Into Caranniam?"

"No, only Red Gorge."

Maghran scowled as if he had eaten something foul.

"Held by dunters," he said.

"We were treated well enough. They knew our value, and so did Caranniam."

"Where exactly was it?"

"In the manor of a warlord there. In their city."

"You could find it again?"

"I can, yes."

"And all the others are still there?"

"I assume so."

"Aladar," Maghran now asked the elf, "why did you not take her back to White Mount directly? Why did you hold her?"

"Again, sir, we were not willing to make that journey across the territory of Red Gorge."

" 'Territory,' " Maghran snorted. "They barely control anything more than a morning's walk from Red Gorge City. You could have skirted east of it unmolested."

"But neither does anyone else control that area," the elf said. "And remember, we cannot be sure of what sort of reception we would get in White Mount, or near White Mount."

"Even with their leader with you?" Maghran demanded.

"Even with Herrar," Aladar answered. "We are no more eager to show ourselves there than you would be to march into Meerglade. But this decision is past, and here we are now. We ransomed her, and we have kept her safe with us, and now you may escort her where you will."

And the elves began to slip back into the woods, while Herrar stood with us.

"Wait," Maghran said. "We want to turn this into a trade."

"A trade for what? We give her freely to you. There is no obligation to us. We ask no favor."

"Yes, well, perhaps we are asking a favor of you," the dwarf answered. "You know this man." He nodded to the baron.

"We do. Baron Laurent. Late of poor luck."

"Yes. We do not need him, and he slows us down. But we would like him kept by—" I think he was about to say "kept by friends," but he caught himself:

"We would like him kept away from his people for some more days. We do not want him informing the army of Caranniam of anything he might have learned."

"The army of Caranniam?" Aladar asked. "They are long gone. You saw. Nothing will turn them around now."

"Well, that is what we hope," Maghran said. "But we favor caution. Would you take this man?"

A few of the elves tilted their heads just slightly, at this. They were silent. One would get the impression that they were communicating with each other, somehow, as they did this, but I don't believe they were capable of doing so. After a moment, Aladar answered:

"We will take this man with us." He now inspected the baron more closely.

"My friends Maghran, and Master Shearer," he said, "it does not seem that you have been feeding this man particularly well."

"You might borrow the pole from the kobolds to haul him with, if he is too weak to walk," Maghran answered.

"Perhaps his horse would be better suited," Aladar said.

"Ah yes, that animal. I had forgotten. But we will want to keep it, for our comrade Shearer, here."

I don't think he would have honored me as a "comrade" if the horse were not involved.

"Very well, keep the baron's mount," the elf said. He stepped up to the baron and took him by the elbow. The baron had been standing, through all this, but had been slumped, and was haggard after his days with us. But now, as the elf touched him, he rallied somewhat. He straightened, and seemed to gain some strength. Perhaps he just considered the elves better company than we had been; fair enough.

"We will hold this man until this current war is over," Aladar said. And then he spoke directly to the baron:

"You understand that you have some incentive to end this war, then, Baron Laurent."

The baron nodded.

"One more thing," Maghran said. "We will want his clothes, again."

"Again?" Aladar asked.

"It turns out that they fit our Shearer quite well. As you would expect for a high-born man," Maghran said. Then he turned to me:

"You must take these, Master Shearer. And then you must help us."

"Maghran, Emmervale is under siege."

"Yes, but three of our brothers are held captive by these beasts. Does Emmervale have any captives held by that dunter army?"

"None that I know of."

"I assumed not, or you would have mentioned it," he said. "Imagine what those three must be enduring. Imagine what their families are enduring."

"We need to get home."

"Red Gorge will not add that much time," he said.

"It's considerably north and west of here, Maghran. What do you need us for, anyway? Three more added to your four will not be enough to storm Red Gorge. And if you are trying to rescue those others through stealth, we won't help that cause either."

"You well might," he said. "I believe it will be useful to have a noble of Caranniam with us."

"In order to do what?" I asked him.

"Perhaps exert influence in Red Gorge."

"Not again," I said. "You want me to march into Red Gorge, into the hall of a warlord, and try to pass myself off as this man?"

"Yes. In order to help us rescue my kinsmen from White Mount. I would be indebted to you, Shearer. All the dwarves of Stenhall and White Mount would be."

"That would be quite a debt to call upon," Hrond said.

But I declined:

"I will not do that again, Maghran. Risking it out in the open, when I was on horseback, was one thing. I will not enter a manor in that dunter hive and try to fool them."

"You could still go in there on horse."

"But it would be much more difficult to flee out of the heart of that city than it was to run, if I'd needed to, from the far edge of the dunter camp."

"You wouldn't need to flee. Who would recognize you? I am sure all the able-bodied men from Caranniam who might have been stationed in Red Gorge will be marching on Varenlend, now that their attack is under way."

"Yes, well. One unable-bodied man from Caranniam could still cause a lot of trouble for me." I shook my head. "I will accompany you to the city, Maghran. But we will find a wiser plan than that."

Maghran stood silent, at this. I think a man might have shaken his head, were he as disappointed as Maghran probably was, but the dwarf was merely still.

After a moment he said:

"Can I prevail upon you to at least take the clothes? Just in the event they are useful. If nothing else you can probably fetch a price for that fine cloth, back in Emmervale."

I knew him well enough to understand this was a joke.

"Very well," I answered him.

"And you will accompany us to Red Gorge, to free our cousins there?" He was asking this of Jed and Britta.

"We will," Britta answered. Jed nodded, once.

"Maghran," Herrar interjected. "Are you certain we need assistance? Begging your pardon."

Her last sentence was addressed to us; it seemed a reluctant courtesy. Herrar, a powerful dwarf, had paid us little attention in the preceding talk.

"They are skillful, and helpful," Maghran answered her.

"But Maghran," I said. "After these other three of your people are free, we must return. I will want to return with a larger force, from your cities and from our town."

"If we free these three of ours—and I will not leave without them—I'll help you myself, Master Shearer. I am not sure about my people."

"I would hope you could talk them into it. Starting with your brother."

"If I start with him and succeed, that would also be the end of the debate, and we would march with you. I will try to have that conversation with him, after we have succeeded," he said. I thought that was as close as I would get to an agreement, at the moment.

Jed and Britta readily agreed to continue with me and the dwarves to Red Gorge.

"You're not obligated," I said. "They would understand if you returned to Emmervale. It's me they expect to perform heroic deeds and the rest of it."

"I want to go," Britta said. "I want to see Red Gorge. What do you think it's like? I picture it as a slaughter yard, a run of mud; but they have industry. I want to see it. And of course they sent their army to attack us; this may be as good a chance as we will get to pay them back somewhat.

"And you know," she continued, "it's probably very fortunate for us that the dwarves are now taking a real interest in Red Gorge. Not just in dabbling in their blasting on the rail line, but traveling all the way to the dunter home. It may well inspire them to do some blasting there, too."

"I'm glad to keep going, as well," Jed said. "But our people will be very worried about us. My family, and Anders and your mother. And of course your parents too, Britta. I wish we could send word to them."

"We could have done so when Ghranam and that other dwarf departed, had we known," I said. "We'll just have to be content that they are not receiving any bad news about us, at least. For the time being." I shook my head. "I am not looking forward to skulking about in Red Gorge. It's unfortunate in the extreme that those dwarves are there. I'd be much more interested in a quick trip back home than an epic rescue."

"We can hope it is epic and also brief," Britta said.

"I wonder what's going on in Emmervale right now," Jed said.

"So do I," I said. "I'm sure Thona is doing well keeping things in line. In any event the three of us would not tip any scale, whatever's going on, if we were there."

"Let's hope there is no scale to tip," Britta said. "It's entirely possible the dunter army is bickering and paralyzed, now."

"Or perhaps marching back to Red Gorge as we speak," Jed said. "Perhaps we'll meet them."

So again we extended our mission. The elves had loaded Herrar with ample packs of food, fortunately, for her to make the journey back with the other dwarves. Even divided among three more of us, we would not need to worry about hunger for a number of days.

I was also relieved that at this time of year, back home, the sheep were not too demanding. They had lambed several months earlier, in the spring, and that was of course also when we had sheared them. But we did need to cut and dry hay for the winter, and that would fall mostly to my two sisters. My mother and father mostly handled our vineyard, and were busy there, so they would have little time to help. We were able to hire shepherds, and some other help around the farm, but none of us was ever free from hard labor. In addition to putting away hay for the winter, and also wheat and other grains we could obtain, there would be predators to worry about; ansarks had come down into the valley over the winter and were picking off sheep. They had also taken one of the mastiffs which we had out with the flocks. Getting rid of the ansarks was going to have been a project for a number of our families together, with many muskets and crossbows, but we had to put it off because of the invasion from Red Gorge.

We rested the remainder of that day, and the next morning left the modest cover of the trees for the journey to Red Gorge. Herrar, who had been away from her home by far the longest of any of us, was the first prepared to begin the walk. She stood gazing north as we finished breakfast; perhaps patiently, perhaps impatiently—it was difficult to tell.

Herrar and Maghran walked at the front of our line, followed by the other two dwarves and then Jed, Britta, and me. I led the horse, which we had loaded with our food.

"I will ride you again, my friend, so don't get too used to these light bags," I told it.

The land was largely level, with gentle slopes here and there, and covered with tall grass. Trees grew occasionally, usually beside one of the small streams that ran through.

Any signs of the dwellers who had populated this land long ago, before the emptying, were gone; either rotted to dust, swept away by wind, or burned in the fire years. We walked into the early afternoon without seeing sign of men, dunters, or anything else, living or dead.

But six hours into the journey we did see a ruined fortress half a mile to our west. It was a few towers mostly intact, surrounded by mounds which were tumbled-down walls.

"I wonder how long it has been since a spider keeping watch in those towers had anyone to observe," Jed said. No one answered him.

*   *   *

During the walk I half expected to see smoke and soot smearing the sky, from the far-off dunter town, but of course we were too many miles away for that.

We stopped before sunset. Once again we found a stand of trees near water. This time it was a small pool fed by a spring. I led the horse to it and we all dropped packs.

"Do you think we can risk a fire?" I asked.

"I believe so," Maghran answered. "We are far enough from Red Gorge, still, and far from the dunter expedition. And I'm sure the Caranniam van is long gone by now. And finally, as much as I grow fatigued with the elves, I think we are close enough to their territory that it is probably safe around here."

The dwarves started the fire and we sat near it and warmed our elven food. Darkness fell and we let the fire burn down to embers.

During our walk we had all talked easily, for much of the day, but it was mostly me speaking with Jed and Britta while the dwarves conversed among themselves. Here, around the same fire, all were quiet. I began to consider it awkward.

"Maghran," I said. "Do you have any stories for a fire?"

He was silent and motionless for a moment, but then rumbled:

"Well. It is yet early, you are right. So then. I suppose I can share this with you. I have a tale about our work, our digging. All of us hear this story as soon as we are old enough to listen. Perhaps your fathers and mothers picked it up while they lived with us, years ago. The story of Twill."

"In all those years I don't believe we spent much time listening to dwarf tales, Maghran."

"I suppose not. So, then. Back in our city, whenever we are below the ground—"

"You are nearly always below, my friend."

"I mean in our ore tunnels. When we are below our halls, in our work tunnels, down there with our picks and shovels and blasters, many of us will leave a coin or two in a crack in the wall. We do this to appease the cobbers, you know."

"Cobbers?"

"The knockers, the strikers. Tunnel imps down below who share the caverns with us."

"Spirits?" I asked.

"Come," Maghran scoffed. "Flesh and blood like yourselves. Knockers—keep your eyes open for them, up the hills beyond your pastures, and you'll see them. Tiny chaps, half the size of kobolds, if that. For us, underground, they sometimes knock near veins of ore, or jewels, to guide us. We seldom see them, but we hear them."

"Why do they help?"

"Why not? They're amiable sorts, and assist when they can. They have been underground neighbors to dwarves since the beginning of time. So we leave them some gold now and again. Gifts for them. They nearly always just leave the coins there, but they like to know they can have them if they wish.

"Well, there was a dwarf a few generations back, Twill was his name. He was stingy, greedy. Even for a dwarf—and that is saying something, isn't it?"

He smiled at us briefly.

"Twill was reluctant to leave any of his gold out for anyone else, even someone who might help him. Or even someone who might have been in a position to harm him, as these knockers were. He did leave something, but he took the coins and shaved off the edges first. Of course the coins had been made with reeding, and an outer inscription, to prevent that, but Twill figured he could cut these few gold pieces and the knockers wouldn't know. Twill was always cutting corners, cutting whatever he could. So he shaved them, tucked away the shavings with the rest of his sad little fortune, and put the adulterated coins in cracks.

"The day after this trick of his, when he was down there for his day's digging, a cobber appeared to him. He was pale—as they all are, of course—and held a small lamp. He was dressed much as Twill was, as is their custom, albeit with rougher clothing.

" 'Twill,' it said. 'You are the hardest-working dwarf down in these mines, and you have earned the right to possess great wealth. Follow me and I will show it to you.'

"This sounded perfectly reasonable to Twill, of course, since he was sure he was indeed the smartest-working and most deserving dwarf down there. He followed the cobber as it turned and started away.

"The cobber walked forward a few paces but then left the passage in which Twill had been working and slipped into a fissure.

Twill had not seen this path before. The cobber apparently knew it well, and after just a few twists he led the dwarf into a chamber that shimmered. The gold ore along its sides was so rich that one could see a trail of flecks of yellow, like the tail of a shooting star."

"That's not usually the case?" Jed asked.

"Almost never," Maghran said. "Outsiders seem to think that these riches we excavate just fall into our laps.

"But these walls, which the cobber showed Twill, had yellow specks like snowfall. And above them, the ceiling of the cave was studded with diamonds. And those were not cut, of course, not as you see them in rings, but nonetheless the raw stones shimmered in the torchlight.

" 'All this is yours, Twill,' the cobber said. 'And you are the only dwarf who knows this place. You may come back and take it all out.'

" 'I can't believe I never saw it before,' Twill said. 'So close. But it may take me years."

" 'It is enough digging for a lifetime,' the imp agreed.

"Twill was beside himself with joy. He followed the little cobber out, via a different path. The cobber got ahead of him, and Twill was left on his own.

"The path out was ten times, twenty times as long. There were many tunnels. Some went up, some down. Others twisted around like a tower staircase. Some went through rock, others through packed soil which had tree roots visible along the walls. Some were cold, but some were apparently so deep in the earth that Twill began to sweat. And then he kept sweating. He was stranded for hours, and then for days. He became so weary that he stopped to sleep. He did this several times as days passed. This rest allowed him to keep walking, but then thirst, of course, began to overwhelm him. He was parched; his very joints inside his body felt sticky to him for lack of water. He began to fear for his life, and was near to giving up—when he came back upon the crack where he had placed the shaved coins. He took them out and put in two whole ones. From there he was out of the mine in minutes.

"He never found his prize cavern again, of course, and he never again cut corners with the cobbers. He did so with us, other dwarves, but never again with them."

*　*　*

Soon we unrolled our bedding and slept. Britta and Inman stayed up first as watch. The night passed quietly, as Jed took a turn at watch in the middle and then I arose well before dawn. At light we moved on.

After some hours, the land began to change. It had a few more rolls to it, and that was one way we knew we were nearing Red Gorge City. As the afternoon progressed the low hills played tricks on us; after each one we thought we would be able to see the dunter sprawl. This went on too long, but then as we came to the top of one easy incline we saw an expanse before us that included agricultural fields and, in the distance, the city. And I could indeed see a smoky haze over it.

"Lower yourselves," Maghran said, but we were already doing so.

"I will call this an arrival," he continued. "Which one of you will lead that horse back?"

He was right; we could not keep it with us this close to the city.

"Britta?" I asked.

"I did it the last time."

"Jed, then," I said.

"Very well. I'll move south to the first trees I come to. You'll tell me the plan?"

"I'll come find you tonight or tomorrow night," I said. "You have food with you?"

"Yes."

"Stay safe. Flee if you must. East, if you do."

"I won't flee; if need be I can simply hide myself behind the horse."

He nodded, took the bridle, and hurried back to our rear.

"From here on out," Maghran said, "we move only at night. We just need a proper place to conceal ourselves."

"Before us, or behind us?" I asked.

"We can press ahead some small distance, at least," he said. "We want to be able to walk all the way in the dark, with enough night left to do some work, so we shouldn't be any farther away than this."

"Would we be better off having only a few of us continue,

Maghran? I would be one of them—I'm not begging off from the rescue—but two or three of us would be less likely to be noticed."

"Of course, when we move in," he said. "But I think we can get closer, all of us, first. Let us find a place, when the sun is down."

We stepped back down that little incline and huddled low to wait for darkness. We kept our eyes open for dunters or any other passersby.

"For all we know, we might see the entire expeditionary army returning," Hrond said.

"We are too far south for that," Maghran answered. "They would come in to the northeast of us."

We stayed low in the grass on that hillside for the rest of the light of day. This passed quickly. We crept forward to the crest, for a survey; nothing had changed. We saw no dunters. In one of the fields, though, at a distance, we did see kobolds at work.

As Britta and I looked toward the city, she asked:

"I wonder how many dunters will have gone? Will this place be empty?"

"Between the army out by us," I said, "and the mass of them by the tracks, there may not be many left here. Plenty of kobolds, but maybe few dunters."

"You're right," she said. "This city may be full of nothing but female dunters, now."

"Although that army out by Emmervale may include plenty of females, for all we know," I said. "I'm not sure I could tell them apart. Even close up."

Night fell. Rahune was high and now nearly full, and quick Rahira was catching up.

The fields around us had been quiet all along, and we moved forward. Britta and I, with Maghran next to us, went first. Herrar, Inman, and Hrond came behind. We traveled in the direction of the city, though there was little to guide us. We were still too far out to see any fires or lamps which might have burned, and there were no such lights any closer to us either.

We looked for a place to conceal ourselves. We crept through one bean field and saw a rambling, low shack materialize in the dark ahead of us.

"Good thing they can't stand dogs," Britta whispered. "We'd have been set upon by now, if this were Emmervale."

"Certainly no Emmervale," I answered. We continued stalking through the plants.

We came within fifty paces of the shack. It was dead quiet and showed no lamps or candles at all. I took it to be occupied, just because the bean plants had not been planted right up to its edge.

"Is that thing a house?" Britta asked.

"Or a barn, maybe? I don't know. A farm house? It seems to have a yard."

"Very sad farmers, if so."

We lay still, watching it.

"If it's empty, it would be ideal," she said.

"But how do we know? I doubt the dunters are in the habit of staying up late into the night reading by candlelight."

We kept watch on the structure for a time. Maghran and the other dwarves had heard our talk but had not commented, which I took to mean that they agreed with us.

Then, from a doorway on the side, we saw a figure emerge. It was a kobold. We all lowered ourselves. We crawled away, without speaking, to search for a safer spot.

Again we picked our way forward over the dark dunter fields. In that night, it seemed as if we were barely even in our own world; for one thing, the dunters and kobolds were clearly in the habit of fertilizing their fields with whatever foul refuse was at hand. The stench was that of a latrine.

We eventually came to another shack, much like the first. Again we watched it, and again we decided to move on, although at this one we saw no movement whatsoever, not even a servant kobold. The place just looked too much like a residence, rather than a barn.

We next passed a pig shelter. We would not have been too proud to stay in it, but again we were concerned we would be discovered inside.

Finally we came upon a nearly ruined wooden building which seemed to be a disused equipment shed. The southern wall of it was leaning inward, and one entire end had apparently been dismantled for the lumber. It looked about to collapse.

"Perfect," Maghran said.

"You might need to shore this thing up," I whispered to him.

"We certainly could. You've picked the right companions if that becomes necessary."

We entered. It was a dirt-floored abandoned shed, nothing more. There were scraps of wood here and there. I also thought I saw the shapes of rats scurrying away as we came in, but I did not look too hard. We dropped our packs, and weapons, and sat down.

"Shall we plan?" I asked.

"We have to hide ourselves all day long," Herrar answered. "We'll have plenty of time to plan then. For now I will sleep."

Britta and I unrolled our blankets next to each other, along one wall, and the dwarves lay down across from us.

"Do you think Jed is safe?" she asked.

"Safer than we are," I answered.

Hrond and Maghran stood watch, and the rest of us slept.

We woke at dawn. Light came in through the myriad cracks in the slat walls, and powdered dust rose and drifted in the beams as we moved about. Herrar dug into her pack and passed around some fine elven food. It would have made for a wonderful breakfast had we not been hiding in a crumbling shack an easy walk from Red Gorge City. We ate silently.

"And now," Herrar eventually said. "How we extract my companions."

"Did you get a thorough look at the structure, when you were taken there?" Maghran asked.

"None at all. I was hooded when I was brought in. In my time there I gathered it was the manor of a warlord. It was clearly a fortified dwelling as well as a dungeon."

"We should see it, then, before we all move," Maghran said. "Master Shearer, we should send in a scouting party."

"I agree," I said. "But how will we find it, if Herrar herself did not see it?"

"They hooded me on my way in, but not on my way out," she answered. "They had me bound up in a cart, when I left, and I could not look back; but I saw the route. And we headed south, so I can tell you what you will see from here. You remember the main road, or track, that leads into the city, which we saw last night."

"Yes."

"This will turn to the west at a cluster of heaps of slag. You shall still follow it until you reach a ruined tower. It is stone, but covered with smoke stains and burns. From there to the north again, and over a low bridge above a stream. The road will weave slightly to the left and right, twice each, with low, poor structures, much like this one, on either side. Then, before the manor, there is nothing; the land is bare. They apparently kept the area clear for sight and line of fire. It was the only such clearing I saw, north of the slag heaps."

"This sounds like a veritable midsummer foray around the meadows of Emmervale," I said.

The dwarves, of course, did not acknowledge this.

"So, Master Shearer, we need a scouting party."

"Yes."

"And we would like it to be you. I understand that men would seldom be seen in Red Gorge, but dwarves would absolutely never set foot there."

"I see," I said. "You know, Maghran, I would call that situation a scout, rather than a scouting party."

"Perhaps."

"Your first description led me astray a bit."

"Yes, but you see our logic?"

"I suppose I do."

"How do you wish to head in? Disguised as our erstwhile companion baron, perhaps?"

"I am still not convinced by that idea, Maghran."

"Very well. But you will travel in, reconnoiter, and then tell us what you find."

"Yes."

"If you do not want to try to pass yourself off as the baron, then I suppose you would want to go on foot."

"Of course," I said.

"This will make you a very good friend to dwarves," Herrar said.

"Even if I don't return, you mean? At least I'll be able to take solace from that?"

We passed the afternoon in the shed, often with our eyes up to cracks and gaps in the walls. We saw no dunters. On three occasions we saw kobolds at a distance; in every case they seemed intent on their work, either carrying tools or struggling under loads on their backs. The farms around us were disturbingly quiet. Even birds seemed to avoid the place. We did see a feral pig rooting around nearby, once.

At one point I found myself sitting next to Maghran, both of us occasionally glancing through the wall, waiting out the afternoon.

"We are very fortunate to have found Herrar," I said.

"Indeed. She is invaluable to White Mount."

"Had the dwarves of Stenhall met with her, recently? Before her latest attempt, I mean?"

He shook his head. "Not in years. Our two branches of our people have had little contact for some time."

"I knew you kept yourselves remote from Emmervale. I didn't know you didn't even keep company with other dwarves."

"We are content in our halls. And if you think we are withdrawn now, we may disappear completely in the years to come, Aiman."

"Why do you say that?"

"Because of those things there." He nodded toward Britta's musket, which was leaned up against a wall.

"The gun? What do you mean? You make them as well as anyone."

"That is true, but everyone is making them better. When firearms first appeared, in my father's time, perhaps my grandfather's time, they were so unreliable that they hardly made a difference in conflicts. But they keep getting more and more accurate. More and more dependable. We have relied on our bravery and our skill to preserve us, in battle. But soon anyone will be able to shoot accurately at a range of—who knows, perhaps one end of your considerable pasturage to the other, Aiman. Any dunter whelp with one eye and a musket will become our equal. We don't want any part of that."

Twilight eventually fell. As it grew darker outside I stood and peered out the doorway. We were now close enough that some fires were visible in the city. I took deep breaths. I felt I must be insane to wander out alone into the dunter capital. I had told my father I would be careful, and now I was about to do the least-careful thing I possibly could.

"I suppose it's time," I told Britta.

"Good luck," she said. "Just get a quick glimpse and return.

Don't press your luck the way you and Jed did out by the railway."

I moved along the farm track in the darkness, keeping to one side so as not to be right in the middle of it. For over an hour, I would say, the countryside was much the same: shacks, and quiet, and the stenches of uncleaned and undrained barnyards.

My first view of Red Gorge was shanties, the dwellings of the dunters. I thought of these, at first, as outlying hovels, but as I walked further I realized that this was the bulk of the city. The shanties did not give way to larger houses. Eventually I would see workshops, and railways, and the rambling fortresses of warlords, but for some distance as I walked it was nothing but flimsy wooden houses.

I do not mean to say that I strolled down these streets and took everything in at my leisure. At the first shack I had stopped, crouched low in a ditch at the side of the road, and just listened. I heard no movements near me, nor much of anything farther away for that matter. For the rest of my walk I would creep ahead one shack, or one dirt yard, at a time. The streets generally had ditches off to the sides, and I used them. They were occasionally strewn with piles of dung, and ashes, and rotting food, but I kept to them as much as I could.

Next to most of the buildings, even the lowliest shanties in some cases, were rough sheds that I took to be tool storage or poultry houses, at first; then I realized they were kobold huts.

I picked my way along, alone but for a few dogs and pigs that roamed the streets. At first I was concerned about the dogs, but they were clearly half-starved curs more afraid of me than I them. The pigs ignored me as they nosed through piles of refuse in the ditches, or along the sides of the street. Several times I saw them flush out rats as they snorted.

I came to Herrar's promised slag heaps, and turned left. I passed many more shacks and sheds, and then came upon the ruined tower. I wondered if enough of it were intact for it to be used as a watch station. Would I be better off skulking by it at some distance, or right along its base? If I moved along its base I might better avoid any dunter above who was scanning the streets, but I'd also be more likely to be surprised by any dunter stepping out of a doorway. How could I know? But the tower looked too burnt to be in use. I crept by it, apparently unseen.

Next I saw what I took to be a fortified manor house. It was not the one where Herrar had been captive, if her description of the route was accurate. But it seemed similar; a high-walled building standing alone about twenty yards away from the street.

And within were lights, the first I had seen. It was clearly occupied, although of course I did not know if the residents were dunters or their kobold caretakers. I could have stood and watched it for some time longer, but I remembered Britta's admonishment and moved on.

About at this point I became, I must say, very confident in my scouting trip. I felt invisible and invincible. I was the first person from Emmervale to set foot in Red Gorge City since we had begun our lives outside Stenhall, and probably for many years before that as well, and it was surprising to me that the jaunt was so easy. We could have been creeping around the city for years, had we known, spying on their progress (such as it was).

I crossed over the stream, moved past the weaves of the street, and was then upon Herrar's prison.

It was a building similar to the first fortified house I'd seen, but larger. The manor, if such a rude pile of rock could be called that, stood atop a low earthwork platform. Sharpened logs protruded from the slope of the platform; several of these were decorated, as it were, with skulls. The skulls were of dunters. It was clear, despite their recent campaign against us, that the dunters did not enjoy peaceful relations even among themselves.

The earthwork was overgrown with vines and scrub. Some attempt had been made to trim this growth, in order to deny concealment to enemies.

The manor's walls were made of massive tree trunks interspersed with black and gray boulders. In a few spots boulders had come loose and tumbled down; these had been repaired very roughly, with horizontal beams spiked onto the tree trunks in order to contain the fill. All the wood in the walls—the trunks and beams—had been coated with something black, some sort of tar I supposed.

I had assumed that the wall was an outer bulwark, with a more polished home within, but I then noticed sections of low roof extending all the way to the edges. This was one giant fortification. It struck me as just a much stronger version of the endless shacks that all the other dunters lived in.

The dwarves were still in there, presumably. They might have been right behind any part I was looking at. I supposed it was most likely they were in a cellar beneath the earthwork.

Rough steps led up the slope to the front gate of the manor. The gate consisted of double iron doors on thick hinges. Each door had a small, barred window.

Again there were a few dim lights inside. I had seen enough. I turned.

I was retracing my route back to our hiding shed, carefully, with every intention of going straight back, when I heard a steam blast some distance to my left. Then came clanks of metal on metal. I stopped, held my spot in a splendid reeking ditch, and listened. I thought, or imagined, that I heard croaking voices off in the same direction.

Perhaps I was close to their rail yard. If so, I might learn something about their industry that would be useful. I could not help thinking that Herrar and the other White Mount dwarves possessed, not so far away from here, a ready supply of blasting charges, niter-glycerol, and whatever else we might need to blast dunter machinery into shards. We might convince them to return to blow up a good part of this miserable city. I moved down the street until I came to an alley perpendicular, and then I headed toward the sounds.

I crawled through more ditches and passed another tedious expanse of shacks. I had hoped the alley would be a straight shot east, but I came to several forks and chose what I thought was the best route. I kept hearing the noises and some activity ahead.

I am not sure how I found the courage, or the foolishness, to keep moving through that city of enemies. I was alone, unarmed, many days away from home, and at least an hour's walk from any friendly face. I think the ramshackle state of Red Gorge helped; had I been in a more orderly enemy city, such as Varenlend or Caranniam, I would have felt like a cornered mouse the whole time, I suspect. But this was such a jumble of hovels and scurrying kobolds, and so empty of dunters (apparently), that I felt comfortable enough wending my way through shadows.

I kept walking eastward. Some of the structures I passed were every bit as sagging as the shed where we had been hiding, and must have been just as abandoned.

At one point the ditch ran up to a berm of earth, and atop it, finally, were the train tracks I had been searching for. These were not upturned rails, no giant symbols of Lord Silvermoor; the steel from the elves had not been laid all the way into the city. The gray line stretched away in the distance toward the noise. I looked around for a landmark, saw a rare two-story building to my right, and started down the tracks.

I had gone not fifty yards when I heard a chuff and screech behind me. I dropped down the berm and stepped into an open area behind a row of shanties. I took cover behind a thicket of scrub.

A throbbing dunter locomotive approached from my left. It was enveloped in an orange glow from its fire and from lanterns hanging off spars. It rolled ponderously but sounded powerful enough; or perhaps I should say that it made an impressive racket considering how slowly it propelled itself.

It was not much more than a giant cylinder on four wheels, with a steaming chimney at the front and a car of coal trailing behind. As it came into view I saw a dunter perched at the front, on a platform atop the cylinder. This platform had an armor wall chest-high. There was a another such turret with a similar dunter guard in back, behind the cylinder where other crew—kobolds, most likely—would feed the fire. Each of the dunter guards held a long musket. They looked grim and long-toothed enough, and certainly wide-awake in this night, but they were smaller and overall less impressive than those I had seen up close weeks ago when they had shot at Jed and me. Perhaps all the meatier dunters had gone off in the expeditionary army, or were working at the end of the tracks, and those left here were the third line.

They had also welded on, or bolted on, two more platforms extending out from the sides of the engine. These were also armored. No dunters stood in these at the moment.

The thing screamed its steam-strokes and rolled past. It was a sooted iron monster. From behind the scrub I smelled oil and imagined I could feel the heat from the fire. The lanterns hanging off spars rocked back and forth as it crawled ahead. A string of red pennants stretched from the chimney back to the rear of the cylinder. Trailing along behind was the coal car. There might have been a few guards aboard that, too, for I saw what looked like two more musket barrels poking up from behind its walls.

I allowed the locomotive to roll past me, by some yards, and then I crept forward to follow it. The dunter in front had turned his glazed eyes my direction as it surged past, but he had evidently not been searching the shadows very hard. I assumed neither of the two guards would. I could imagine they thought themselves completely secure here in Red Gorge City. And they were, of course; but I was glad to at least bring Emmervale eyes, if nothing else, into their sprawl. I wanted to see what they might be going to meet up with, on this hardened locomotive of theirs.

I followed the orange blur through the city, perhaps another quarter mile. I kept low, sticking to the bottom of the berm. The steam and churning wheels of the machine were loud, but occasionally I heard dunters aboard shouting to each other, and yap speech from kobolds.

Then I saw fires along the sides of the tracks, further down. I veered a bit further away, then, keeping in shadows, and saw that the locomotive had almost reached a rail yard. I got close enough to see that there were several side tracks on which stood dozens of cargo cars. Small fires burned among these, and I saw dunters huddled around them.

In front of one fire I saw a cannon which must have been intended for Stenhall and Emmervale. I went nearer and saw more of them—four, six, ten, twenty. The first one I had seen, in terms of size, was respectable, and some of the others were much larger yet. They were fat, wide-mouthed guns that seemed waiting impatiently to be put to work, straining their wooden mounts. They looked large enough to—well, to blow down a dwarven gate.

Past them I saw stacks of wooden barrels and piles of crates. They rose into the air twice a man's height. This was a depot of material and arms for the expeditionary army—the stockpile that was supposed to have been sent out by train on their new rails. Everything had been frozen in place, now, by the trick of the elves. But the dunters had not moved any of the supplies; it was all still ready to roll. I supposed they would do it with oxen and carts, now. A slow job, but the material would get out there just the same.

I had seen enough, now, and turned. The dunters had labored long to accumulate the supplies in that yard. As I walked I could think only about how high into the sky we might blow it all if the dwarves were willing to assist. We could walk to White Mount and back in a week with enough blasting sticks to level that depot and hobble Red Gorge for years.

I retraced my way along the tracks and then down the roads. I shuddered through a few moments of dread when I realized I had paid much more attention to finding my way into the city than remembering the way back out. I also kept second-guessing myself because I made very good time. I realized that in cautiously picking my way along I had moved very slowly, and now I was able to cover ground more rapidly.

I made it down the tracks, then through the alleys, and back to the main road. The city was still quiet. I wondered if most of the activity of those dunters who remained was centered around that rail depot.

Eventually I was back onto the country road, which now seemed welcome despite its dark and smells. I made it to the shack well before dawn. Britta and Hrond were standing watch and welcomed me in.

"You are a fine stalker," Hrond said. "I noticed you just a moment ago."

Britta touched my arm to guide me in, out of the doorway.

"Was it as Herrar said?" she asked.

"Exactly. I can't believe how easy it was to move about. I believe I was seen only by their vermin."

The others awoke, although it was still early. I told them what I had seen: The manor, the earthworks, the logs, the boulders, the dunter skulls. I stopped there, since I knew the dwarves were thinking only of their imprisoned cousins and not the stranded war supplies. They sat perfectly still as they listened. In the darkness I could barely make out their faces: Britta's fair hair and skin, Herrar's weathered features, and the eyes of Hrond, Inman, and Maghran above their high beards.

When I was done speaking, Herrar said:

"I believe I have the plan, from your description of that manor."

"I'm sure," Maghran agreed.

"What would that be?" I asked.

"Well, Master Shearer," Maghran said, and leaned back. "We'll have all day to discuss this. So let me ask: What do you think our plan might be?"

"Well, I do hope to sleep, and not discuss this all day long. But I do not see any obvious approach. The manor itself might be lightly defended, but any assault on it would draw attention from the whole city, I believe. I was able to move around, but I was quiet; I was not trying to shoot my way into a jail."

"Such an approach would certainly draw attention," he said.

"My first thought was that you share some of your arovis with these dunters, just as you did with the kobolds for that baron."

"I'm afraid three dwarves held by dunters implies a much higher price than one fool held by the dog men," Maghran answered. "I did not bring a pack full of jewels. And furthermore, this is not exactly neutral ground, here, conducive to haggling."

"Of course. You had also spoken about me using Baron Laurent's robes to try to talk my way in there, and then back out, something I would rather not attempt."

"So be it. I'm not sure even the real baron could talk three prisoners out of there."

"Perhaps you're thinking of infiltrating," I said. "Prying up a bit of roof, or managing to breach the front gate quietly."

"That could be promising," Maghran said.

"Indeed," Herrar said. "And the hill this fortress sits on, it is not natural? You're certain?"

I nodded.

"It's an old dirt rampart. Obviously dunter work. And uniform. Square, or rectangular perhaps, and level."

"It did not look to you like a rock hill that has been built upon?" she asked.

"No. The surrounding area is quite flat."

"Then we could dig in," Herrar said.

"Clearly," Maghran answered. "It will be half an hour to get in, at most. We'll go tonight and we'll all be off by the morning."

"You'll just walk up with shovels and start excavating?" I asked. They did have two shovels; Herrar carried the spade, and Maghran had kept the one he used when we buried the explosives by the bridge.

"Essentially. You mentioned some barred windows. Were they placed all the way around the walls?"

"I saw only two of the walls. I believe they wrapped around both, though, yes."

"Well. We'll check the sides you didn't see, but even if they are there, we will stay low and dark."

"Will you need us?" I asked. "Britta and me? We won't be any help to you, digging. And you won't need a fake baron, either."

"I don't think there will be much for you to do, no," Herrar answered. "But you should come along. The route out of the town will be shorter heading northward, once we're free of that fortress."

"It will be? How can you know?"

"They did not cover up my eyes, on the way down here, until we were on the outskirts of the city, to the north. And judging from the amount of time it took you to walk, we'll be just as close to the north side of the city as this side. We'll want to escape straightaway to the north, is my point."

"Rather than return here and then head around the city to the east or west."

"That's right."

"How well do you know the roads up there?" I asked her. "This far south of White Mount? I think Jed should take the horse and ride around the city to meet us."

"Ride far around it, you mean."

"That's right. We can do it if we have a place to meet."

"The roads, you say. But there is only one, heading north. Barely a road to speak of. It leaves this pit of a city and leads toward White Mount. Some miles north of here it crosses another road, or the shadow of one; and an old, ruined town sits there. Your friend could find that. It's small, but there is nothing else in the area."

"I'll tell him. It's deserted?"

"Yes. Since the fires. It was once called Midwall."

One question nagged me:

"Herrar, you were not able to dig out of the cell while you were in there. Are you certain you will be able to dig into it now?"

She nodded.

"They kept our hands chained. That's why we could not tunnel out. We were on a stone floor, but we could have pulled it up easily.

146

It was the chains that stopped us."

For the first time, now, I understood the privation of Herrar's captivity. She had not been merely locked away, but chained.

"I hadn't realized. That's terribly cruel," I said.

She shrugged.

"We would have broken out, otherwise, and they knew it." She seemed to hold no grudge against the dunters for this detail of their captivity; once the decision was made to hold dwarves—she seemed to acknowledge—the restraints were a given.

The dwarves were satisfied with the report, and their plan, but I went ahead and told them of the locomotive and rail yard. I related my views of the cannons, the other stacks of materials, and the few dunters guarding it all.

Maghran raised his eyebrows.

"We might have preferred you not take that risk in surveying the city, Aiman. Had you been lost, your knowledge of our kin would have been lost with you."

"It was quiet," I said. "I was cautious. I saw nothing that came close to a threat."

They did not answer.

"And," I added, "I am here now. I made it."

"Well," he said. "At any rate. This new machine of theirs sounds like an improvement over the last."

"I would say so," I agreed. "It's slow, but strong. They must trust it, or must have trusted it, to haul all of that out to Stenhall."

Hrond and Inman actually jolted a bit at that. They may not really have been thinking, until that moment, about all this dirt and stench of Red Gorge transported to their front gates.

"Must they," said Maghran. "But they won't be hauling anything anywhere anytime soon."

"Not with that locomotive over the elven tracks, no. But they'll try to get those supplies out there. I would assume they are making a plan to do so right now."

"It could be."

"We can't let that happen. And in any case, it's a gift to us. I mean the fact that they have stockpiled it all. We could go in and blast it. A few sticks of yours, next to their powder barrels, would probably level a quarter of this city."

"We don't have any such materials," Maghran said.

"You know we sent what we had back with Ghranam," Hrond added.

"But you could get it from White Mount. We could be back here in a few days. And we could destroy their new locomotive also."

"Once again you have very grand designs on the home of the dunters," Maghran said. "And once again I'm afraid I have to say that we should not get ahead of ourselves. We still have dwarves to free. And I don't believe we will very easily be able put a stop to all of the progress, if you want to call it that, which the dunters have engineered. But again I, personally, understand your inclinations, Aiman Shearer."

He said no more. Herrar had nothing to add, and did not look at me.

The sun had now risen, but with nothing else to do in that shed, I slept. I woke at midday, and Herrar again shared the elf food with us all.

"I'll need to go tell Jed," I said to Britta.

"And here we are again talking about the horse," she said. "How attached are we to it?"

"I know," I nodded. "It might be simpler just to release the thing. But Jed can ride around the city and meet up with us to the north. That will be safer for him. And that way, at least one of us will be at a good distance from here, and mounted. If anything goes wrong with the rescue, he'll be able to get to Emmervale eventually and relay what happened."

"If that strikes him as the safer option," she said, "he'll probably want me to do it. Or you."

"I'm sure. But we don't both need to walk down there to see him, right now. That's too much of a risk. So he'll be arguing with only one of us. And I think it should be me who sees him; and that means he'll be the one to ride, since I'm the great friend to dwarves around here. I don't think he'd choose a dwarf rescue over a long, easy ride."

"You are ready to dig into that manor?" she asked.

"I hope it goes as easily as they say. Then we get out, and we can get back to our own affairs. At last. I wish these dwarves were more receptive to attacking this city."

"I agree," she said. "What will we realistically be able to do, when we are done here? We don't have the power to defeat the dunter army right outside Emmervale, much less take the fight to them here. Not alone."

"We could do it if we had allies, but I don't know who that would be. The elves would be glad to be rid of the dunters, but they wouldn't cooperate with us. And if they had ever felt it was worthwhile to attack Red Gorge, they would have done it already without waiting for our suggestion."

"They probably feel they have already attacked Red Gorge, with their sabotaged rails," she said. "And Varenlend will have no interest in helping us, even now that their alliance with Caranniam is over."

"That's right. Their hands will be full with Caranniam's attack."

"It's unfortunate the Duchess isn't really duchess of anything."

"And now you are truly reaching," I said. "I'll go tell Jed what's going on."

I told the dwarves my errand and walked out of the shed into daylight. I could not wait until twilight, since we would all be moving north into the city that evening as soon as we could. Again I kept low to the ground, as I moved through the farm lands, and eventually crossed the same low ridge behind which we had waited on the first day. After that it was not long until I came upon the first stand of trees beyond, and Jed stepped out.

"You're alive," he said.

"Of course."

"You left me waiting quite some time for news, my friend."

"I apologize. We have been busy. Or, honestly, I have been busy, and then have held others in rapt attention as I spin my tales."

"Well done, then."

"Yes. We know where these other three are, and our dwarves have a plan to rescue them."

"What is it?"

"Dig them out."

"As we might expect," he said. "Will it work?"

"I think it will. The city seems mostly deserted, and we know how quickly these dwarves dig. But listen: after the other three are free, we are heading due north when we escape. So we want you to take this horse and skirt around the city, and meet up with us to the north."

"I'll just get rid of the horse now and accompany you, Aiman."

I shook my head. "That's what we guessed you would say. But you may as well proceed without the risk, Jed. Britta and I won't have much to do during the rescue, and you wouldn't either. And there's no need to have a larger group in there and run the chance of drawing more eyes."

"Hmm." He looked down at his boots and drew a circle in the dirt with his toe. "Well, I think I could find something useful to do, if I went with you. But I see your point that a smaller party will be better, in there. Although you're going to be such a crowd with those new dwarves, one more body wouldn't make much of a difference. But very well, I'll head around. I'll have to cross their rail line, east of here."

"Yes. But I doubt they are devoting much energy to watching it, given the state it's in."

"How will I meet you, once we're all north of the city?"

"The dwarves said that on the other side, a bit to the northeast, there is a road, and along it some distance is a ruined town. Wait for us there. You should easily get there first."

"That's all they said? I'll be able to find it?"

"Herrar says it's obvious. There is only one road north, and it crosses an old east-west track at the ruins."

He shook his head.

"I would much rather just go with you and Britta, Aiman."

"We don't need someone your height trying to sneak through that city, Jed. Just head east, and around, and we'll see you in two or three days."

"Very well."

"And," I added, reluctantly, "if anything happens to us, you'll have to return to Emmervale and tell them. And tell them everything we've learned."

"Now you have me worried again, you idiot," he said. "Yes, I'm sure everyone in Emmervale will be perfectly content if the Marshal's grandson and handsome Britta are lost, but good old Jed makes it back." Again he shook his head. "Be careful. I'm still not sure we should be all the way out here, after so much distance and so many days, helping these dwarves in the first place."

"These dwarves can be an enormous help to us, Jed."

"If they choose to. And who knows what they'll choose to do. We could carry their three companions out of here on a litter and that doesn't mean they'll repay us. Be careful."

I assured him I would be. It turned out, however, that I was not nearly careful enough.

Eleven

I turned and started to walk back to the shed, to rejoin Britta and the dwarves. I had progressed well out of sight of Jed, so he could not have been watching me; he would have been lying down to pass the remainder of the afternoon before he left, or perhaps he had ridden off already. In any case I was alone, and once again trying to keep low in the tall grass. For this entire journey I had been thankful for the tall grass of summer, to help conceal my movements—but I neglected to consider that it might in turn be hiding others.

Kobolds sprang up around me and pounced. There were six, and they had me surrounded. They must have seen me walk out from the shed, earlier, and had either waited for my return or been pleasantly surprised by it.

The two in front of me smiled horribly and snarled, but did not move. They kept their arms out somewhat, like ridiculous little brown bears. (East of Emmervale, up in the heights at the feet of the mountains, there are such bears; when they stand up, it is much more impressive.)

But these two did not need to do anything to catch me. Four behind me and to my side were rushing in. They did not scream or yelp, but I heard their growls. I turned on them, attempting to draw my knife, but then the first two darted up. The group was attacking me just like trained dogs might: one or two would draw my attention and stay out of reach, and the others would close in.

I turned once more, and then three of them hit me and knocked me down. The other three were on top of us all in a moment. I struggled, but together they outweighed me considerably. I tried to yell, but one climbed atop my head, pulled my jaw shut, and then wrapped a furred arm around my face. He was remarkably strong; I felt his muscles harden into rocks. His rough fur pressed into my mouth and nose.

Another then reached under this one's chin, which was grinding into my head, and slipped a blindfold behind my ears and then around my eyes. Others followed with ropes around my wrists and ankles.

I felt I was being trampled by one enormous, dirty, panting, powerful dog. They pinned me to the ground and took away my knife. They then pawed me to find anything else of value. I had left my pack and sleeping roll back with Britta, fortunately. This was likely good not only because it kept me from losing much, but because it made me look like just a foolish wanderer. Had they seen all my supplies they might have realized I had a plan for their city. This in turn might have made them search harder for Britta and the dwarves, on the assumption that I was not working alone.

But they bore me off toward the city immediately. They moved to their left some distance, and then turned north. This path kept them away from our shed. The others would have no idea what had happened to me.

They half-carried, half-dragged me along, and of course I thought of the satisfaction Baron Laurent might have felt had he seen this: I was being dragged by kobolds just as he had been. And my trip was much longer. They ran nonstop, seeming to drop me in the dirt and drag me every hundred yards or so.

At one point they paused. They released me to the ground, and I rolled half a turn and came to rest against a wooden wall. I guessed they had reached the first shacks of the city. They began chattering with each other, then, with rushed and quieted voices. Their language sounded like strings of yaps and dog moans. All six seemed to speak, at first, but soon the argument—for that's clearly what it was—fell to two speakers. Each seemed have a different plan for me, from their tone.

One of them prevailed, and I was picked back up. They hustled me through the streets, then, more quickly than before. They did not drop me, this time; but this was because they were in a rush, not because of any concern for my welfare. From time to time my head would be snug up against a muscled kobold abdomen, or hip, and I felt their exertion. The dog smell became more and more pungent as they ran.

Eventually the sound of the ground below us changed. One of the kobolds barked a loud order, then, and I heard a gate creak open. They ran me into a building, out of the sunlight. We rounded one corner, more orders were barked, and then I was dumped onto a stone floor.

The one who had been giving the orders now spoke in what I recognized as the language of the dunters. His voice still had a yap to it, but he was clearly speaking dunter and also sounded more respectful.

The kobold touched me twice with his foot, as he spoke. He must have been using me as an illustration of his tale. Then, suddenly, I felt a hand tug at my blindfold, and then it was off.

I saw that I lay amid the knot of kobolds who were presenting themselves and their prize to a dunter. The dunter looked older, with some grey hair and also a few of his teeth snapped off short. His red eyes glared at me. I now felt, impossibly, some camaraderie with the kobolds who had taken me; they seemed a much more pleasant lot than this new host.

The dunter stood before a chair in which he had apparently been sitting when we entered. We were in a room with a large fireplace, and tools hanging from the walls. There were no windows, and the walls were rough-hewn rocks. In a corner was a rude table with a helmet; it was a battered old piece and seemed to be an ornament or trophy. Overall I took the room to be a dunter's formal parlor—as well-appointed a room as one might find in Red Gorge City, I guessed.

The dunter pointed at me and snapped a question at the lead kobold, who bowed his head and answered. The two of them went back and forth. The dunter seemed more content and calm as the conversation went on, and I looked up and saw that the kobold, for his part, was narrowing his eyes. He was a touch larger than the others, and he had an unusual black patch of thick fur atop his head.

The dunter then stepped toward us, reached into his coat, and pulled out a purse. He fished out three coins and tossed them to the kobold leader. This one caught two of them, snatched up the other from the floor, and then all six hustled out as quickly as they had come in. The leader looked back at me once, on their way out, and then they were gone. I was alone with my captor.

The dunter now walked over and circled me. I could see him, but was still bound.

He spoke at me in his language and looked me in the eyes. I

don't know that any humans anywhere learn that language; certainly I had never met or heard of anyone in Emmervale who did. But he kept jabbering, apparently just content to be upbraiding me or whatever he was saying. As he spoke he kept his eyes focused on me, alternately widening them and squinting.

Then he switched to Valley Lower:

"And why do you visit Red Gorge City, human?"

"I live in the plains, east of the city," I said. I had already decided to take on the identity of Korben, the man Maghran and I had met along the train tracks weeks earlier. Or even better, I thought, I would pretend I was a neighbor of Korben's, just in case he himself was known here as the crazy hermit down by the river.

I added: "I was just walking here."

"No one lives east of here. No one between us and the dwarves, and the flower-pickers of the hills."

Flower-pickers; that would be Emmervale.

"A few do," I said. "A few of us who want to live alone."

"Why would a fine young man like this one want to live alone?"

"I was outlawed," I said.

"An outlaw. From where?"

"From Emmervale."

"Outlawed by the flower-pickers. I suppose they will outlaw for anything. What did you do to them—snare a bird? Butcher a deer?"

"I ran into trouble with the Shearer family," I said.

"And who would they be?"

"Some consider them the main family of Emmervale."

"And what did you do to the shearers?"

"I stole one of their sheep," I said.

He nodded at this.

"Believable. Well, sheep-thief. That theft has cost you much."

"Indeed."

"Because you will have no family to care about you, or hear about you."

"My family remembers me," I objected. I did not like the turn this was taking.

"No one to ransom you," he continued. "Better you were in one of those main families yourself. We would treat you well, in that case. But an outlaw . . . an outlaw. I must think about how you would be most valuable to me."

He walked in a straight line now, away from me, apparently immersed in thought.

"Do you forge?" he asked.

"What do you mean?"

"Do you work metal? Tools, dies?"

"No."

"Do you know steam?"

"I do not."

"Do you gunsmith? Do you mix powders?"

"Again, no. I can shoot."

"Anyone can shoot," he said. "You will have to wait while I consider you. Outlaw sheep thief."

He shouted down a hallway to the side of the room, then, and returned to his chair to sit. Soon a kobold came trotting in. He looked older and more ragged than the strapping young group that had abducted me; again I found myself half-missing them. This one was dressed in one battered tunic, and looked at me in confusion. The dunter gave orders to him, and he then ran back up the hall.

"Not my usual servant," the dunter told me. "My finest two are out serving the dunter force outside Emmervale. Be glad; they may soon take revenge for you on this sheep family you spoke of."

I did not dwell on this threat to the nefarious Shearer family. It struck me, instead, that in this city of dust and offal, as I lay on a rough stone floor in this jumbled mess of a front hall, the dunter seemed concerned that I might take away a poor opinion of his estate because his kobold slave was feeble and poorly dressed. I thought about telling him that the bent old servant should have been the least of his worries.

But mostly I wondered if I should share news about the breakup of the combined dunter-Caranniam-Varenlend expeditionary army. Perhaps this dunter had heard of it already, but perhaps not. I could not decide how much to say, however. I wanted this creature to treat me well, and to accept any chance to release me, but I didn't know what might best accomplish that.

The old servant returned with others, five total, and they again picked me up and carried me away. Kobolds did not seem to trust captives to walk on their own.

We moved through two hallways and then dropped down stone

stairs. This was now the lower level of the fortress. Of course I hoped that this would be the same manor I had reconnoitered, the one where the dwarves were held. I had no way of knowing if it was, since we had come into the city by a different route and I had been blindfolded.

I was despondent when they brought me to a single, empty cell. I was alone down there. I would be left stranded in a dungeon unknown to Britta and the dwarves.

But I then saw that the cell had bars on two sides, and past the set to my left was a longer cell holding three stocky lumps. These were the White Mount dwarves. They were dozing, or otherwise idle. Two were sitting up against the far wall, and the third was lying in the middle of the floor. One of the two against the wall rose at the noise of my entrance.

The five kobolds set me on the floor, and then four held me as one cut the cord at my wrists. They all then backed out quickly, slammed the barred door, and left.

"Man," the standing dwarf said. This was his greeting. He did not bother to say "welcome."

I stood, carefully, with my ankles still bound. I could see, because the cell had a tiny window, with bars of course, at the top of the outside wall. The dwarves' cell did not have one. The window was partially obscured by vines on the outside; this was why I might have missed it, had I seen this side of the fortress in my visit the day before. The window was no bigger than my head, but I could see out. There was a street, and I saw the cleared no-man's land and shacks beyond.

"I don't suppose you see any friends out there you might call to," the standing dwarf said. There was a clink, as he spoke. I looked over at him, and saw a chain around his right arm. It was anchored to the wall. All of them, I learned, were bound in this way.

"No friends yet," I said.

"Not yet," he repeated, and I could hear a smirk. He continued:

"I suppose you managed to fall into the hands of these dunters outside Emmervale?"

It sounded as if he thought little of anyone who could be captured by dunters; yet here they all were, themselves. I did not challenge him with this.

"Why do you say Emmervale?" I asked.

"We know the dunters have headed out that direction. And all the few men between here and there have enough sense to keep their heads down."

"What do you know about dunters at Emmervale?" I asked him. "You've been in here some weeks, I believe, or months even."

"And how do you know that?" he demanded. The other two were both also looking at me, now; the one on the floor had sat up.

"Listen, I have come here with Herrar, and with a group of dwarves from Stenhall. They are intending to break you out of here. Tonight."

At this, all three stood. It was a pathetic scene, as they rose on stiff legs. Their chains were long enough to allow them to approach me a few paces.

"You? Have come with Herrar?" the dwarf asked.

"Yes, and with Maghran of Stenhall. And a few others. Elves presented Herrar to us a few days ago."

"So that is how she left! Elves! And they did not bother to take out the rest of us, when they bought her freedom?"

"They tried," I said. "The price was too great. It was more than they had."

"More than they were willing to part with, you mean. And you know this how?"

"From the elves. I was there. We were a small group, and I stood beside Herrar and Maghran during all this. They spoke with Aladar Silvermoor."

The one speaking seemed to regard me for a moment and think to himself. I could not see his face well between the dark, the distance, and his beard.

"You have spoken with Herrar," he said. "You would have no reason to invent this story."

"I would not risk raising the hopes of three dwarves and have them dashed," I said.

"I suppose not. And how are they planning to rescue us? Have they shared that with you?"

"Of course. They just plan on digging in, at night."

If he thought this an unworkable plan, he didn't mention it.

"I am Hostenback," he said.

"Aiman," I answered. "Aiman Shearer."

My name did not seem to mean anything to them. I found it a relief.

They introduced themselves. The one chained up beside Hostenback was Ferlingas, and the third, on the floor, was Tam Shanter. Shanter seemed quiet and in very poor spirits. He seemed young. Hostenback and Ferlingas, for their parts, seemed to be holding themselves together with defiance, sarcasm, and hope.

The White Mount dwarves did not keep their voices swallowed up in the backs of their throats quite as much as those of Stenhall did. There were none of the rough -gh's among their names, as I heard with Maghran and Ghranam. They also did not speak with what so often sounded like, among the Stenhall group, ornery growls. But they were just as caustic, just as often. Hostenback queried me:

"How did you get captured?"

I told them about my walk to see Jed, and the kobold ambush. They asked how I had joined up with Stenhall dwarves in the first place, and that led to the long story of the attempted demolition of the railway.

"And it was you who approached the dwarves of Stenhall, for this?" Hostenback asked. "You yourself?"

"Yes."

"And why was that? Do you speak for Emmervale?"

"We all speak together. I just volunteered to walk up the mountain."

He let it go.

"And finally," I concluded, "we were hoping that we would dig you out, and be on our way. And I hope we still will. If all goes well, I will still be able to meet this man Jed in a day or two."

Hostenback shook his head.

"You should have stayed with the group. This companion of yours would have been fine. Away in safety, and with a mount no less."

"He would not have known where we had gone."

"He would have figured it out. You would have been reunited back in your town at some point."

"Perhaps six months from now," I said.

"Come," he said. "This dunter siege can't last that long. Stenhall won't allow it."

"Well," I said. "Stenhall volunteered to blow up railroad tracks, it's true. But apart from that I don't think they have much concern for Emmervale."

They made no answer to this. We were all silent for some time.

"So tonight," Hostenback resumed, "is when they come."

"That's the plan."

"We shall prepare our fond farewells to this elegant place, in that case."

"How strong are those chains you are in?" I asked. "I know they're intended just to keep you from digging—Herrar told us that —but from the sounds of those links, it seems they may bind you to these walls even when your kin arrive."

"They will have tools," he said. "These chains will not slow them down for long."

I heard a door groan open, down the hall, and then footsteps. Two kobolds brought food. They were scrawny young ones, and both were chewing on something as they arrived with the iron trays; apparently they felt free to nab anything that looked appealing from our meals. Little of it did. There was bread that was edible, but otherwise the trays were piled with not-too-thoroughly-washed roots and tubers that had been fried in lard that was well past its best days. The kobolds slid two trays through a gap beneath the bars in the dwarves' cell, and left. One then returned with a clay jug and one more small tray for me. As I inspected the fare, he departed, and then both returned once more with three of the clay jugs for the dwarves.

I lifted the jug. It smelled of the same lard and bread as my tray, but fermented.

"Bread beer," Hostenback said.

"Do they bring water?"

"Never. This is it. And from the way the kobolds handle it, and the dunters we see, they seem to think they are being good hosts in sharing it with us. Quite sad."

The bread was tough, dense, but the least-worst of the meal, so I concentrated on it.

"You think they consider this proper food?" I asked.

"Perhaps," Hostenback answered. "At the least, it's clear they don't want us to starve."

"Are there many other dunters here?" I asked. "I saw only one."

"We've seen only a few. Most seem to be out in the army, or armies. There's Crotchet; that's what we call the lord of this manor."

"He would be the one I saw."

"He welcomed you, eh? And one other, an even older one, we call Auntie Fang. And we've seen a flaccid young one who was apparently too dissolute to join the raiders. That seems to be all. There must be other females around, also, but we've seen none."

"You make it sound like breaking out of here would not be difficult, if you weren't chained."

"It would not be, no. I suppose Crotchet would probably get a shot off, and old Fang too. I don't think we'd have trouble from the young one, but the older two could at least raise an alarm. But we'd have to mind the kobolds, also. They have quite a fear of their masters and serve them faithfully. But when Herrar and Maghran make it here, we'll be out quickly."

I listened to the dwarves pass around the trays and jugs. I had finished what I wanted of the bread and hoped I would never become hungry enough to eat the food as eagerly as they were doing.

The light had failed out the little window. The dwarves did not speak, after their dinner, but I knew they were still awake. Time passed.

"I will not be able to sleep, with your news," Hostenback said after a long silence.

"I don't know at what time they might be here," I answered.

I sat with my back to the wall, and eventually dozed. I might have tried to stay awake for longer, but I had had a long day of travel and capture. I nodded off hoping to be awakened by dwarf spades smashing up out of the floor, or through the wall; or by Britta or Jed peering in through the window to tell me to ready myself to leave.

I woke in the morning. Light from the overcast sky entered the cell. I had lay down fully on the ground at some point. As I sat up again, and felt my stiffness from the hard floor, I noticed equally hard dwarf eyes staring at me.

"Good day," Hostenback said. "It seems we are still here."

I glanced over at them; it was a grim sight. All three sat gazing at me. I stood and looked out the window, as if I might see something. Of course I did not.

"I don't know what might have held them up," I said. "They intended to come last night."

"You're certain this group of saviors exists," he said.

"Of course. Come, Hostenback. I could not fabricate a story about Herrar."

"You knew of her already. You certainly could have."

"She was nothing more than a name to me, before I met her. A few weeks ago I would have assumed that she never left White Mount."

Tam Shanter shook his head and grumbled, at this.

"Perhaps the plan was put off because of your capture," Ferlingas said. "It may be that your carelessness will keep us holed up here."

"And how would that be?" I asked.

"The rest of the group might be waiting for you. Or searching for you."

"You think so," I said. "Let me ask: Are you telling me that you, if the situation was reversed and you were free while Herrar was imprisoned, would put off the rescue because a man from Emmervale had gone missing?"

He may have muttered something, to this, but he slouched over and said nothing aloud.

Breakfast, such as it was, came at midmorning. Down the hallway a door creaked again, and the same two kobolds wandered up with the same food. After we had eaten—I again limited myself to the bread, but now had to drink some of the syrupy beer—the dwarves lay down and slept.

"You'll pardon us, Shearer," Hostenback said. "We did not sleep last night. Unlike you. Please do let us know if anyone shows up to free us."

There was nothing to do during that day, and what became the several following days. I listened for the urban sounds of Red Gorge, but heard little. Occasionally a shot or two was fired, some distance away, and several times I heard the steam and screech of a train.

The dwarves were not very talkative, even after their anger with me about the first night's missed rescue dissipated.

They did tell me the story of their capture, months ago. It was just as Herrar and Maghran had described it: they had been on their way to visit Stenhall when they fell into magic.

"We were working our way over a crest, quite high in the hills," Hostenback said. "High enough so that little grew, and there was no cover for any enemies. And of course we were close enough to the lands of Stenhall—or in them, actually—that we thought we would be safe. At one point our path passed next to an outcrop of rock. The mages were there, making themselves invisible before it. They blended into the stones. One moment we were walking, and the next it was as if we had fallen into a sand pit."

"That's what Herrar told us," I said.

"Our legs would barely move, and then stopped altogether. As if bogged down in mud. We were awake, well aware of everything, and by then could see the mages."

"How many of them were there?"

"Just two. But after we were immobile, they called more. In order to carry us. They had four of them for each of us. They tied us to stretchers and hauled us down the way we had come, and then eventually here."

"You were awake the entire time?"

"Alert, yes. As we came down the hills the effect wore off, but by then they had bound us. A few days later, we were here. Those Caranniam scum were walking through this city as if they stayed here all the time. Now we know why it suits them well."

"I wonder why they did not take you to Caranniam instead."

"It was part of the plan to put together that combined expeditionary army, I think. Caranniam wanted to show the dunters that they were good allies, so we were a token of that. Quite a prize."

To stanch the boredom I could gaze out the window, of course, but I did not do so very often. For one thing, there was seldom much to see. Two kobolds pulled a rough cart piled with what seemed to be trash, once; that was the height of the entertainment. I heard two or three dunters passing by, at various times, and stood to look at them. But I was reluctant to get up too often because it seemed so unfair to the dwarves, who were chained and windowless while I was free to look out. Hostenback did get in the habit of asking me, after each poor breakfast:

"Why don't you take a look and tell us what is new in the world outside today, Mr. Shearer."

And I am sure he was doing so as a kind gesture to me, since he knew I was avoiding the view. Nonetheless, nothing was ever new in the world that I could see.

The dwarves seldom spoke. I wondered if they had been more talkative, weeks earlier, and were now too gloomy to converse. Maghran and certainly Herrar were not eager speakers, but these three made them seem like Bollard and Jed rambling in a tavern.

We did not see the chief dunter, Crotchet, again, but at one point a pair of others shuffled down the hall past our cells. One was young and heavy; the other, coming behind him, was stringy and old. They were on some errand, it looked like, and the older one was not happy with the younger one's speed. It leaned forward as they walked and smacked the young one on the back of its head. I realized the smacker was a female.

"That would be kind Auntie Fang," Hostenback muttered.

At this the old dunter stopped, produced something sharp from her clothes, and hurled it at Hostenback. The dwarf made a half-effort to dodge, but the shard of glass struck him. It bounced off. The dwarves looked on, somewhat amused I think. Any one of the dwarves could have torn both dunters apart barehanded, were it not for the chains and bars, and it was going to take much more than a bit of glass to do them any harm.

"It must be pleasant to carry around shattered trash in one's tunic," Ferlingas said.

Meanwhile the young dunter, still hurting from the strike from Fang, looked back at her, crossly, but did pick up pace.

The dwarves would stand and take few steps around their cells at regular intervals.

"We'll tighten up like knots of scrap iron if we don't keep moving," Ferlingas told me.

The chains were long enough to allow them into a rude alcove that held their latrine, also. This may have made the dungeon relatively luxurious, as such things went in Red Gorge. For my part I had a hole in a corner near the outer wall.

Our kobold jailers provided some diversion. In addition to those who brought food, we occasionally saw others passing down the halls with loads of firewood, bottles, sacks, various other things. One of them seemed to be a tinker, several times hurrying past us with a toolbox and a hammer in his hand.

"These creatures keep busy even if few dunters are left," I said once.

"Indeed," Hostenback answered.

"They may do most of the work around here."

"Especially with the absences. But I believe the dunters run them quite hard all the time, no matter what."

"Do you know any of their language?"

He snorted at this.

"I have had no inclination in my life to learn the dog-men's tongue, no."

But I tried to. They often came in pairs, and the ones who brought our food always did, and I listened to them speak. As usual, their speech sounded to me, at first, as nothing more than strings of yelps, snarls, and menacing growls; but if I paid close attention I could sort out words.

Ragan, or something close to it, seemed to mean either "over there" or "put;" they said it when they were discussing the delivery of our meals as they nodded and pointed. Simple enough.

One benefit to eating the same food every single meal was that the three words for it were not hard to grasp. *Shinga* was clearly the bread beer; *rach* or something like it was the bread; and the greasy roots were approximately *arangrang*.

I decided to test my learning on the third day. The two porters stopped at the dwarves' cell first, as they always did since that's the direction they came from (on their way out of what I could imagine was a marvelous kitchen).

As they bent down with the dwarves' trays, I moved to the hallway bars of my cell. I reached my hand out through the gap between them, and said:

"*Ragan.*"

The two of them went silent and stone-still. Both stared at me.

The dwarves glanced over, also, but the kobolds ignored them. Their eyes bore into me as if I had called them by name.

"*Shinga*," I then said.

They stood still a moment longer and then blew up with laughter. They bent over, and *shinga* actually sloshed out of the jug as one clutched it to his side. The laughter sounded like a pack of dogs on fire.

One of them finally got control of himself, straightened up, and walked over.

"*Zhirnga*," he said. He seemed to be correcting me. "*Zhirnga, rafa.*"

"*Rafa*," I said, and pointed to myself.

"*Rafa*," he repeated.

I pointed at the dwarves and asked him:

"*Rafa?*"

He shook his head and said:

"*Shenken.*"

He thrust the jug between the bars and the two of them walked away. I had wanted to ask him what he called himself, but he didn't turn back around.

Hostenback said:

"I don't know why you waste your time with that growling."

"I never know whom I may need to talk to," I said. I did not point out to him that the kobolds' speech, in terms of being a growl, was not so far removed as the accents of the dwarves from Stenhall. Perhaps he would have agreed with me had I said so. In any case he and the other *shenken* just ate their food quietly.

After dinner each night, for three nights, the dwarves rolled their eyes (to the extent that I could see them) and brought up the planned rescue again.

"I suppose you believe tonight may be the night," Hostenback said on one of these evenings.

"Again, their intent was to get us directly. Get you, rather."

"Well, I am going to sleep tonight, rather than keep vigil."

"I just hope they have not been harmed," I said.

"I suppose I must, too," he said. "Pardon my flippancy. If Herrar and other dwarves are really out there, I do hope they are taking care of themselves. They are far from home. And on the wrong side of this miserable city."

One morning, after my customary look out the narrow window, which as usual revealed nothing, a racket down the hall announced the approach of Auntie Fang. I heard her screeching, plus the whiny voice of the flaccid young dunter, and also yelps from a kobold. I reflected that it was truly sad I had been down here long enough to pick out these three noises accurately before I could even see them.

Auntie had the kobold by an ear, pulled downward, and was pushing and kicking him along the hall. Each kick meant that his ear was stretched, of course, and he craned his head to try to provide some slack. She was repeating something over and over, following it with kicks in rhythm. Meanwhile the laggard young one shadowed her, imploring her with something. His voice was always a whine, but his speech now seemed more pathetic than usual. Was he begging on behalf of the kobold? Did he own it?

The three of them came to the door of the dwarves' cell. Auntie looked at them, thought a moment, and then kicked the kobold a few more times to get him down to my door. She produced a key, opened the door, and threw the kobold in. She was strong enough to launch him into the air a bit, and he landed with a thump at my feet.

She slammed the door shut and left. She and the young one shrank down the hall noisily, something like the creaky dunter locomotive I had seen.

The kobold rolled over, looked at me in apparent fear, and backed away. He slid back on his behind without getting up. I could see that Auntie's grip on his ear had done real harm; the skin was angry red, and seeping some blood. She had not been too far from ripping it off.

He was a typical ragged kobold of Crotchet's manor, barely wrapped in dirty clothes and clearly ill-fed. I would have given him food, or clothing, had I had any to spare. As it was all I could think to do, to at least put him at ease, was to open my hands to him: No threat here. I backed away from him and sat down, myself.

"So are you being punished by being housed with a kobold," Hostenback called over, "or is it being punished by being housed with you?"

"Fine question," I said. "She didn't want him with you, for some reason."

"That she didn't."

"Have you seen this before? Kobolds locked up down here?"

He nodded.

"Not unusual. It only lasts for a day or two, and then we see them doing their chores again. Just light punishment, I suppose."

" 'Light.' She almost tore his ear off."

"I'm sure that happens too," he said.

When food came there was an extra lump of *arangrang* for the new prisoner. The two jailers chatted with him a bit; he seemed understandably glum. From the tone of their voices they seemed to be encouraging him to keep his chin up. Later in the afternoon they returned, one with keys and the other with a short sword. The one with the sword made a point of waving it at me as the other opened the door to my cell.

"You can take him, Shearer," Ferlingas said. It was in jest. "Never mind that knife of his."

"I assume they are clever enough to call for help and keep me down here," I said.

My erstwhile cellmate left, the door slammed back, and the dwarves and I resumed . . . doing nothing.

Twelve

I had just learned that the kobolds who brought us our food were named Dororg and Rarakan when we were indeed rescued. It was my fifth night in the place. As it happened, that day was the first in which I had resigned myself to a long captivity. I had finally accepted that something terrible must have happened to Britta and Herrar and the Stenhall dwarves.

That evening, after dinner, I had exchanged names with the kobolds by calling myself "*Rafa* Shearer" and then nodding to them. The first said Dororg; I gestured to the other and repeated the word to see if he was telling me his name, or their word for kobold. He said:

"Rarakan."

Dororg and Rarakan. I could tell them apart when they were standing next to each other; Dororg was shorter and broader. I had also noticed that, although both were mainly dark brown—no surprise with a kobold—Dororg had a bit of dark gray fur beneath his eyes, and below his chin. Rarakan's face was more a solid color.

I then pointed to myself and to the dwarves in turn, and said:

"*Rafa; shenken.*"

—and then pointed to the two of them.

"*Kororen*," Dororg said. Somewhat close to "kobold," it turned out; our word might have come from theirs.

And finally I wanted one more word, one more lesson. It might have been the word for good, or brave, but I'd decided those were too difficult to convey. Instead I lifted my arm, brought in my wrist, and made my biceps bulge to the extent I could. Britta, and big Bollard, would have laughed at the attempt, I'm sure. But I clenched my teeth and growled a bit and pointed to the muscle.

"Strong," I said.

They were amused; they laughed in yelps. But they told me the word:

"*Akag.*"

"*Akag*," I repeated. I then nodded to them. "*Akag kororen.*" Strong kobolds.

"*Koror akag*," Dororg corrected me. "*Kororen akagen*." So *kororen* was plural, the noun came first, and there had to be agreement with the adjective.

Rarakan, for his part, flexed his own biceps—rather more impressive than mine, pound for pound—and they left.

The kobolds had finished bringing us our evening food. The dwarves and I ate and then settled down for another night. Of course, "settling down" was a generous description, since all we could do was sit or lie down on hard rock. At any rate, we all lay still. Perhaps the dwarves were still waiting on a rescue; I had given up.

Long before I noticed anything different on this night, compared to the preceding ones, the dwarves roused themselves. I heard scuffs as they came to attention. They sat up straight, and cocked their heads to listen. They muttered to each other quietly. Finally I head Hostenback speak:

"There is work going on."

"What sort of work?" I asked.

"Earth work. We felt it. Now we can hear it."

And then I, too, heard muffled sounds in the earth behind the rear wall of the dwarves' cell. Soon the scrapes of shovels became clear.

I stood, and so did all the dwarves. I looked out the window and saw nothing. I hoped that Britta and whichever dwarves were not digging were well concealed, and not merely out of my view.

The shovel scrapes grew louder, and then I myself could feel the digging.

A moment later, the wall tumbled down. A heavy-footed form stepped out.

"Greetings, all. Some light."

A match flared and then a lantern illuminated the cells. It was Maghran. He gripped a shovel and was covered in dirt. Behind him now emerged Herrar and Inman. They sized up the prisoners, and each dashed to one of them.

"You return," Hostenback said to Herrar.

"At length. Maghran and Inman, of Stenhall." This was the extent of her introduction.

Hrond then dropped out of the hole in the wall. Only Britta was missing.

I noticed something:

"Hrond," I said. "Your musketoon?"

"Outside," he said. "Didn't want to shove it along before me through that dirt. Inman left his gun out there also."

"Just sitting out there? Hidden, I hope."

He nodded. "And we don't intend to be in here very long."

Herrar meanwhile pulled a pair of heavy pincers from her pack. Inman produced an iron pry bar and set to Hostenback's metal cuffs.

And then Britta climbed out of the tunnel. She set Hrond's gun by the wall, gazed around, saw me, and shook her head at the bars between us.

"More digging," she said.

"You joined them in that tunnel?" I asked her.

"Better than staying out there," she said. "And we all needed to push dirt." She was as soiled as the dwarves.

Meanwhile Inman gave up using the pry bar on Hostenback's shackles.

"This is too large," he said. "Nothing to fit into."

"Then open their door," she said. She was squeezing the pincers she held on a link of the chain that bound Ferlingas, but that also seemed to be slow work.

"We will need the keys to these shackles," she said. "As reluctant as I am to admit it. If I had all my tools you'd be free already."

"Do you know where the keys are?" Maghran asked.

"The kobolds keep them," she answered. "So open that door. We'll go find them."

Inman moved toward the barred door on the dwarves' cell and braced the pry bar between it and the wall. He hauled on it; this produced creaks but nothing more. Hrond joined him, then, and they pulled together. They strained. I thought the bar might snap, but the door gave first, and its bolt popped out of the wall socket. The two dwarves stepped out. Hrond had his musketoon with him.

At that moment Dororg and Rarakan came running down the other end of the hall, to my right, toward the commotion. They froze, right in front of my cell. They might have retreated, but Hrond swung the gun up to aim at them.

"Don't shoot!" I yelled at him. I reached out through my bars with both arms to put my hands in front of them.

"Might these two have the keys?" he said.

That was a kobold word which I had not, of course, learned. I looked at them, however, and made a key motion with my fingers before the lock of my own cell. Rarakan nodded and left. Dororg seemed to understand he was staying behind as a hostage, still covered by the musketoon.

"Would the first really care if I blasted this one?" Hrond asked. "I'm not sure this will guarantee his return."

"He'll come back," I said.

Ferlingas called over to Hrond:

"This human friend of yours is a friend to these kobolds. Talks to them. I'm sure it will be back with keys."

As he said this, Inman stepped back into the cell toward Hostenback. He crossed to the wall and smashed the pry bar into the blocks over the mounted end of the chain.

"They're coming with keys," Hostenback protested.

"I'll believe that when I see it."

"What, you mean for me to carry that chain with me when I'm out of here?"

Inman answered without turning away from his work. "I'll explain to strangers that you're an upstanding gentleman, until we get it off."

Herrar, meanwhile, winced at one final press on her pincers, and the link of Ferlingas's chain broke. She moved on to Shanter while Ferlingas stretched his right arm around freely for the first time in weeks.

Britta came to my bars.

"Do you think the kobold will have keys for your cell, too?"

"I would guess so."

And then Rarakan returned, back down the hallway to my right, with a bright ring of keys.

"Open those shackles," Hrond ordered, and held out his wrist as an example as he nodded toward the dwarves' cell.

"Don't worry, Aiman," Herrar called over to me. "We won't forget you. Although perhaps we should."

"I let down my guard," I said. "Did my capture cause your delay somehow?"

"No," she said. "There have been forces of Caranniam walking the city at night. That's why we held off."

"But they're not out there now?"

"Not tonight. We think they have left with a dunter force to haul some of those supplies which were to have gone on the train."

"That same stockpile I saw."

"Yes."

"One of you watched the city at night?"

"Britta."

I looked at her and shook my head.

"The palest one here, most likely to be seen," I said.

"I covered my hair," she said. "I was almost completely shrouded."

"How were they hauling?"

"With oxen. Just as you saw, weeks ago."

"They moved the cannons?"

"Cannons, barrels, more muskets. Much material," she said.

As we spoke Rarakan moved through the cell and keyed open all the shackles, except for those of Hostenback. Inman had chiseled that one free of the wall.

Herrar now came to my cell, tested the door, and then yanked it open with a single pull.

"You did not try that?" she asked.

"I don't believe I ever did," I answered.

She shook her head.

And then a tremendous explosion some blocks away cracked through the air and shook the fortress. Dust fell from the ceiling as the dwarves braced themselves. The explosion took some moments, like a long roll of thunder ripping down the sky into the distance.

Herrar seemed to have been expecting it. She stood firm while the blast roared and echoed.

"That's our diversion," she said. "Move."

"Let me get my chain off," Hostenback said.

"We have no time," Herrar said. "Get through that tunnel, all of you."

"I can't wear this," he objected.

"We'll be back at White Mount soon, we'll remove it there," she said. "We have to move. If you get left behind, we're not returning."

Hostenback raised his arm again to display his chain, and began to object once more, but shouts down the hall cut him off.

Auntie Fang appeared with a raised pistol.

We all ducked. What went through my mind was that I would be the largest target of all of us down there. I got face down on the floor.

Fang fired. The boom cracked down the hall, but I heard the bullet clang off one of the bars. I wasn't sure whom she had aimed at.

"Those slobbering kobolds sounded an alarm!" Maghran shouted.

"The kobolds are right here!" I answered.

Hostenback took advantage of the confusion to snatch the entire key chain from Rarakan.

Meanwhile Fang looked at her pistol with her scowling eyes and seemed at a loss. I did not see that she had any other weapon, and even with a sword or knife I doubt she would have rushed us.

She turned and shouted toward where she had come from. Now her pudgy nephew (as we fashioned him) arrived. He held two more pistols.

I turned toward the escape tunnel to see Herrar disappear into it. The others followed in a rush: first the captives Hostenback, Ferlingas, and Tam Shanter. Then Maghran, Inman, and Hrond. The seven of them all darted in like one long and dirty rabbit.

The Stenhall dwarves had done the captives the courtesy of allowing them out first, but they hadn't waited for me or Britta. We looked back at Fang and the other dunter, who were fumbling with the pistols; it seemed that Fang wanted to take the shots herself.

"Go!" I yelled, and I pushed Britta into the hole. I followed. Another shot banged as I stepped in. The bullet slammed into the earth behind me.

The last thing I saw in there was Rarakan and Dororg standing together in the dwarves' erstwhile cell, dumbfounded.

The tunnel was not long, heading straight out into the earthwork surrounding the fortress. When Britta and I slid out, the dwarves had already taken off down the road. I felt that shock waves from the explosion and the pistol shots still coursed through the air; it must have just been my head ringing.

I ran next to Britta, down the street.

"What did they blow up?" I asked her.

"They found a small arms warehouse. They were hoping it might set off a secondary explosion, from the powder, and it must have."

"Is that sort of diversion smart? Won't it just draw dunters?"

"We thought there would be an alarm as we left. I still think there will be. So we hoped this would distract them."

We trotted through the dark.

"A warehouse," I said. "How long did they have to spend searching for that?"

"Not long at all. We were lucky enough to hear a few gun shots in the night, and we followed them, and there it was."

"You came in for that?"

"Two nights ago, yes."

"You've been busy. And Jed?"

"We didn't see him again. I assume he moved north, and he's waiting for us up there. Or searching for us. You're all right?"

"I could do with a pot of stew and clean water, but yes."

She was carrying my bag and handed it to me as we ran out. The dwarves were all ahead of us. We sprinted straight down the side of the street.

A dwarf sprint is a thing to behold. They move quickly enough, but it requires a furious amount of pumping of their short legs. I was glad Jed was not with us, for he likely would have shown off his pace by overtaking them with half their strides.

Britta told me now:

"I am hoping that the dunters took still more of their able-bodied with them when they moved out with those supplies. It would make this city even quieter."

The street was much the same as the ones I had seen south of Crotchet's fortress: surrounded by rough houses that seemed nearly empty, and kobold shacks, and abandoned structures and lots. I was hoping the sprawl would start to look like outskirts, soon, but we still had blocks of battered Red Gorge City before us.

"This place looks much more lovely at night," I said.

"The light does it no favors."

"We're just running the whole way out?"

"That's the plan. We hope that blast draws all the attention."

We continued up the street, Britta and I following the seven bobbing dwarf heads. We could not tell, yet, if the explosion of the dwarves had actually drawn any dunters or kobolds who might otherwise have seen us; and of course we did not pass any organized fire companies rushing tankers down the streets. Our several nights of skulking about Red Gorge City had been possible because it was so unthinkable to the dunters that such a party would try such a thing. I was sure that after this escape, and the explosion, the city would now be guarded. For a moment, though, we were still able to run through it unchallenged.

I did notice some eyes on us. A head appeared at a window here, a door cracked opened over there. But all seemed to be kobolds, as far as I could make out as we dashed past. Down alleys, I might have seen a form of another or two of the dog-men. But no one emerged to block us, or chase us. If they noticed, and realized that we were outsiders, it seemed none was eager to wake up its master and point us out. The dunters could get the kobolds to work for them if they drove them with whips, and rationed food, but these methods would not turn servants into useful guards.

But then suddenly the dwarves drew up short, ahead of us.

"Off the road!" Maghran snapped in a gravelly low shout.

The seven of them dropped to their left, into a ditch, and we followed. Not far up the road was a group of dunters, perhaps fifteen or twenty. They carried lanterns, so we could see their forms, and they were well-armed. They held long muskets and were swinging them back and forth slowly as they walked. They pointed them variously before them, and off to the sides, and behind.

"We can't just hide here," Maghran said. "They're searching. We go back, or through one of these walls." Next to the ditch was a long wall of a shanty, with others on either side.

"Do they all have guns?" Herrar asked. She rose up a bit to look.

It was a foolish move. Light from the dunters' lanterns must have glinted off the circlet she wore. They instantly shouted, brought other lights to the front, and ran toward us.

"Many guns," she said.

Tam Shanter and Ferlingas immediately trampled us and ran down the line of the ditch back toward where we had come. Herrar and the other dwarves, except Hrond, clambered out of the ditch and slammed themselves into the wooden wall of the structure behind us. Hrond held his ground, aiming his musketoon at the oncoming group. I don't know what good he thought his single shot would do before the dunters overtook us. I was torn between following Tam and Ferlingas, and trying to help the other dwarves breach that wall; I think Britta was, too.

Herrar, Maghran, Hostenback, and Inman loosened a board in the wall through their body blows and kicks, but then shots roared from the street. Bullets hit the wall, and splinters flew. The dwarves dropped to the ground.

"Not enough shots," Herrar said. She meant that the dunters had been smart enough not to all fire at once. The shooters could reload while the others blasted us in a moment. The dwarves might have risked a hand-to-sword fight against twice their number, but they would not walk into musket fire.

Hrond fired. The dunters shouted at this, and held up a moment, but it wasn't clear that any of them had been hit.

We all ran, then, following Tam and Ferlingas back the way we had come.

We stayed off the road, which slowed us. We high-stepped through the filth of the ditch. We could hear the screams and even the boots of the dunters on the street.

More shots boomed, and this time we were hit: Hostenback took a bullet in the back of his left shoulder. He was in front of me, and I saw him yanked forward like a marionette. He stumbled a step, and fell. Herrar and Maghran reached down, barely breaking their short strides, and hauled him up.

And now another shot, and another. I heard one bullet whistle past me.

"Alley ahead," Tam shouted in front of us. He darted up the embankment and we followed. It was not an alley, I saw, but just a gap between two fences. We ran into it nonetheless.

We hustled perhaps twenty yards into this channel and then crashed into each other as Tam hit the end of it.

"No outlet!" he yelled back.

The fence on either side was at least eight feet tall. Britta and I might have been able to jump up and pull ourselves over, but there was no way the dwarves could have.

"Do we jump?" she asked me.

"They're going to shoot us in here like bears in a cave," Herrar said.

Hostenback, who was still between her and Maghran, grunted

now and leaned back against the wall. He was holding his left arm before him, across his midriff. He tried to stretch the arm backward, and straighten, but shuddered in pain at the attempt.

The other dwarves again started trying to knock a hole in the wall, somewhere, anywhere. The dunters would be at the entrance in a moment.

But then a gate between us and the road swung out. I had missed it, running past; it was made of planks just like the rest of the wall.

A kobold leaned out and looked at us with bright eyes. We saw his white teeth in the night.

"Aimaaan," he said.

I confess it took me a few minutes to tell which one it was—Dororg or Rarakan—in the dark, and the rush, and the confusion, but soon I settled on Dororg. He had the bit of black on his face.

He beckoned us in the through the gate.

The dwarves stood stunned for a moment, but Britta and I did not need any more invitation. We squeezed past them, past the kobold, and into an open yard beyond. We then heard the dwarves following behind us.

Hrond was the last one through, and when he cleared the opening Dororg slammed it shut and threw a bar across it.

In an instant the dunters on the other side reached the gate and began shaking it and screaming. The entire wall shook.

The kobold pointed toward the far end of the yard and shouted at us:

"*Kayan!*"

So that meant "over there." We ran. Dororg overtook us, running up and stepping in front of me and Britta. He looked back and smiled, with his tongue hanging out.

"*Dunteren,*" he said, nodding back behind him. I looked, and saw half a dozen of them topping the wall and beginning to drop down on our side.

But quickly we rounded a corner, passed a shed, and then took another right. This path led only a few yards before bearing left, and we hustled down another gap between fences. With Dororg as our guide through the maze of back lots we seemed to separate ourselves from the dunters, judging from their dwindling noise.

Dororg made another right. Here we ran a few more strides,

but then he pulled up short. He motioned to a crack in another wooden wall. It was small enough to not be noticed as a passage, but big enough for us to fit through. Dororg reached up to put his furred hands on Britta's back and push her through the gap.

"*Woondala sala*," he said; who knows what that meant. He was gentle as he guided her, so maybe he was telling her to take care.

I followed. It was easy for me, but I wondered if all the dwarves would fit. Now they stumbled up to us, ran into Dororg, and took my advice from the other side:

"Hostenback!" I said. He was first, with Herrar right behind him. "Come through here."

He squeezed through, wincing, and one by one the rest followed. Hrond fit easily; some of the others did not. The ones who had been captive just now were thin, from their meager diet, but Inman and Maghran got caught between the fence planks.

We had a lead on the pursuing dunters, thanks to Dororg, but now we again heard them nearing. They were shouting, and howling, and a few of them were firing off their muskets at who knows what.

Inman made it through the crack with Ferlingas pulling on his arms as Maghran pushed from the other side. Maghran, last, then began to wiggle through. Dororg helped him with shoves and then a few kicks, into which he may have put more energy than absolutely necessary. One more kick and the dwarf dropped into the darkness with us.

"Curse that dog, he milked those kicks," he said; but he turned and watched through the opening, his face held back in shadow, as Dororg shot up the alley to draw the crowd of dunters.

It worked. We saw them all run past, frenzied. There were perhaps twenty, hurrying in single file. The last two held muskets carefully which were presumably still loaded. They disappeared, and the night became a bit quieter.

"The hound did it," Maghran said. "Let's move north again."

"Hound" was a respectful dwarf term for a dog, I knew. It was all Dororg would get from Maghran, but remarkable nonetheless.

We were able to cut through three or four quiet yards before we came to a small alley and cautiously took to the streets again.

"I think we covered some distance with Dororg," I told

Maghran. "We can't have far to go, now."

"I agree."

"Is Hostenback able to keep up?"

"You've seen he is."

We clung to shadows off to the side of the street. There was no more movement from dunters or anything else. The city began to dwindle as we forged north. Buildings became—not more modest, exactly, because even in the center they were ramshackle firetraps, but smaller. We moved further away from the street, which out here was becoming just a narrow track, and picked our path between buildings. We passed what I might have called the boundary of the town—the last of the massed shacks—and entered another agricultural area like the one to the south: dark, and stale, and barely populated. We left the road and cut slightly to the east. We did this as soon as we could see we'd no longer be troubled by any ditches or fences.

And soon we walked out of the last cultivated field. By the time dawn rose we were in untouched open country. It was an enormous relief to be out of the orbit of Red Gorge City. With no sign of the dunters or their filth, the land could have belonged to us just as well as to them. I felt a bit lightheaded walking through that country, overwhelmed by the freedom. And I had been around their city only a few days; I could imagine how glad the White Mount dwarves must have been. Or perhaps they were just longing for their mountains, and anything else was all the same to them.

They trudged ahead. Hostenback with his shoulder wound tried to move as smoothly as he could, I saw.

We crossed an expanse of a tall grass, and then one of shorter turf and wildflowers, and came to a stretch of woods. We stepped in and rested beneath the trees.

Britta and I were the last to sit down, not far in. Hostenback came up to peer behind us.

"No one trailing us," he said.

"No."

Maghran asked him:

"Shall we look at your shoulder?"

He nodded. I noticed that his arms were free.

"You got those shackles off, at least."

"Early on. I keyed them open on the street as we ran," he said.

"I dropped the ring, then. Maybe that kobold chap will find them. He seemed helpful."

"Very," I said.

"I've had much good luck today." He said this as Maghran pulled out a knife and cut through his jacket, and then his shirt. It was wet with blood, and beneath it the flesh of his shoulder was red and swollen. The bullet hole was a small black pit.

Maghran peered at it.

"Should we reach for the slug?" he asked.

"With what?"

"That, I don't know."

"If no one has pliers, or anything else, let's wait," Hostenback said. "If your plan is to dig it out with a knife, I fear you'll just slice me up more."

"Can you feel the bullet?"

"Yes. It's not stuck in the bone. Perhaps next to a bone, but behaving itself."

"Very well." He lowered his hands.

"And now, off to Midwall. Do you know the place, Shearer? Do your people know it?"

"No."

"But you think that friend of yours will be able to find it?"

I rolled my head at this in exasperation.

"Herrar assured me he would!"

"Of course," he said. "It's the only stretch of such ruins in the area. The ruins don't stand out, but if he circles around he'll find the road.

"The town there," he continued, "was a way station along the highway centuries ago. It was a highway at the time, I should say. Not much left now. This was before the rise of the dunters and Red Gorge City; the men who used that road did not have to worry about protecting it, but rather just having a bed and a roof and a watering hole. Once Red Gorge grew, it became a garrison town to protect the highway against them. But it was gradually abandoned as the dunters expanded their reach. Then during the plague and then the dragon years it was abandoned altogether when they fell back."

"Did dwarves use the road?"

Hostenback answered this:

"Seldom. You know we've never been much for traveling. But we quarried much of the stone in this stretch. Our White Mount ancestors, I mean, of course. Ancient Nemeya paid them well. They were powerful men, with that road north from Searose and then all the way east almost to your Emmervale."

"I'll look at those stones when we get there," I said.

"I believe they're long buried."

Herrar walked up to us.

"It has been a long night," she said. "And now the morning already. But we want to push on to Midwall."

"Is it far, now?"

Maghran shook his head. "Not at all. Perhaps two hours. We can spend the day there, and you will meet up with your companion."

"That's our hope," I said. "And Maghran—once we are reunited, we want to speak with you to determine if the dwarves of White Mount will join us to march on Red Gorge City."

"We shall," Maghran said. "I plight you that. Perhaps it would be possible to stage an attack from Stenhall on the force outside Emmervale. And at the same time have White Mount come down here. I imagine the dunters out near us would flee toward here, and we could crush them in the middle, out on the plains."

"That's an ambitious plan, and adventurous," Herrar told him. "Two dwarven armies out in the open, and fighting alongside men."

"The time may have come," Maghran answered. "We have seen how busy the dunters are, here. And we have seen the aid from Caranniam. Now might be the time."

We gathered ourselves and left the woods. Maghran and Herrar led the way, followed by Hostenback, Ferlingas, and Shanter, and then Inman and Hrond, and finally Britta and me. We again checked behind us to confirm that no one was pursuing from Red Gorge City. The land was flat, here, and had no ridges or hilltops from which to scout the countryside, but there was nothing to worry us. Only grass fields stretched away to the south.

"If they had sent anyone, they would likely be on the road west of here," Maghran said. "And I assume they would travel as far as Midwall. But we'll approach from the southeast, and be able to see anything amiss there."

We marched over more grassland. Only a few of the party had dozed in the woods, and barely, but I think we were all alert between the new dawn and the possibility that we were being followed.

I had assumed we were still at some distance from the old fortification, because I saw nothing to speak of ahead of us. But suddenly Herrar spoke:

"There it is."

And then I saw. Midwall was a low jumble of broken-down buildings. Tall grasses and scrub trees had grown up around the remains of an ancient wall, which was more collapsed than whole. Only a few sections still reached up to their original height, topped with crenelations. Inside the wall were a few structures, again mostly fallen.

"And this was once an outpost of proud Nemeya," I said.

"Indeed," Herrar answered. "A landmark for travelers, at one time. Including my ancestors, on occasion. Not much of a welcome here for anyone now, but we can spend the day. And meet your companion and move on."

The ruined town was small, and as we approached we saw the road from Red Gorge City coming in on our left. It was empty.

Herrar nodded to Britta and me.

"One of you tall ones should get up on those walls, as high as you can, and tell us if you see anything."

We came to one of the sections of wall that remained standing, and stopped at a gateway. The gate, which may have been timber or iron at one time, was long gone. Over the gap a keystone had been placed with the crest of Nemeya: a dragon in profile, its wings upraised. Little did the Nemeyans know that it would be dragons who would largely destroy this outpost, centuries on.

A voice inside spoke:

"Welcome to my palace."

The White Mount dwarves all startled at this. It was Jed, of course. He walked out from behind a mostly-intact building. It was good to see his prankster face and upraised eyebrows.

"You arrived," Britta said.

"Days ago. I was getting concerned. I actually rode back out of here once, wondering if I had taken the wrong road. But I went quite a distance to the west and saw no other. What happened to you?"

"We were delayed by some activity in the town," I told him. "Forces of Caranniam were moving about."

Britta snorted at this, but Jed answered:

"But you made your rescue." He nodded to the three new dwarves.

"Indeed," Herrar said. The others did not acknowledge him.

"And Aiman ended up among the rescued, also," Britta said.

"What?"

"I was taken by kobolds and thrown in a dungeon," I said. I reflected on this and added: "But somehow that makes it sound worse than it was. It was the same one where these White Mount dwarves were, fortunately."

"So you enjoyed the dunter hospitality?"

"I've had enough for a lifetime, now."

"How long ago did you escape?"

"Just earlier this morning. Or very late last night."

"They dug you out? Or did Britta bend bars with her bare hands?"

"They dug us out."

"And then you just marched out of there?"

"There was some pursuit, but we managed to evade them. Between hiding and running, we made it out."

"You haven't stopped moving since?"

"Briefly. Under some cover. But we wanted to get here and rest. Then tomorrow, we'll decide what's next."

The dwarves moved in among the ruins while Britta and I stayed with Jed. I lowered my voice.

"Supposedly these friends of ours are going to have a serious talk about attacking Red Gorge. Attacking both the expeditionary force and, perhaps, the city itself. Maghran seems to be in favor, now. I don't know about Herrar, though. She and her dwarves are very close to home, at this point. And they've been away for some time. And that railroad was not aimed at them, so I doubt they'll feel any danger from Red Gorge the way the Stenhall dwarves might. But we shall see."

"I wish the dunters would just wander off of their own accord," Jed said. "But that's not their way, we know. Speaking of them—should we set a watch?"

"Yes, we should."

"I've scouted a bit. This building right here is the sturdiest. We could head up and look out those windows."

The building had likely been built as a guard tower, and may have predated the wall. Its four corners were fat columns made of slabs of stone. The walls between them were brick and mortar, with tall and very narrow windows on the bottom level. The building had an upper story as well, quite high and offering a good view.

We entered through the open doorway. Again any door it once had was gone. Inside, the floor was packed dirt. Perhaps there were paving stones beneath. It was littered with ashes and half-burnt logs and bones from apparent dunter encampments over the years. The ceiling was high above us. Two sets of stairs along the walls led up to the top floor. One of these had crumbled into rubble, but the other looked sound. The beams above—the base of the top floor— also seemed intact.

The three of us climbed up.

"So just one day here, and then home tomorrow?" Jed said.

"That's the idea. But if the dwarves decide to attack the dunters somehow, we might be extending our excursion once more."

We reached the top floor and walked over to its windows. We looked out over the shells of buildings and the fields beyond. The landscape was more or less flat out to the horizons, and nothing moved. The east-west road was obvious even though it was grown over. It was a ribbon of flat turf stretching away in either direction.

"This must have been an impressive highway in its day," Britta said.

"We'll put it on the list of things for our grandchildren to take back and renovate," Jed said.

Down below us on the street we saw Maghran walk into view. Herrar followed him, and behind her the rest of the dwarves. He looked up at us as we peered out the window.

"You see nothing, I suppose?"

"Nothing."

"How far this highway has fallen. At one time someone in your shoes might have seen a thousand horses marching down that road and not even remarked on it."

Now he lowered his eyes and looked over the building.

"Good stonework, here. In this one, at least. Perhaps we built it for them."

"Perhaps."

"May we join you up there to eat?"

"Of course. You are giving us title to this house?"

"To the extent it's mine to give, certainly."

The group entered and climbed up. As they appeared, one by one, I found it was good to be holed up in a room of sullen dwarven faces. I again smelled the leather and stone dust I always associated with them. They stumped around on the wooden floor, their wide backs to me as they moved to the windows. Their tools and weapons dangled from their shoulders and packs: the battle axes of Hrond, Inman, and Herrar; Hrond's musketoon; Inman's long musket; the small shovels of Herrar and Maghran.

Hostenback sat down with his shoulders against a wall—well, he leaned back against it with his good shoulder—while the others spread out and took their own turns looking down at the roads outside.

"This will do for the day," Herrar said. "We will set out at night again. And then that will be the last time I hide my journeying for a long time, I hope."

"I suppose we do not risk a fire," Britta said.

"No," Herrar answered. "We don't know what eyes may be out here. And we are barely armed."

Once again I wondered if this little group of dwarves might have been willing to risk a battle with a force from Red Gorge, had they only had more guns with them. Perhaps they would have hacked down the scrub trees around the walls and set up a bonfire, just to attract a fight. The thought made me glad that they had in fact lost most of their weapons. I kept this to myself, of course.

"We should sleep," Maghran said.

"Especially you," I answered. "Those of us in the dungeon slept some of last night, at least."

"Hm, not much of a trade. I'd rather be free and up all night than sleeping in that hole. Someday we will make the dunters pay for that. A nighttime rescue teaches none of them any real lesson. I think of them wandering unmolested at our border, and then past our border, taking you," he said, nodding to Herrar. "We must make them pay. Protect our bourn after the fact."

"The dunters had help, don't forget," Herrar answered. "Making

Caranniam pay will be more difficult."

Maghran just grunted at this. After our recent ordeal, and Hostenback's shooting, it was understandable that he was thinking of revenge on the dunters more so than on the wizards who had helped abduct Herrar and her escort.

Hrond and Inman now sat on the floor, fatigued from their night digging and running. Shanter and Ferlingas, for their part, seemed to look each other over and then decide against sitting. Ferlingas asked:

"We saw no water, in our little walk just now. Have any of you?"

That's why they were not yet settling down: they were filthy. I had never known them without their being covered by dunter grime, I realized, and it had not occurred to me that they likely preferred to have less dirt and stink about them.

"There is a spring on the north side of town," Jed said. "One street over, then all the way up. It has a short stone wall, you can't miss it."

They gave him short nods and headed toward the stairs.

The rest of us sat. The dwarves unloaded their hardware with thumps on the wooden planks. Jed and Britta seemed to float down like autumn leaves, compared to the noise and scuffs of all of them.

Maghran spoke.

"Master Shearer, you owe me a story. I told you about our unfortunate Twill, and the cobbers."

"Indeed. Do Herrar's companions know that story?"

"Of course. But in White Mount they claim his name was Dvill. And I believe he used larger coins." He turned to Herrar.

"Old Dvill put out shaved half-weights for the cobbers, is that right?"

"That's so."

Maghran snorted at this.

"Twill, as we tell it, put out something smaller—just a few rounds. Pennies, you know. Everything is bigger in White Mount."

I saw Herrar barely, barely turn up a corner of her mouth in a smile, at this.

"But now to you. You must have something, Aiman."

"Well, I know one. Our own work story. About the shepherd. The first one, you know. The first shepherd who was able to gather sheep and tend them. But Britta tells it better." I looked at her.

"Shall I?" she asked.

"Please," Maghran said.

"The shepherd, then," she said. She straightened up a bit where she sat, and drew in a breath.

"This was when the world was young. In fact it was soon after the first winters began. Because you know that back in the beginning, the world was always in summer. You do know that?"

"Very well," he said.

"But then the giant bears came, and with them their winters. But that's another story. This woman I speak of, the first shepherd, gathered sheep for their wool—now that there was a use for it, with the cold—and watched them, and eventually sheared.

"And she kept the flock together with a wooden whistle. She learned that they would listen to the sound, and she used it to guide them. The whistle was just a simple tube, and it played only one note. But she sounded it beautifully, and it spoke to the sheep.

"Now back then, Wolf was always close by."

"Wolf."

"Wolf, the first. Yes. He was not a large creature, barely larger than those today, but he was smarter. And he stood up straight; many of our animal enemies were more like us, back then. Bear, Snake, thieving Crow; they walked and used hands, back in the beginning, because all of them were still vying with humans to rule the earth, and we had not yet beaten them down as we would.

"Wolf had learned that he could never defeat the shepherd in a fight. The shepherd carried a spear, or a bow, always some weapon, and she was able to defeat Wolf every time. So Wolf learned to skulk, and hide, and move around the edge of the flock, always waiting his chance to take one by stealth. He seldom got any, because the shepherd was too smart for him. She was always watching her sheep, staying between them and Wolf, and using her whistle to guide them.

"But one day a lamb ran away from the main flock, and the shepherd ran to find him. Wolf then did something very clever; unusually clever. He could have moved in and taken a single sheep, while the shepherd was away, but he thought better of it. He could have sheep for a lifetime.

"Because he saw that she had left her whistle behind when she ran after the lamb. It was lying on the ground to the side of the flock, near a fallen tree where she had been sitting.

"Wolf ran up to it. He grasped it, put it across his knee, and tried to snap it in two. But the whistle was made of thick iron-wood, and he couldn't break it. He tried again; nothing. Then he looked to his right, and left, and behind him. The shepherd was still far off. He had a sharp stone knife with him, so he began to use that as a drill. He set about ruining the whistle. He worked all day to run it through with holes, so it would no longer sound. He drilled as many holes as he could into it; he had time to punch six of them through. Then, just as darkness was falling, he saw the shepherd returning with her lost lamb. Wolf dropped the perforated whistle by the fallen tree and ran off.

"Wolf was indescribably pleased with himself. He had used his smarts and controlled his hunger long enough to wreck the shepherd's prized whistle, and now he would have the edge. Her flock had barely moved, and Wolf did not take one with him. He knew he could eat a sheep the next day, and the next and the next, when the shepherd's sound failed her.

"But of course the shepherd picked up the whistle and learned to play it with the holes, and now it was a flute. She was able to play entire songs, not just the one note. Within a few days she was nearly able to make the sheep dance with her music. It became even harder for Wolf to molest the flock, and eventually he was forced to drop to all fours so he could try to outrun rabbits and rats.

"And that is how we shepherds learned to use flutes."

Britta finished with a nod. The dwarves murmured at this end of the story, and they applauded—even Hostenback.

It was still broad daylight outside, and there was nothing to cover the windows, but still most of us slept. We unrolled blankets and covered our eyes. Tam Shanter and Ferlingas came back, then, wearing cloaks and little else as they carried their wet clothes in their hands. They wrung them out and laid them over the window sills. Jed and I stayed awake, keeping watch.

"Tomorrow we can finally head home," he told me. We spoke quietly.

"Yes. Finally."

"I wish this were over. It's been quite a journey. Especially for you. You don't suppose Thona and Bollard will have mopped up the dunter problem by the time we get back?"

This was a grim joke, of course, but I shook my head. "Quite a problem still to deal with. And now they have a load of cannons heading out as well. All of our work these past few weeks will be just the first piece of saving Emmervale, I'm afraid."

"You think the dwarves will really join us?"

"It sounds like it," I said.

"That would be good. But this will still be a nightmare, Aiman. Many of our people will get hurt when we push those dunters out, no matter how much help we have. I'm afraid we're going to see a terrible battle out on that plain. Something no one from Emmervale has seen since—who knows how long."

I could only nod along, slowly. I wished I had something better to offer.

I then slept for a few hours. Jed woke me, too soon.

"Aiman, Britta," he said. "Get up. People are coming from the east. People in white and gray, at speed, and more in red behind them. All are coming right here."

"Varenlend and Caranniam," I said.

"It must be."

I sat up. I shook sleep off and then slapped Maghran on his back as I stood up.

"Visitors," I told him. "Coming from the east."

Britta and I moved with Jed toward a window.

Some distance away from us, out to the east past the ruins, I saw the two groups as Jed had described. The Varenlenders kicked up dust, but through it we could see the red Caranniam pursuers behind them. Perhaps two dozen horses in the first group now approached the remains of the east side of the town wall. They were galloping hard. A few carried carbines.

As they reached the wall they rode around it and turned to face their pursuers.

Behind them came fifty or sixty riders from Caranniam. They ran hard, also, but seemed more methodical. As they neared the town they spread out to be able to outflank the Varenlenders on either side.

The riders in white and gray mostly dismounted and crouched down behind sections of the broken-down walls. Their backs were to us, as they faced the red line.

Maghran and Herrar now came up to us.

"Much excitement here for a deserted outpost, Maghran."

"I wonder if these Varenlenders are remnants from the ambush outside Emmervale," he said. "Maybe they have been pursued all this time."

Now one of them shot at a rider outside the wall. More shots followed. And then the mages of Caranniam responded, not with shots of their own but with magic: A few of them waved their arms, and the air in front of them flashed and then blurred. I guessed they were stopping Varenlend bullets.

And then a man in gray reached out his hand, from atop the wall, and the land before him cracked and shook. Two of the pursuing riders were knocked from their horses, and stayed down.

"I thought it would be all lightning bolts and the like," Jed said.

"Not even the best wizards have the power to keep that up for long," Herrar answered. "That's why they carry carbines, and blades."

It continued like this, a battle that was a combination of musketry and wizards' blasts. I saw one Varenlend man load his musket with powder and ball, replace the ramrod, and then snap his hand; fire ripped away toward a line of the Caranniam horsemen. They flinched, and then he raised his gun and fired.

"We should get down while we can," Maghran said. "It's all well and good if they have at each other out there, but if the Varenlenders retreat we'll be in the crossfire."

"Or in their sights," Herrar said.

Everyone was up, now, and gathered blankets and equipment. Shanter and Ferlingas snatched their still-damp clothes and threw them on. We were the last three to head down; Britta and Jed went first.

But when I reached the steps to descend, the floor changed. It became one solid slab of stone, somehow, and suddenly there were walls close around me. I turned around to try to see what had happened. I wondered if the little building had collapsed, and if this was my addled mind's response.

But behind me stood a woman, looking momentarily as surprised as I was. She was dressed in the white of Varenlend.

"How do you know this place?" she demanded.

"I don't," I told her. I don't know why I felt I needed to respond, but I answered her. "I was in a building in Midwall."

"And you still are. But you found the inner passages."

"I was just standing on a second floor."

"Indeed. That's how one starts." She regarded me suspiciously. "I've never known anyone to just stumble upon our portal. But again, you may have a gift."

Now I recognized her:

Annelle.

She looked much the same as she had seven years before. Her jaw was lower now, and broader, but she had the same black hair, gray eyes. And of course she was still young. I had assumed she would have no idea who I was, but she recognized me instantly.

"Aiman, it is you," she said. "It's no surprise you were able to enter."

"Enter what?"

"This place. This is a hidden plane in Midwall."

"A plane?"

"A place apart. Outside of your usual horizon, and used by my people for hundreds of years. Few can find their way in. But you are talented, still. The scion of Emmervale."

"We've no position like that," I said. "What is this passage?"

I looked past her. We were standing in a narrow room, or perhaps a hall, and beyond her it continued and looked less like stone and more like glass. There was light, past her; some source of illumination, somehow. There were gaps in the walls that might have led to more rooms.

"A hall in the other plane," she repeated. "There's no other way to describe it. It is space between the spaces out there. In here we are not visible to anyone outside."

"Varenlend has always known of this?"

"Yes. It has been a meeting place for us. And a refuge."

"Why not bring all your companions along?"

"Not all of them can know this. If we all used it, Caranniam would learn. So here we can hide for a moment." She shook her head. "It was much better circumstances for all of us when we met years ago, wasn't it."

"I would say so."

"We should have pressed you harder, Aiman. We could have used you. We still could. We had a plan, then. A plan to elevate Caranniam and Varenlend, together; and it would have helped Emmervale too. Lovely Emmervale with your fields and your old ways. It would have worked. But Caranniam talked us into another plan, and now we have their treachery. You know Sokran is dead, and Annira also?"

"No, I did not know that. We haven't heard."

"Killed outside your town, when Caranniam struck us in the night."

I did not consider offering condolences, of course, and she did not seem to expect them.

"So you were there, too," I said. "Outside our town."

"I was. We were all to assist in the attack on Stenhall. But now that alliance is over, and again I want you to contribute your power to us, Aiman."

"You attacked us. You sent dunters into our streets."

She shook her head dismissively at this.

"That was only a foraging raid of theirs. Our target was Stenhall."

"People were killed, Annelle." My voice was sharp.

"You were never our target. We could have taken Emmervale had we wanted to."

I began to object, but she shook her head quickly and continued.

"We could have. But we did not want to. And we never wanted to attack Emmervale, nor even wage a direct battle with Stenhall. We had a different plan, Aiman. We should have carried it out. You can still help us do so."

"We're not interested in harming Stenhall."

"It would not be harming anyone as much as protecting yourselves. You, simple people in the hills, far from industry"—she spat the word—"would gain. As would we. We would put dunters and dwarves back two hundred years."

"I don't know what we would provide you to help with that."

"Not your town; just you, Aiman. You have the power to assist."

"By doing what?"

"Channeling power. Wizarding."

"I have no such ability."

"Yes. You did when I saw you seven years ago. And here you are. You have not lost it."

"Because I turned some grass brown, back then."

"Yes."

"I decided afterward that must have been your doing in any case." This was not exactly true; I had never wielded magic again, but I always remembered the feeling I'd had of working that change there on that hillside years ago.

"It was your work, not mine."

"What is it you want to do?"

"I can share it only if you promise to help us."

"Annelle, you chose a very poor way to ask. I will only help Emmervale, and I will do it directly. And I will help these dwarves if I can."

"Will you?" she said. "You will help dwarves? If you can forget what they did to your people, you should be able to think of your interest with us and collaborate for your own good. But you have spoken."

I realized this was a question to me.

"I have spoken," I repeated.

"Well. You bring up the dwarves. They will soon need all the help they can get."

"Why?"

"The main force of Caranniam marches toward White Mount."

"White Mount? Why? What happened to attacking Stenhall?'

"White Mount is closer to them. And it is more vulnerable, since its leader is gone."

"Herrar."

"Yes, Herrar. She was captured weeks ago. The dunters have her locked away."

I almost said something, to this, but caught myself.

"How do you know this?" I asked.

"It was always their plan, and our scouts have seen them moving. Varenlend is not defeated yet, and we have eyes on them."

"And what does Caranniam hope to achieve, destroying White Mount?"

"They gain more time. A respite from steam, and iron, and gunpowder."

"And how can they hope to conquer White Mount? To conquer dwarves? I wondered the same thing when the attack on Stenhall was rumored. The dwarves can withdraw into the mountain, who knows how far. Who would want to go in after them? Would you?"

"They do not plan on gunfire and swords in the tunnels, no," she said. "The dwarves could collapse tunnels on top of them, if nothing else. Caranniam has other plans."

"Such as what? An army could besiege them, and eventually starve them out, but I don't think Caranniam has the personnel."

"No, not that. Their plan is to make the tunnels unlivable."

"How would they do that?"

"I don't know exactly. They would not share the ideas with us. We believe it has to do with poisoning the air within, in some manner."

"Despicable," I said.

Now we heard shots closer by, outside. The sound was muffled, where we stood, but still audible.

"They are pushing us back," Annelle said.

"Can you tell me the plan of the dunters?" I asked her. "You were with them, and they are still outside Emmervale. I believe they still intend to attack Stenhall, even without you. And even without their railroad."

"I would not be surprised," she said. "The dunters needed to be led, but once they set their campaign in motion—I think they will continue. They are greedy for Stenhall, for one thing."

Now more guns outside. The shots still sounded unreal, in our dream space there, but I knew my companions could be under fire, and under spells as well.

"I have to leave," I said. "My group can't get caught in this fight. Am I able to go?"

"Just step forward, the way you were heading," she said.

I did so. With one step, the stairs became visible again.

"Go," she said. "We will see each other again."

With one more step, I was out of that plane—whatever it was—and starting down the stairs.

Once outside the building I glanced left quickly and saw a man from Varenlend trotting toward me sideways. He was looking behind himself as he ran, keeping his musket pointed back at the pursuers from Caranniam. I caught glimpses of them, red forms down the old street. The ruins were filled with smoke and the smell of burnt powder. I hurried around a corner of the building and then headed the other direction.

There were more gunshots as I ran, and more sounds of magic from the battle. These were mostly rumbles like thunder, but quick and close. There were also shouts as the Varenlenders coordinated their retreat, and the Caranniam force advanced.

I dashed past buildings and rubble and reached the broken western wall without seeing anyone. The dwarves might have left me, but Jed and Britta, at least, would have waited.

I found them all on the far side of the last bit of wall. The dwarves were on the verge of breaking away. Jed held the horse, with Hostenback mounted on it.

Britta asked me: "Where were you?"

"I entered," I began to say, but dropped it and started over. "I saw that Varenlend woman I met years ago. Annelle. She is here, with these fugitives."

"We leave, now," Maghran said. The dwarves headed away, and we followed. We ran due west.

"Did you collar her for invading Emmervale?" Britta asked.

"I was not able," I said.

"I know, I said that in jest. I'm sure she would not stand still for a collaring. Do you think she'll survive? Will any of them?"

"She seems like a survivor," I said. "And she was well concealed."

We ran, putting Midwall behind us. Again I was able to watch dwarves attempting to sprint. They all must have done more running in these few weeks than was normal in a lifetime. Hostenback, meanwhile, seemed in pain as he held onto the horse. The animal was only trotting, not very quickly, but he was still jarred.

Eventually we ran up a gentle hill, partway down the other side, and halted. We looked back at Midwall. There were flashes of light, and a visible cloud of dust had risen around it.

"Still going at it," Jed said. "I wonder they haven't run out of powder, or become worn out with their magic."

"They may be at knives soon," Maghran said.

"Do you think we are far enough away to turn north?" I asked.

"I believe so. Do you agree?"

"I do."

"And then we shall soon move east," he said. "Aiman, we've decided to attack that dunter army at the foot of our hill, and outside Emmervale. If it is still there. And if not, we'll march out there so we can find it. Herrar and I have been speaking. She agrees it is time. And we think this would be a good opportunity, since all the erstwhile dunter allies are busy at each others' throats, as we see."

"But Maghran—" I started.

"We shall head now to White Mount," he continued, "gather troops, and then head east. And then Ghranam will not say no when he sees that Herrar is along."

I considered withholding what I had just learned, but of course I could not. First, I would not have felt right doing so. Second, had the dwarves ever learned that I knew what I knew and didn't tell them, that would have made them enemies of Emmervale for a hundred generations.

"Actually, Maghran, Caranniam is going to attack White Mount."

"What?"

"I just spoke with a leader of Varenlend, back there. That's why I was detained. I met her years ago."

He looked at me, incredulous. I explained:

"She came to Emmervale years ago and spoke to my family, Maghran. Because of who we are. And she was there just now. Running with the rest of the Varenlend group. I don't know why she told me, but she did. The main force of Caranniam is on its way to White Mount."

"How would she know?" Herrar asked.

"It had been their plan, she said. They shared it back when they were cooperating. And she says her countrymen have seen the Caranniam army on the move."

"I can't believe they would dare," Herrar said.

"For one thing, they think you are not there," I said. "All of them believe that. Including this woman I spoke to."

Herrar exchanged solemn looks with Ferlingas, Shanter, and Hostenback. Hostenback had sat up straight on the horse, again, as he listened to me.

"You didn't correct her?" she asked.

"I did not. I thought it was just as well if they are mistaken."

"Indeed," Herrar said. "Then we go home, now. As we planned.

But if this news is true, we will stay there."

I nodded at this. The four of them gathered, then, to talk with each other. I took this moment to pull Maghran aside.

"If what you say is true," he told me, "we must assist our cousins. And then we'll likely send to Stenhall for even more help."

"Of course. I understand. But Maghran, I have a plan of my own. We can take down Red Gorge City."

"Now?" he asked. "What do you mean? That's the last priority for Stenhall, with what you've just told us."

"I know. But we don't have to do it ourselves. I've had an idea for some time, and our escape yesterday confirmed it. All we have to do is set allies on the path."

"Allies? Who are you talking about?"

"The kobolds."

He blinked. "The dog-men? The servants? To do what—carry manure buckets with their left hands instead of their right?"

"They can take over that city, Maghran. And they could cripple that expeditionary army as well."

He shook his head. "Kobolds? Aiman, I am not sure you are thinking straight."

"They could, Maghran. Think of how many of them there are. They could shut down the city, and cut down that expedition, just by all the kobolds walking away from their work."

"Stopping work? I don't think that will give them firepower they need."

"It's not about firepower. The kobolds do everything for the dunters, Maghran. Think about what we've seen. They farm. They transport everything. They lay track. They shovel coal. They hold the keys, even; they literally hold the keys to Red Gorge City. And I would be surprised if they don't clean the muskets, cut the wads, cast the bullets, and mix the gunpowder."

Maghran was quiet again.

"They do seem to do everything," he said. "And you're right about the farming. And they keep the livestock. And they do the cooking, such as it is."

"They do the cooking," I repeated, nodding. "In addition to the farming. They could starve the dunters in a week."

"The dunters would slaughter them. Or try to."

"I don't think the dunters could, if they're not having their muskets handed to them and their powder carried for them. And without Caranniam or anyone else to lead them."

"So you mean an uprising. All the kobolds working together to take power."

"That's right."

"How would they get the chance? How would they put that together?"

"Think of how empty that city is right now," I said. "There wouldn't be enough dunters around to stop them. There are probably not even enough of them to notice anything going on."

"I suppose the kobolds might be able, if they wanted to," he said. "But these kobolds have never thought this way. And it would be up to them to do so; we couldn't instigate any such thing."

"We couldn't, no. But that clan we saw by the Duchess could."

"That clan?"

"The warren, yes."

This made him stop again and think. He was silent a moment as he considered.

"I remember them well, of course," he finally said. "Perhaps they could pull this off. If they were here. But they are far away."

"That could be fixed."

"You mean bring them out here?"

"That's right."

"How would you do that?"

"Just tell them how wide open Red Gorge City is. They seem ambitious, and it's theirs for the taking."

"Ride out there and invite them?" he said.

"Exactly."

Maghran lowered his brows and looked painfully consternated.

"You are serious," he said.

"I am. You saw how proud they are. You felt their ambition, didn't you?"

"Well. That little warren was well-armed, I agree. And they seemed organized. But there's no way they have enough arms to win a full battle against these dunters."

"It would be kobold guns against dunter knives, if the kobolds took a night to prepare. If the local kobolds are raised up in a rebellion by their free cousins—think of it."

"You would ride out to that warren directly?"

"Yes."

"So that's why you were studying their language. You were planning this?"

"I had the idea, yes. And now we saw from my jailer that they are willing to take risks for themselves, and even for us. I think they just need a kick, Maghran. And those others we met can give it to them."

"You think they'll be willing?"

"Willing to set themselves up as rulers of Red Gorge? Yes. And they've probably been ranging about, so they'll know I speak the truth when I tell them the dunters have largely departed, and have left the city weak."

"Well. Aiman Marshalson, if this works, you'll overtake your grandfather in fame."

"Fame." I laughed. "I'd be glad to live my days as an unknown if we can put King Kobold What's-His-Name on the throne of Red Gorge. Do you remember his name, by the way? Their leader?"

"Korf."

"That's it, Korf. I'm going to talk to him."

"Good luck to you, Aiman. Do your companions know?"

"Not yet."

"Good luck convincing them, also. I'll tell Herrar. I don't imagine she'll think it wise."

"I would suspect not."

"And I'll get Hostenback off that horse." He turned away, but then stopped and spoke to me again.

"And Aiman," he said. "If this all works, and you put Korf in charge of Red Gorge."

"Yes?"

"And he expresses any gratitude to you."

"Yes, what?"

"Try to get my axe back from him, will you?"

"Certainly."

I turned back. Britta and Jed came up to me as Maghran went to speak with Hrond.

"What was that all about?" Britta asked.

"I'm going to have to take the horse. You two must head back to Emmervale."

"Why?"

I told them the plan, as I had told it to Maghran. These two accepted it more enthusiastically. This was because of our own history.

"That Chief Korf can lead his people out of servitude just like the Marshal took us out of ours," Jed said.

"Exactly. What we went through looks like a mountain holiday, compared to how these kobolds suffer. But look, you two have to move quickly to Emmervale. And somehow, if you can, you need to make sure that dunter army stays put. I hope they have not moved yet."

"Stays put?"

"We need Red Gorge City empty when I come here with Korf and his clan. We don't want that army to come back here."

"Very well, but what can we do to encourage the dunters to stay camped outside Emmervale?"

"Well, don't attack them, for one thing. I hope it hasn't happened already. I'm sure Thona will not have done anything rash, but who knows. With all the men from Caranniam and Varenlend gone, she may feel confident enough to organize an attack."

"There were still many, many dunters without the men," Britta said. "I doubt we would have struck them."

"I hope not."

"Perhaps we can send some sheep their way, for lunches," Jed said. "That might encourage them to stay, and not return home."

"That's actually not a bad idea," I said. He rolled his eyes and shook his head.

"I was joking," he said. "But I assume the dunters will still be waiting for those wagons of supplies we saw ready to leave Red Gorge. I don't think they'll have moved."

"It will take us days to get there," Britta said.

"I know. Just move as fast as you can."

"We won't need to sleep."

"Rest as much as you need to stay safe," I said.

The Kurtenvold was a long way off, and unfortunately I would have to take a roundabout route, initially, to get there. The shortest ways would have been due east or due south, but the first would have taken me through Midwall again, where the wizards might still be fighting, or where perhaps victorious Caranniam would be camping. The second route, due south, would have taken me through Red Gorge City. So I headed further west, and then south.

Once again the horse seemed glad to have a proper rider—as opposed to packs, or a wounded dwarf—and an apparent direction to go. He had looked at me with some anticipation before we began, I thought, and I now patted him on the neck. I rode alone through the grasslands, trying to keep watch around me in all directions at once. I wished that my companions were with me, but we had only the single mount and I needed to get to the kobolds as fast as I could.

In the afternoon I first noticed, far in the distance, patchwork colors of cultivated fields. I thought of the patient work the kobolds of Red Gorge would put into their wheat crop, so they could eventually harvest it, and ferment it, and make great batches of their awful *zhirnga*. I turned the horse a bit to the west so as to avoid these outskirts of Red Gorge City.

Moving around the dunter home in this way took a depressingly long time. I did not want to get within eyeshot of even a single kobold field worker, so I gave the crops a wide berth. I kept them far on my left, barely visible. I thought about chancing a closer approach, and getting around the city forthwith in order to turn more quickly east toward the Kurtenvold; but I remembered I had made enough mistakes already in this adventure. I could not get myself captured again. And even before that particular slip I had almost been taken by dunters, while with Jed, and had lost track of a baron of Caranniam for a few vital minutes. Not to mention getting accosted by surprise by the group of elves by the railroad tracks.

I rode with caution.

Gradually I realized that I was indeed turning slowly to the left, making my way around Red Gorge. I wanted to at least get some distance away from it before I rested the horse for the night. After a few more hours I was finally heading due east.

I kept going into evening. Eventually in the twilight I came to water, a small wet depression in the endless grassland that held some shrubs and, past them, a pool.

There were no trees, so I tied the horse to the thickest bush I found. I spread a blanket and sat down.

I had seldom felt so alone. I had monitored sheep for many, many days of my life, of course, but while doing that I was never far from our house and my family. All my travels so far after our eventful spring had been with the company of Jed, at least, and often Britta and others. Even in the dunter prison I had had the sullen dwarves for at least some conversation. Out here there was no one.

I felt scared as darkness fell. What if dunters stumbled upon me? Or kobolds? There were no ansarks in these lowlands, but what of other predators? What had I done? I would have to sleep with no watch; who could tell what might befall me?

Fortunately I was so fatigued that sleep overtook worry.

I woke in the morning to the hoots and twitters of grouse nearby in the grass, although I did not see them. After my lonely despair of the previous night, it felt as if they had been sent to keep me company—and possibly to jeer at me. I stood and gathered my sleeping roll.

I began to pull some food out of my bag, but thought better of it. I climbed onto the horse immediately; I could eat as I rode. The horse seemed glad to get going.

I headed southeast, moving farther away from Red Gorge. The sun came up behind me and rose over my shoulders. I was prepared to ride hard all day and keep going into the dark, but I would not be able to push the horse that much. In the midmorning I came to a stream and stopped.

I had seen nothing but the monotonous prairie in these hours. I was still wary of a chance meeting with roving dunters—but it then occurred to me that I was now near the territory of the elves. Red Gorge would be reluctant to come this far south, and it was likely I was being watched myself.

I found myself gazing off to my right as I picked up the ride again. I imagined I could see the elven woods off on the horizon. I felt more secure, now—whether or not I had any real reason to—and the distance passed more easily.

I thought now of Annelle and our meeting in Midwall. All along I had had a lingering feeling of disappointment, about our talk, but I hadn't had the time to put my finger on why. I could almost feel a burn in my heart about her—a sense of loss. Not so much for a person, since I barely knew her, but for an idea. I felt as if a plan, a vision, had fallen through. I realized that all these years since I had met that beautiful, beautiful young woman, there by my home, I had expected that sometime we would meet again and perhaps stay together. There was always time ahead of me; I still had the opportunity to leave Emmervale and move closer to her orbit if I wanted to. And I pictured her as a wise and kind young noble, all along.

When it had become obvious that Varenlenders were part of that dunter camp, I had hoped that she was not there. I couldn't imagine she would have been. I assumed she would be back in her city, shaking her head at the greed of her peers.

I had nothing much to base this on; one meeting of fifteen minutes with a girl, seven years before. And perhaps bits of news I had heard now and then about the calm of Varenlend and its competent leaders. Annelle developed in my mind as a potential partner.

But she had been in that camp, and had countenanced the dunter raid on Emmervale. My dreams of anything otherwise had been broken. I could not now ever imagine collaborating with her, much less having any other sort of relationship.

On the afternoon of the next day I reached the western outskirts of the Kurtenvold. As I saw the ribbon of dark green appear to my right, my heart suddenly raced as I faced up to my plan. I would be walking alone into a clan of armed and proud kobolds who were keen on taking outsiders for ransom. I reflected that it was fortunate the baron had been the obvious notable during our last encounter, and that Maghran had done most of the talking; the kobolds would likely barely remember me, and I hoped it wouldn't occur to them to try to imprison me for a payoff.

I remembered the Duchess, too, and our visit to her keep. I would have enjoyed seeing her again, and telling her the results of our altered message, but I did not want to spend the time doing so.

But as I finally neared those woods, there she was.

From some distance away I had noticed a form among the trees, but had assumed it was just a sapling. As I neared, it looked more and more like it could be a person. For a moment I became very wary about this apparent stranger staring at me, but then I recognized the blue of the robe. When I was close enough to shout to her she finally strode out.

"Aiman, you return."

"I do. I am glad to meet you on my way."

Again I was struck by her strength, and her solemn eyes. She gave the appearance, at least, of a genuine Duchess of the Kurtenvold.

"Were you coming to speak with me?" she asked.

I shook my head. "I am very glad to. But I was going elsewhere."

She nodded very slightly at this, and I believe she looked disappointed. I would have been very surprised if such a hermit would have any interest in speaking with me twice in the course of just several weeks, considering that intervals of years went by between her visits to us in Emmervale. But her face did seem to fall a bit.

"But I am pleased to see you, Duchess," I repeated. "I could use your advice for my errand."

"What is it?"

I had reached her, now, and dismounted.

"I am going to speak with Korf, and his clan."

She did not seem especially shocked at this.

"Concerning what?"

"Well," I said. "My companions are doubtful of my plan. But you know that Red Gorge City has been nearly emptied out of dunters."

"Yes."

"And it is full of kobolds. The dunters depend on them. I don't think they can live without them."

"You intend to lead those kobolds back here?" she guessed.

"No, I intend to take Korf there and install him as their leader. I am going to encourage these kobolds to seize Red Gorge City. They can do it if they raise all the ones that live there."

She stood silent and considered this.

"A slave rebellion, then," she said. "That is what you are considering."

"Yes."

"The dunters and many others believe that the kobolds are born to serve, you know. And that they can do nothing else."

"Well, Korf and his group here disprove that."

"Indeed." She nodded. "It's quite an idea, Aiman. Remarkable. There have been other such events in history, you know."

"Have there been?"

"Yes. The state which became Nemeya depended on slaves, and

there were revolts. And long ago, Caranniam had its own rebellion of indentured servants. I've never heard of an outsider instigating one."

"Korf will be an insider," I said. "Or close enough."

"Good luck to you."

"Duchess, do you know their language?"

"I do not." She seemed reluctant to admit this; this was the first time I had seen such a reaction from her. "It never occurred to me I would have any reason to learn it. Do you?"

"No. Just a few words."

"I only know what every other student of speech knows," she said. "Their quirk."

"And what is that?"

"What they cannot pronounce."

"Which is?"

"So you have not learned that. It is P," she said. "They cannot formulate it."

"Hm. Now that I think about it, I never heard that word in their jail. Too much dog in them, I suppose."

"You were in a jail?"

"In Red Gorge, yes. Held by dunters, of course, but in reality it was the kobolds who did all the real work. Just as I said."

"I am glad you escaped."

"So am I. I ended up getting help from the kobolds, in doing so. That's one reason I believe this will succeed."

"You are heading to their tunnels now?"

"Yes."

"Shall I show you the way?"

"That would be helpful, thank you."

"I will take you just to within view of their hideout, and then I will leave you alone. I would offer to accompany you all the way in, but I don't think it would be for the best. Two of us."

"I agree," I said. "Two might be a threat. If it's just me, I think they'll listen for at least a moment, with their guard down."

She led me through the woods. She did not talk any further, and seemed busy taking in the sounds and slight movements. A bird here, a breeze on a leaf there; she looked left and right at these things. In time we came to the thick growth of trees and brush that concealed their buildings and the entrance to their tunnels.

"Good luck to you, Aiman."

She slipped away into the trees.

I led the horse around the wall of brush, and came to the opening we had burst into, weeks before. I spoke to the horse:

"You're going to be seeing a lot of dog-men in a moment." I touched my hand to its neck. "Keep your senses."

I moved in.

The small clearing with its sturdy little houses was evidently empty. I had assumed I would be accosted by a guard, but no one was visible. Once again I marveled at the construction of all the stone walls and sloped roofs.

I did notice a pen behind one of the buildings, still filled with pigs. The kobolds must still be around somewhere.

I stood a few moments longer. I tied the horse to a tree and then walked further in toward the buildings. I stood still and gathered my breath. The pigs ate, and the trees swayed very slightly in a breeze; no one seemed to be around to pay me any mind in the quiet clearing.

"*Kororen akagen*," I called out. "Korf *akag*." Strong kobolds, strong Korf. I hoped that would get their attention.

A few pigs which had been rooting around in their pen stopped, for a moment. Beyond that, nothing moved.

I waited a short time, and then shouted again:

"*Kororen akagen*. Korf *akag*."

Still nothing moved. Would I have to go to the top of the stairwell and yell right down into it?

But then a very confused-looking kobold stepped out of one of the houses. He was a young male, possibly one of the group that had stolen the baron from us, but he was not attempting any heroics just now.

"*Kororen akagen*," I repeated one more time.

He just stared at me. His ears were cocked up as if I had two heads.

"Listen," I said, "will you get the translator for me? Or get Korf? Tell him this *rafa* wants to talk."

"Korf," he said.

"Yes." I nodded. "Or someone."

He then rattled something off in his language, none of which I caught.

"I'll need the translator," I repeated.

Now another kobold appeared and sidled up to him. Both kept their eyes on me. The second one was also a male, a bit younger than the first.

"*Kororen akagen*. Bring me the one who can talk to me."

They spoke to each other and then the second turned and dashed into the house which had the entrance to their tunnels.

The first kobold and I stood there, just looking at each other. He clearly did not take me as a threat, fortunately. Within a few minutes, the translator emerged. This was the same one who had spoken to us before; mature and with a narrow gaze.

"You were here before," he said.

"Yes."

"You ask for Chief Korf," he said.

"I do."

"Why?"

"I need to tell him of a plan. Many other kobolds need your help."

"Kobolds where?"

"In Red Gorge City."

He dropped his head and narrowed his eyes further. His expression was plain disbelief.

"I have been there," I said quickly. "I have met these kobolds. They helped me. I went there with the *shenken*, and I was given *zhirnga* and *rach*. I know. I must speak with Chief Korf."

Now the translator crossed his arms, still staring at me.

Soon I stood before Korf, again in the large hall where he held court up on the stone stage. Only a few kobolds joined him, this time. The chamber was nearly silent, quite a contrast to the first time I had been down there.

Korf was again wearing chain mail and a black stone circlet. I noticed he did not have the axe he had taken from Maghran; I guessed it was held for safety further back in their tunnels. He was also accompanied again by a few strong and tough-looking kobolds who must have been his personal guard.

Korf spoke to me. The translator relayed it:

"The Chief would hear more of your stay in Red Gorge."

"I thank him for the audience," I started. "Red Gorge City is nearly deserted of dunters. I spent some days there, and I met kobolds. I think they could rise up against the rule of the dunters, but they need the idea. They need a leader."

I had paused between each sentence to wait for the translation. The translator passed along everything I said, and—although I was no expert at reading the expressions of kobolds—he seemed to shrug as he talked, acknowledging to Korf that I was speaking borderline nonsense.

Then I added:

"I am hoping you will march up to Red Gorge and liberate the kobolds, because it will cut down the dunters. They are still camped outside my city, and I want them gone. They cannot operate without the kobolds. That's why I am here."

Chief Korf seemed like a smart and no-nonsense leader, to me. That's why I admitted exactly why I was looking for him to act. I thought he would be impressed that I was not claiming to be there out of concern for the enslaved kobolds of Red Gorge. I hoped to make it clear I was treating him as an equal, and not attempting to hide my motives.

He was silent a moment, evidently considering what I had told him. His eyes seemed more wise than wild, now that I focused on them. His face was marked with scars, I assumed from fights, and his canines protruded from his top lip a bit. This was not the case for all kobolds, but with him there was a dignity to it.

He finally spoke, and the translator asked me:

"Who are you to speak for your people? The dwarves ordered you around. And you served that man in red."

"I worked with the dwarves then, but they are not here," I answered. "And I do not serve Caranniam. We only wanted to keep that man alive, for our own reasons."

Korf spoke again:

"Our warren cannot raise an army to invade Red Gorge."

"I know. It will take only a few to raise all the kobolds there. You and these guards of yours could do it yourselves."

Korf made a sour face when he heard the translation of that, and I guessed he did not appreciate this obvious pandering. He spoke:

"We cannot raise an army," the translator said, "but we would take as many of our capable warriors as we can reasonably spare. Chief Korf will not walk into Red Gorge City with just his four cousins."

So that's who the guards were. I answered quickly:

"Of course. But my point is that the kobolds do all the work there, and they are practically alone. They are sitting atop enormous power, but they just need someone to show them. I can't do it."

Korf asked a question:

"Are you certain the expeditionary army of dunters has not returned?"

"As of a few days ago, they had not."

"And some others are busy transporting supplies, again outside of their city."

"That's true."

Korf spoke a few more words to the translator:

"We will leave in the morning," he said.

I was amazed. Apparently when this kobold chief felt he had all his information, he did not dither making a decision.

"Very good," I said. "I would like to accompany you, if you will have me along."

"Yes. You may sleep up above, with your horse."

Korf, who had been leaning slightly forward in his chair all this time, now leaned back. He kept his eyes on me and said no more.

I slept alone in one of the buildings aboveground. One was filled with sacks of roots the kobolds had dug, and I was concerned it would draw mice and rats; another was next to the pig pen, and I didn't fancy those neighbors. The building which had the entrance to the tunnels I avoided for fear of being trampled in the night. I found one small shed which was used as an armory, and I rolled out my bedding there. It was filled with spears and a few swords, and many bare handles waiting for use. Had I not seen their tunnels I might have wondered why they kept this many weapons seemingly unguarded; but having seen their halls twice now, I knew they had plenty of better equipment down below.

In the morning I woke at dawn as the clearing began to fill with kobolds. I gathered my kit and watched them file out of the tunnel house.

Again I noticed that they were well-outfitted. All wore boots. Each had a helmet slung behind his back or tied onto a gear pack. Most wore leather armor; some had plate metal waistcoats. Only Chief Korf wore chain mail. They carried mostly spears but also swords, pistols, and a few short muskets.

Korf, I noticed, was carrying Maghran's axe at his side.

Eventually around forty of them had gathered around Korf, and no others emerged. He then spoke to them briefly. They listened intently and often nodded and growled their assent to whatever inspirational speech he was delivering.

The translator approached me.

"We leave now."

"Very good. What is your name, by the way?"

"Arken. And you?"

"Aiman. Aiman Shearer."

"We plan to move quickly."

"I will ride along."

Korf looked over at us then, and nodded. The kobolds began filing out of the clearing.

They marched through the woods in a single file. They were quiet, but that changed when we left the trees and entered the fields. They all gathered in a knot and began to chatter and occasionally bark as we all continued to move.

The horse seemed a bit put off by the big pack, and their noise, but he kept up with them. I rode to their left, leaving a gap between.

Before the sun had risen very high they had gained speed. We passed through field after field, and then I saw something new to me: Some of the kobolds would drop down and run on all fours. To do this they would close their hands into fists and run on their knuckles. Only those who wore their weapons across their backs ran this way, and they were the younger ones of the group. Korf and the rest of the older, larger soldiers seemed to disdain this, and they trotted proudly upright. Once I even saw Korf bark what must have been a quiet reprimand to one who had begun to gallop on all fours, because the one singled out instantly resumed his trot on just his legs. He was not young; apparently Korf didn't mind the youth running like that, but expected more from his older members.

We stopped for only one break, during the early afternoon, and it didn't seem as if any of them really needed it. Korf may have just been cautious about them wearing themselves out with their enthusiasm. A number stood around for some minutes, hands on hips and panting with their tongues out. Others kept trotting, but in circles, and a few pairs sparred with each other with swords or spears. Loud conversations between kobolds continued, just as they had during the march.

I noticed that they were much louder when they spoke than any of their kin in Red Gorge City had been. These adventurers had the pride of their freedom and their mission, I supposed, whereas the dunters' servants were constantly subdued and wary.

Korf looked a bit annoyed that so many of his followers were not resting, but he just shook his head and we resumed the march. We kept on until nightfall and the kobolds decided on a fire. I helped gather wood.

Later Korf, a few of his older guards, and Arken the translator sat with me next to the fire. Korf gestured toward me and spoke.

"Chief Korf asks what your plan would be for us in Red Gorge City," Arken asked me.

The question took me by surprise. I had not suggested any plan before the group departed the warren, and I did not think they would be much interested in anything I did come up with.

Korf just stared at me with unblinking eyes. He looked powerful, even at rest, although a bit tired. He was relatively old, and this journey may have been harder on him than on the younger kobolds. I'm sure the heavy chain mail he wore and Maghran's weighty axe, on top of his other equipment, did not make it any easier.

I paused to think, and then Arken continued to relay our words back and forth as Korf questioned me.

"I believe," I started, "you should make yourselves known to the local kobolds, and give your message to a few of them. Tell them to rise up against their masters. Tell them to take keys, take weapons, and join you."

"And how exactly are we to do that?"

"When we were there we frequently saw kobolds working in the fields, or doing other errands outside the city. I would think you would start with them."

"And do they have a leader we would ask for?"

"I don't know. I'm not aware that they do. I assume you would know better than I if those kobolds are set up in that way. Do you happen to know?"

Korf ignored this question and asked something else:

"How do you think the dunters will respond to this attempt to seize control of Red Gorge?"

"Not well," I admitted. "That's why I think it will be important to coordinate and take their powder, disable their weapons as much as possible, and stop their food supply. All of that should be done first."

Korf and his guards watched me as I spoke, with little expression on their faces.

I wondered what the point of these questions was. Were they having second thoughts? Had they really marched out of their warren with no plan, and were only now trying to come up with ideas?

But this seemed unlikely for them. They were clearly an organized group, and able to plan ahead. I seriously doubted they would have taken up the campaign had they not been confident of their moves.

"And what will happen," Arken now asked, "to the dunter army that is outside Emmervale if we succeed?"

"I suppose they will return to Red Gorge," I said. "You'll need to be ready for them of course. But again, it would help if the kobolds who are out there with that army, just like those who stayed behind, took measures to hobble those dunters as much as possible."

"This will all be difficult."

"I agree," I said. "I will be around to provide any help I can. Although I'm not sure how much I'll be able to do."

Now Korf glanced at his guards, and then back at me. He gave me a brief nod and spoke a few final words.

"Chief Korf says you are a level-headed young man," Arken said.

This gave me the impression that all these questions had just been a test, somehow.

"Well," I said. "Thank him for me."

Arken duly told the chief this in his language, but Korf was already standing up and looking away.

That night I slept by myself, near the horse, some distance from the remains of the fire. The kobolds, for their part, slept in one large group, arms and legs splayed over one another. They were not quiet sleepers. Throughout the night I heard them yelping to themselves and growling softly in their apparently heroic dreams.

We traveled the next day and another night, about the same amount of time I had taken to round Red Gorge and get to the kobold warren. Eventually we neared the dunter capital again. I felt I was getting to know the place; I recognized the same grades to the hills, the same views of the horizon. I wondered how few men alive could claim the dubious skill of being able to identify the outskirts of Red Gorge City.

The group of kobolds and I cleared the top of a hill, and there it was—the smoke and sprawl. The cohort grew quiet, for once, gazing out at the unhandsome city.

We were near the rambling crop fields. In one, off to our right, there were four figures. They were kobolds. Arken pointed them out to everyone else, and then the chatter of the expedition resumed.

The kobolds spoke to each other and gestured toward the farmworkers. In a moment they were all nodding, apparently having come to some sort of agreement.

And then I watched a very interesting exercise:

They formed up into lines; six of them, of six kobolds each. Korf and one of his lieutenants stood off to one side, near me. They all must have practiced before, because they did this quickly and seemed to know where to go.

The columns formed a small block. There was enough space between each of the six lines for a kobold to fit in between, and I soon saw why:

They started trotting toward the field. I spurred my horse and followed.

As they ran, they all chanted some sort of marching song, or I should say running song. I could not make out a word of it, of course, but it sounded disciplined and kept them all in step.

After a few paces, the kobold in the back of each column trotted up to the front of his respective line. Each line did this, so six kobolds moved at once. Then they all took a few more steps in formation, and the new batch of six who were in back repeated the move. They kept doing this little running drill all the way across the field. The song they sang broke into a sharp eight-count refrain every time the ones in back hurried up front.

It was very impressive. Between their outfitting, their sturdy health, and this marching maneuver of theirs, the kobolds looked sharp.

I also noticed that the drill made it seem like there were more of them than there actually were. Perhaps someone watching would have assumed there were fifty, rather than the actual thirty-eight— it was not a huge difference—but still, it seemed to fortify their numbers.

And I realized furthermore that this small phalanx would be ten times more impressive to the kobolds of Red Gorge than it was to me, because they would have never in their lives seen anything like it. Strong and well-armed kobolds. And trotting in formation straight into the heart of the dunter territory; the story would race through the city.

By the time we reached the middle of the field where the Red Gorge kobolds stood, the four of them were gaping. They had been hoeing but now stood motionless with their tools idle. I noticed they were dressed in miserable rags.

The phalanx came near them and stopped, all on cue. Korf then spoke loudly to the four. He sounded confident, and they listened intently. He asked them a few questions, and one answered.

The phalanx stood silent as he spoke.

Then he nodded toward one of the fieldworkers, who promptly turned and ran off toward the city. Korf looked over to me and then began pacing in front of his soldiers.

Arken had wound up at the back of one of the six lines. He now stepped out and walked over to me.

"What did he say?" I asked.

"As you can guess. He told them that the dunters have deserted the city, and they should take it. He said we are here to help, and to wake them up. Then he told them to go bring their important ones."

"Important ones," I said. "Do you know if the kobolds here have leaders? He asked me about that. I didn't know the answer."

He shook his head. "They do not. Nothing like a chief. Korf

just wants to speak to the oldest, the smartest, the strongest."

Soon other Red Gorge kobolds began to arrive. We could see a trickle of them making their way through the fields. They walked up cautiously in ones and twos and eyed the phalanx of their kin as if they were looking at a giant new locomotive. Korf spoke to them, and his audience grew. The new arrivals looked either older or larger than the average kobold, so these indeed must have been the "important ones" he wanted.

All of them that approached only glanced at me, and did not seem to concern themselves with my presence, until one particular pair walked up. They looked at the phalanx, and then at Korf, and finally at me—and they stopped cold.

They were young males, looking lithe and sinewy. They did not take their eyes off me, and then I recognized one of them: he had a black patch of hair. These were two of the group that had captured me and handed me over to Crotchet in his manor. They looked as I remembered that small group—young and alert. They regarded me silently for a minute or two, and then resumed their approach. They came up to the Kurtenvold kobolds and ignored me.

After awhile the crowd had grown to several dozen local kobolds. Korf called out something to Arken. It went on for a moment and included a nod toward me.

"We go forward, now," he told me. "They have told us of an empty fortification. We stay there, and then Korf wants to talk to you."

The kobolds moved toward the city, but quietly now. The Kurtenvold group kept its shape but no longer trotted or performed its line changes.

The abandoned fortification the local kobolds brought us to was not much closer to the city than the disintegrating shed the dwarves and Britta and I had used as our own base. It had walls of boulders and logs, jumbled together like a pile of debris a flooding river might have left behind. The structure did have a turret, however, rising a man's chest height over the main roof.

The building had been placed, just like old Crotchet's manor, on a shallow earthwork that elevated it somewhat above the surrounding fields. Also like that manor, this one had a few dunter skulls placed in the outer walls. It was a rambling construction with several corners to it, not just four; and one of these had tumbled down. If the local kobolds had been using it as a meeting place for very long, the disrepair must have suited them, because they had made no attempt to fix it up. It occurred to me that they would have left it that way no matter what, so as not to draw attention from their dunter masters.

The various kobolds walked into the old manor, clambering up the embankment and disappearing inside an open door. Soon I saw a few of their heads pop up over the walls of the turret. The Kurtenvold kobolds surveyed the fields while the locals seemed to look proud of themselves.

Arken walked up to me.

"Safe house for us," he said. "You can see the signs."

He nodded toward the bottom of the doorway they were all using, and I saw what he meant: a stick figure of a kobold had been drawn at the bottom, near the ground. It looked something like a kobold with its arms spread. Next to it were two circles interlocked.

"Safe, and seldom visited by dunters," he explained.

"A code," I said. "The kobolds here must be more organized than I thought."

"Nothing hard to make signs," Arken said. "But we can—teach them. Bring them together."

All the other kobolds had now gone in. I still stood outside, with the horse, unsure. I had never felt so far from Emmervale; not when Jed and I had been surrounded by dunters, and not when I had reconnoitered the manor and locomotive on my own in the city. Not even when I had walked down into the kobold warren in Kurtenvold. Always in those instances I had been with a companion or companions, or at any rate not far from them. Even in Kurtenvold I felt that I knew those woods somewhat, and I was near the odd but clever Duchess at least. But here, I was risking my skin again on the outskirts of Red Gorge City, and this time I had no one nearby. My closest companions at this point were kobolds who had once fired a pistol at me; my other kobold allies included a few who had abducted me. Beyond this group lay nothing but filth and dunters. I supposed I should have entered the manor with the rest of them and downed some *zhirnga*, but I did not want to. Even the horse seemed reluctant to get any closer.

Chief Korf now saved me. He walked out, unexpectedly. He spoke to Arken.

"We must head out," Arken then told me. "The chief wants to move. To the force near your home. We cannot have them—" he searched for a word—"whole, to come back here."

"When? Do you mean right now?"

Arken nodded. "Chief Korf wants to get out there as soon as we can. And we assume you may not be interested in joining us in our grand hall for—fellowship."

I was about to protest out of politeness, and insist on entering, when I noticed a look in the kobold's eyes; it was, oddly, exactly how the dwarves looked when they made their rare and unexpected jokes.

"You know I miss my own people, Arken, and I want to see them. So I am willing to leave now, of course. But this horse needs rest."

"Could you ride it just until dark? Not long now."

"Yes."

"Then Chief Korf wants to. It is not wise for us to have a man and a horse with us here. We will not draw attention, as just more kobolds, but you will."

"Very good."

Now Korf turned and gestured toward the manor. He barely waved his hand, and directly three kobolds emerged and trotted over.

One of them was a lieutenant I had seen before, one of Korf's cousins. The other two were locals, and sure enough I noticed that one was of the pair that had kidnapped me; the leader, with the black hair. I rolled my eyes, which Arken saw.

"You know them?" he asked.

"I know one."

"How?"

"You can ask him."

Arken spoke with Korf, as the three reached us, and then the chief had a conversation with my captor. It went on for some time.

Eventually Korf turned to me and spoke.

"So you have met Wukk, here," Arken relayed.

"Indeed."

"Must you fight him?"

"What?" I wondered if Arken was mistranslating. "Fight him?"

"For your honor."

"No, Arken," I said. "He will be one of the ambassadors?"

"The what?"

"He will come with us, now."

"Yes."

"I accept that. If Korf wants him."

Korf spoke further, then. Arken told me:

"The Chief says that Wukk is a kobold with ideas. He leads. He used the money he got from you to keep these kobolds together."

"I understand."

Korf said more, and gave me a wry look.

"The Chief says you should have been more careful concealing yourself."

"Indeed."

Now I looked more closely at my new colleague, Wukk. He wore a simple gray robe, but had a belt with a fine studded leather scabbard and sword. I had not noticed these before. He certainly had not had such a weapon back in Crotchet's hall. I realized that the Kurtenvold kobolds must have brought it along as a gift. I guessed that the other Red Gorge kobolds serving the expeditionary army out near Emmervale would likely be impressed that Korf was able to share such equipment with strangers. It had been a very strategic present.

I was surprised when Wukk now spoke to me, and more surprised that he addressed me in Oppidan.

"I am glad you are well," he said, in the wizards' language. "We knew that Earl Satrafy would not harm you. You would have been worth too much to him."

"Earl Satrafy. So that was his name," I said. "Yes, he treated me well enough."

"He is a thief who must die," Wukk added. "A punisher of kobolds."

He said this without changing his tone, but his anger was clear.

"I think Chief Korf here can help you take over," I said.

"So do we. Why are you with him?"

I realized they apparently did not know that this entire liberation journey had been my suggestion to Korf. I decided it was just as well; let them think that Korf had planned it all himself.

"I am from Emmervale," I said. "My people hope to work with Korf. I am an envoy."

I was portraying him as a ruler, fit to receive diplomats! Korf owed me, now.

"How," I asked, "did you come to speak Oppidan?"

"I was a slave in Caranniam. I was sold to Satrafy some time ago."

"But now you are free?"

"I am no longer owned," he answered. "But none of us is free."

Soon we moved. I learned from Arken that the lieutenant was named Karrar, and Wukk's companion was his brother Agarak. I don't believe Agarak was one of my captors, even though he was family with Wukk. Agarak, just like Wukk, wore a new sword at his side which was a gift from Korf.

The six of us headed east. This time it was Agarak who would sometimes drop down and run on all fours; the rest of them were older, too proud to do so.

We stopped just past nightfall, and the next day continued. We headed east-northeast, and I felt indescribably glad to be returning toward Emmervale for what I hoped would be the last time. My mood brightened even though I was still surrounded by kobolds.

Korf, Arken, and Karrar all took turns leading our group, although Agarak sometimes dashed ahead for a short distance. Wukk usually stayed behind the three from Kurtenvold.

On the second day we came near enough the ruined dunter railroad, off to our left, to be able to discern the circular rails. The kobolds took in the sight.

"You have heard of the work of the elves?" I asked.

Arken nodded. "Chief Korf was told. But none of us have seen this."

"It runs east and west like a river," I said.

"More like a ruined train track."

I shrugged. "The shapes and the color remind me of rolling water. I was there when they bent, you know."

"Were you?"

"Yes. I was held by elves at the time."

Wukk addressed me in Oppidan, then:

"This is the work of Silvermoor. We had heard of it."

"I am sure you did," I said. "Your people did most of the work building it."

"My people died building it. Dunters ran them so hard. To death."

Again I could hear fury in him even though he spoke steadily. His face was like stone.

"Do your people have a plan for what to do with the dunters?" I asked.

"It is really Korf's plan," he said. "Ours, now. We will turn them out. We do not want a battle with them. Enough of us have died already, over the years. We can simply take their food, spike their guns, seize their powder. We will make them wander. This will be enough."

He looked at me.

"You have never been a slave. We want our freedom. Our former masters will have no hold on us. They will not even have our hate."

He was right that we had never been slaves, but of course what he was saying was similar to what older Emmervale residents, like my father, said about the dwarves in Stenhall after our own breakaway.

"Wukk," I said. "My own people were nearly servants of the dwarves, for decades. We were trapped in their halls. Indentured."

"Why?"

"It was during the time of the dragons, the fires. The dragons hit our town Emmervale over and over again. Our grandfathers sought refuge in the tunnel halls of the dwarves. But once they were in, it was difficult to get out."

"Indeed it is."

"We had lost our fields, our stores, our supplies. There was virtually nothing to go back to. We became dependent on the dwarves. We had always purchased our tools from them, and what firearms we had. That was a mistake, of course. But we had always had our crops, livestock, barns, so we believed we could trade and remain independent. After those were exhausted, or outright burned, we had virtually nothing.

"And toward the end of our time with the dwarves, factions of them manipulated us. They set us upon each other by awarding some of us powerful jobs. They separated families to ensure members would not leave. They kept us in debt, always working to pay off a loan but never getting ahead."

"Some of this is what we live."

"And some of us thought we would never escape. But we did. And then we let the dwarves go from our memory, just as you say you will with the dunters. I think that is wise. We suffered enough under them; we did not need to allow them into our minds."

Wukk moved along silently for a time. Eventually he asked:

"Your people, how long were they held by the dwarves?"

"Our stay in their tunnels stretched to nearly thirty years."

"We have been slaves to the dunters for hundreds. We will have to see whether or not we can heal ourselves as you have."

We kept moving northeast, coming closer to the ruined rails on our left. We had decided to follow them, since we knew they would be a straight path toward the encampment.

"I have some elevation here to see any dunters," I said from atop the horse.

"We can smell them sooner than you will see them," Arken answered.

But it was I, not the kobolds, who did notice the crawling mob of the supply party an hour later.

It was the caravan of the cannons and piles of barrels and crates that I had seen in Red Gorge City. Loaded into many wagons, they were treading heavily on the other side of the railway. I saw them first as dark shapes on the horizon, and we came up level with them—while keeping a safe distance away—surprisingly quickly. I had forgotten, as I rode, what good progress my group of kobolds made on foot.

To avoid being seen, we drifted away from the tracks; still moving generally toward Emmervale but veering to our right. Before we lost them from view I studied their line:

One enormous ox-cart formed the heart of the caravan. Even from our distance it appeared huge, a weighty frame on enormous wheels. It had been only a speck as we approached, but grew larger and larger. It was hauled by a number of oxen, perhaps six or eight. Even at our distance I thought I could hear the ponderous plods of hoofs, clanking axles, whips, perhaps dunter growls across the prairie. The power of the thing crescendoed as we cleared it. We kept tacking due east, dropping more and more to the south of the caravan. The ox-cart and the rest of the procession shrank into the far distance, and any noise I had heard, or had imagined I heard, faded and then vanished.

"Do you think they could take Stenhall with all those arms?" I asked Arken.

"I do not know their arms, and I don't know Stenhall," he said. "From what you've said of the arms, it seems they could take your town, at least."

"I'm afraid so."

He shook his head.

"We'll beat them by a day or more. They'll never have a chance."

After some distance we again cut further north, judging that we must now be ahead of the dunter weapons convoy and far out of its sight. We soon again came upon the ruined railway, and followed it northeast again.

Korf spoke, and Arken asked me:

"Much further?"

"It shouldn't be, no."

And shortly we came to a ruined farmstead: a burned stone house flanked by the remains of a barn. It was, I realized, the very same spot where I had handed my message off to the dunters and then been questioned by the men from Caranniam, weeks earlier.

But instead of a dunter or a man, now, we saw a kobold round the corner of the house.

A kobold carrying a small keg; it looked to be a powder keg.

We stopped and watched the fellow take the keg to a pile of similar ones on our side of the house, and set it next to them. Only then did he look up, notice us, and freeze.

Korf and the rest of my party started toward him. I stayed behind. The kobold stood there dumbfounded as they approached.

Korf spoke to him, and then they all talked for a few minutes. I noticed the new kobold look at me and gesture in my direction several times.

Now Korf turned and waved me over. I dismounted and walked

up to them.

"This brother of ours does not believe us," Arken told me. "He thinks we all must be your slaves."

"You told him why Korf is here?" I asked.

"Yes. But he thinks you will order us away."

"Wukk doesn't know this one? Nor Agarak?"

"No."

"I'm standing here," I said. "Do you think he understands now?"

"Probably."

The new kobold was now eyeing me in some surprise. Just to make sure, I spoke to him. I pointed to Korf and said:

"*Zhaka* Korf." Chief Korf, that would be. It was another word I had picked up.

The kobold bounced his gaze between me and Korf a few times, wide-mouthed, and seemed convinced.

"You know, he has stolen this powder," Arken told me. "He and some other kobolds from the camp."

"From the dunters?"

"Yes."

"You are serious?"

"Yes."

Korf seemed to be following our conversation somewhat and spoke to me. Arken translated:

"Rebellion seems to be in the air, Shearer. You chose a good time to get us. The kobolds with this army say they have grown tired of the camp. There is little food. Only a few roots they can dig, and also some occasional sheep and goats that your Emmervale cousins do not keep an eye on."

Those animals, I guessed, were almost certainly sent out intentionally at the behest of Britta and Jed to keep the dunters in place. If so, it had worked. Or at the least it had not hurt.

"Little food," Arken continued, "and the dunters make sport of them. But the dunters have become careless, and the kobolds have been stealing from them. The dunters are keeping close track of their food, but not so much their weapons. The kobolds made a plan to take away their powder, and flints."

"Rebellion is in the air, indeed," I said.

Later, after that summer was over, I wondered at the coincidence that the kobolds serving the dunters' expeditionary army had decided to mutiny at the exact same time the rest of their people, unbeknownst to them, were seizing Red Gorge City. What were the odds of that happening? Could we be sure that they had not communicated, somehow?

But they hadn't. Part of the explanation, I came to see, was that the dunters had never before taken an army so far away from Red Gorge for so long. Had they done so, they likely would have seen the same dissent from their kobold servants. They did not have such a strong hold over their slaves as they had assumed, but it took the distance from Red Gorge and the weeks of privation for the kobolds to assert themselves.

And perhaps another part of it was that rebellion was indeed contagious. There may have been some kobold independence in the air, that summer.

That evening Wukk, Agarak, and Karrar moved down into the dunter camp. They spoke quietly with their acquaintances, relatives, and kobold bosses, and spread the word of Korf's uprising. That night the true rebellion began, both out here and, as Korf had arranged, in Red Gorge City itself. In the darkness of midnight, kobolds began filing out of the camp, melting away like snow in the spring. Now, in pairs and in small groups, they moved quietly to the farmstead where Korf, Arken, and I had waited.

There were dozens of kobolds, then hundreds, and finally well over a thousand, I would say.

How had they crept off without the dunters noticing? With care. It was crucial, of course, that the dunters had not bothered to learn their language. Had they done so, some of them would have picked up on even the hushed conversations of their slaves. But as it was the kobolds waited until dark, dropped whatever they were doing—they certainly had no belongings to gather—and escaped.

Gaping kobold after gaping kobold passed by me behind the burned house. I think all thousand of them in turn stared at me, tried to make sense of me, and then stared at Korf to do the same. Korf was in his mail, of course, a large leader standing firm and welcoming each newcomer with a word or a grunt. A single torch burned in the darkness, and its light flickered on Korf's armor.

Arken and Karrar stood by him, demonstrating that he had a team. Wukk and Agarak could speak of the garrison back in Red Gorge City, if needed, and my presence showed these kobolds that Korf had at least one ally. The throng seemed convinced, and they were waiting to be led.

Eventually Korf turned and lifted his arm for them to follow. They seemed satisfied that all their number had left the camp. We moved southwest.

The kobolds carried away all the kegs of powder and other supplies they had lifted from the dunters. Here and there I saw one carrying an actual dunter weapon, but these were few. Mostly they had not dared to steal anything the dunters might notice right off; but their masters had nonetheless foolishly trusted them to handle vast amounts of vital food and equipment.

The crowd of kobolds, who walked perhaps eight or ten abreast, made their way across the prairies. They struck me, as I rode off to their side, like a river, again, just as the train tracks had. A furred river wending its way westward just like the Walsing.

It was impressive to watch, and I enjoyed myself for some time. But this could not go on. I had achieved everything I had wanted to, and I was moving farther and farther from Emmervale. I felt confident that the kobolds would easily take and hold Red Gorge City. I rode up to Korf and Arken, who were at the front.

"Chief Korf," I said. "I must beg a moment."

He and Arken stepped aside and let the rest of the kobolds press ahead, led by his kinsman Karrar.

"I have come far enough," I told them. "I need to go home. From here I can circle back around the dunter encampment."

Korf listened to this and then spoke through Arken:

"The Chief says you should come to Red Gorge. One more time."

I shook my head. "I have been away for weeks."

"Once more," Arken said. "You must see the kobolds of the city rise. It is only a few more days."

"It will be a sight," I agreed. "But we still have that dunter army outside my city. And they will be hungry soon, from the looks of it."

"Shearer, the Chief says that you have inspired this. You had the idea to call us from our home. We would not have done this without you. You should be the first to see Red Gorge run by the *kororen*. You must come."

I sighed, and smiled. It was difficult for me—impossible actually—to ignore a request like that. Once more I extended my journey.

On our way to Red Gorge City we had something to take care of, of course. Korf took us straight along the ruined railway heading southwest, and as daylight was coming I saw, far off on the horizon, the dunters' crawling convoy of the cannons and everything else. I could barely discern the dark forms, but there was nothing else they could be.

"Here they are," I told Arken. He had asked me, earlier, to let him know if I saw the convoy. I then dismounted.

Arken barked something to Korf, who instantly brought our column to a halt and began growling out orders.

Almost the entire crowd of kobolds immediately wheeled and headed south, like a swirling flock of birds. About two dozen remained behind, quickly gathering into a huddle with Korf. I noticed that all of them carried sacks, or powder kegs.

Arken came to my side to explain, but the plan was obvious even without the narration.

"He is sending just a few out to them," Arken said. "The ragged ones, not himself or Karrar or me. They will take some of the kegs of powder along, and some of the food. They're going to say that they were sent from the camp with the supplies."

"Will the dunters believe them? Do the kobolds ever get sent anywhere without dunters along to lead?"

"We think it will work," he said. "Our boys will carry no weapons, and the food will get the attention of the dunters in the convoy. The dunters won't ask questions. We should be able to get at least a few of the kegs of powder into the wagons, or the carts. They will light them, drift to the back, and then leave. In the confusion they should get a head start. And they will run away to the north, not draw the dunters to us here."

"It's a brave mission."

Arken shrugged dismissively. "They can outrun the dunters if need be. You know, Shearer, this is the second time in one day that the dunters will suffer for having kept us so empty-handed."

"You mean those kobolds have nothing to carry. Just like in the dunter camp when they all walked away so easily."

"Nothing to carry, nothing to slow them down; and nothing, literally, to lose."

Korf now spoke his last words to the group and hurried toward us. The two dozen kobolds in the demolition squad resumed their walk toward the oncoming convoy. The five or six out in front all carried the sacks I had seen.

"What is in the bags?" I asked.

"Roast mutton. They will go first."

This meat might well have been from our farm, of course. I shook my head and smiled a bit, but said nothing.

Korf led all of us due south, then. The mob of kobolds was uncharacteristically quiet. There was no chance the dunters on the wagons would be able to hear any of us, as far off as they were, but the crowd proceeded with caution regardless. We cleared some distance, and then I jumped back onto the horse. Korf took us a good way south before resuming the march west toward Red Gorge.

Soon after our turn to the west, we heard a series of terrific explosions to the north. The first report was modest; that would have been one keg of powder going off. This was followed by more blasts, though, as wagon loads exploded in a chain reaction.

I looked to the right. We all could feel slight percussions along with the noise. Soon we could see smoke rising, also, from what were now the remains of the dunter convoy. I wondered how far the cannons had been thrown.

Arken just glanced at me and nodded. Korf, for his part, was out in front again, and did not even look back.

Thirteen

My last entry into Red Gorge City, with Korf and his mustered kobolds, was unlike any of the previous. Instead of creeping in quietly from the rural outskirts on the south side, Korf led us straight into the eastern edge of the sprawl. We followed the ruined tracks, the double line of Alden Silvermoor's glyph, all the way to where they met the old dunter rails. These were intact, although they extended just a short distance outside the city.

Ahead of us began the usual weathered shacks and scrabbly yards of Red Gorge, but I noticed an immediate difference: atop the first structure by the tracks stood a knot of kobolds, on watch.

They cheered as they saw us, a loud chorus of yells and barks. We must have looked impressive: Korf out front with some swagger, chest thrust forward in his chain mail. Next to him, his respectful advisers Arken and Karrar. Behind him, the long line of kobolds liberated from the expedition encampment. Next to all this, me on my fine stolen horse. Once again I felt like a lone ambassador to a young, new nation.

We walked into the town, filling the street. Red Gorge City did not look festive—it was much too weathered and soiled for that—but it did look far more alive than I had ever seen it. Kobolds emerged from shacks and alleys to welcome their returning kin and to cheer for, and gawk at, Korf.

"The city has been taken," Arken told me.

"That's what it looks like," I said. "Even from the entrance."

We eventually stopped in the rail yard which I had seen weeks earlier. I got down from the horse. All the crates and cannons were cleared out now, of course, and it must have been one of the broader expanses of open air in the city. A good place for a conquering army to congregate.

Hundreds of kobolds poured in. Some embraced members of the group that had returned from the expedition; others engaged in mock bite-fights with them, which was apparently one way young male kobolds greeted each other. Others were passing around jugs of what I guessed was *zhirnga*. I pitied them that they thought that stuff was special enough to celebrate with.

Korf advanced through the center of the yard, and the crowd respectfully drew away to give him room. Then one local kobold walked up to him. It was Wukk's companion, of the group who had taken me captive. It looked as if he had been a leader here while we were away. He was larger than average, I noticed, and wore a metal armband over his right elbow.

He did something then which I had never seen, but which seemed normal for the kobolds: he licked Korf's face. Korf just nodded at this, saying nothing.

Wukk's companion then began a report.

"He says that the remaining dunters are mostly locked up," Arken told me. "He says many jails and dungeons have been put into use for this. He says it must seem—ironic? It must seem ironic for the dunters that the abundance of jails they built are now being used against them. It sounds, Aiman, as if the dunters locked up these kobolds often."

"They did."

"So that has changed around. Other dunters, he is saying, have been placed in irons. And they are not being fed. We have gathered our grain and our animals into a few captured manors and a few yards where they can be guarded. Dunters are left to fend for themselves. Those few who can still move about are trying to catch rats and other such creatures they can find in the ditches around the city.

"And now he speaks of the return of the dunters who are away. All roads and alleys into the city are guarded, now. Our next work will be to build walls. We will take apart many of the dunter manors to do this. This is a large city, but we are many. And we are used to hard work. That is what this kobold tells Korf," he concluded.

Korf turned to the crowd around him, made a fist, and shouted something. They all cheered.

"Red Gorge City is now ours, he says," Arken said.

"I didn't need translation for that."

Korf turned to us and approached. I was still taller than he was, of course—he had not literally grown—but he seemed a larger leader now than when we had met him back in the Kurtenvold.

He spoke to me with his hands on his hips.

"Are you glad now that you came in here with us?" Arken translated.

"Indeed I am," I said.

"And now you should go. Your family must be waiting for you."

"They are."

"Chief Korf says you will always be welcome here," Arken relayed. "You could bring back your comrades who visited us in the Kurtenvold."

"The dwarves?" I asked.

"I believe the Chief was referring to your companions, the man and woman."

"Very good," I said. "Arken, there is one thing I have to ask before I go."

"What?"

"One of the dwarves I was with asked me to do this. Maghran, the one who spoke for us. The one who handed over the stone of arovis. And the axe."

"Yes?"

"On his behalf, I want to ask for that axe back," I said.

I waited while Arken translated this for Korf. The big chief listened and then stood still a moment, ruminating.

Korf then spoke to me, but he did so in a loud voice so that all the kobolds around him could hear.

"This man has asked a question, he is saying," Arken told me. "Maghran, brother to the ruler of Stenhall, has requested, through this man here, that I return my axe to him."

"That's right," I said. I hadn't expected Korf to know exactly who Maghran was.

"This is the dwarf who came to visit my people in our warren, and who paid me for the release of a prisoner. He paid me with arovis." Korf now took the axe and raised it in the air. "He had to pay the additional price of this dwarven axe," Arken relayed.

Korf turned around with it. The kobolds watched him, waiting. He turned back to me and spoke again, loudly:

"Tell Maghran and Stenhall," Arken continued, "that I am pleased to do so. Tell him that Korf and the other kobolds who rule Red Gorge City are glad to send back his axe. And that we wish him well, and we hope to confer with Stenhall soon."

He raised the axe high in the air. He turned it once in the sun, so it glittered, and then handed it to me.

The crowd around him went absolutely berserk. They jumped, they howled. It was even louder than the scene underground in their warren outside Kurtenvold, weeks earlier, when he had obtained the axe in the first place—and this despite the fact that we were now outside, not in an enclosed space. They seemed to understand that while it took a great leader to haggle a prize axe away from a dwarf, it took an even greater one to hand it back.

Fourteen

"They melted away," Jed was telling me.

"Melted? It was that easy?" I asked him.

He and Britta and I were standing once again by the fence outside the paddock between our farm and Britta's, just as we had so many weeks ago before we set out on our journey which had become so long. Our farms were still well-tended, even after all this. The land had ignored the fighting and the marching armies.

"The dunters just picked up and headed west," Jed said. "They apparently woke up to find themselves without food, and also without some of their weapons and nearly all their gunpowder. They were not in the mood to attack us with swords and knives."

"We wondered if we might have to push them out," Britta said. "But they drifted away on their own."

"Drifted? Did they march out in any order?"

"They did not. Their mob just broke up and headed west in clumps. We've been watching them. Some did not apparently even head toward Red Gorge; they went north, up to the borderlands between White Mount and Stenhall."

"Where they came from in the first place," I said.

Britta nodded. "Long ago. I can't imagine they'll find much there. But most will wander into Red Gorge City, or try to, in fits and starts. They won't be welcomed, from what you have told us."

"They will not be, no," I said. "I'm surprised they did not at least march together back toward their city. Even if it were just a mob."

Jed shrugged.

"They had a hard enough time organizing themselves even when Caranniam and Varenlend were guiding them. And now they've lost that, and lost virtually all their possessions also. It's no surprise they are adrift."

"Jed," I said. "You almost sound sorry for them."

"Please," he said. "We can't joke about those murdering fools. But it should come as no surprise that they are wandering now. They've had their servants and virtually all their supplies taken from them. What would you do? If you had nothing?"

I smiled. He had realized the answer as soon as he asked the question.

"Indeed," he said. "What would we do if we had nothing. Well, the dunters aren't up to it, I know. But we would walk down from the hills and rebuild our home, wouldn't we."

Also by Tim Craire

The Pennants of Larkhall - Prince Harlan ascends the throne of Larkhall when his father falls beside him as they fight to save a village from a horde of northerners. Harlan instantly inherits the invasion and its imminent siege of his castle; meanwhile his kingdom is disintegrating from a blight which swallows entire farms and will starve his people even if they repel the siege.

Tropic of Labrador
Three stories:
-2080 brings dustbowls and mass migration northward -- but on the bright side, there's also the Fourth Annual Jellyfishburger Cook-Off on the warm beaches of Labrador!
Plus:
-In the 2030s, a real football fan doesn't just support his team; he seizes it
-A national security agent running out of people to spy on hires an expert

Made in the USA
Middletown, DE
31 January 2020